KiM REAPER

GRIM BEGINNINGS

AN ONI PRESS PUBLICATION

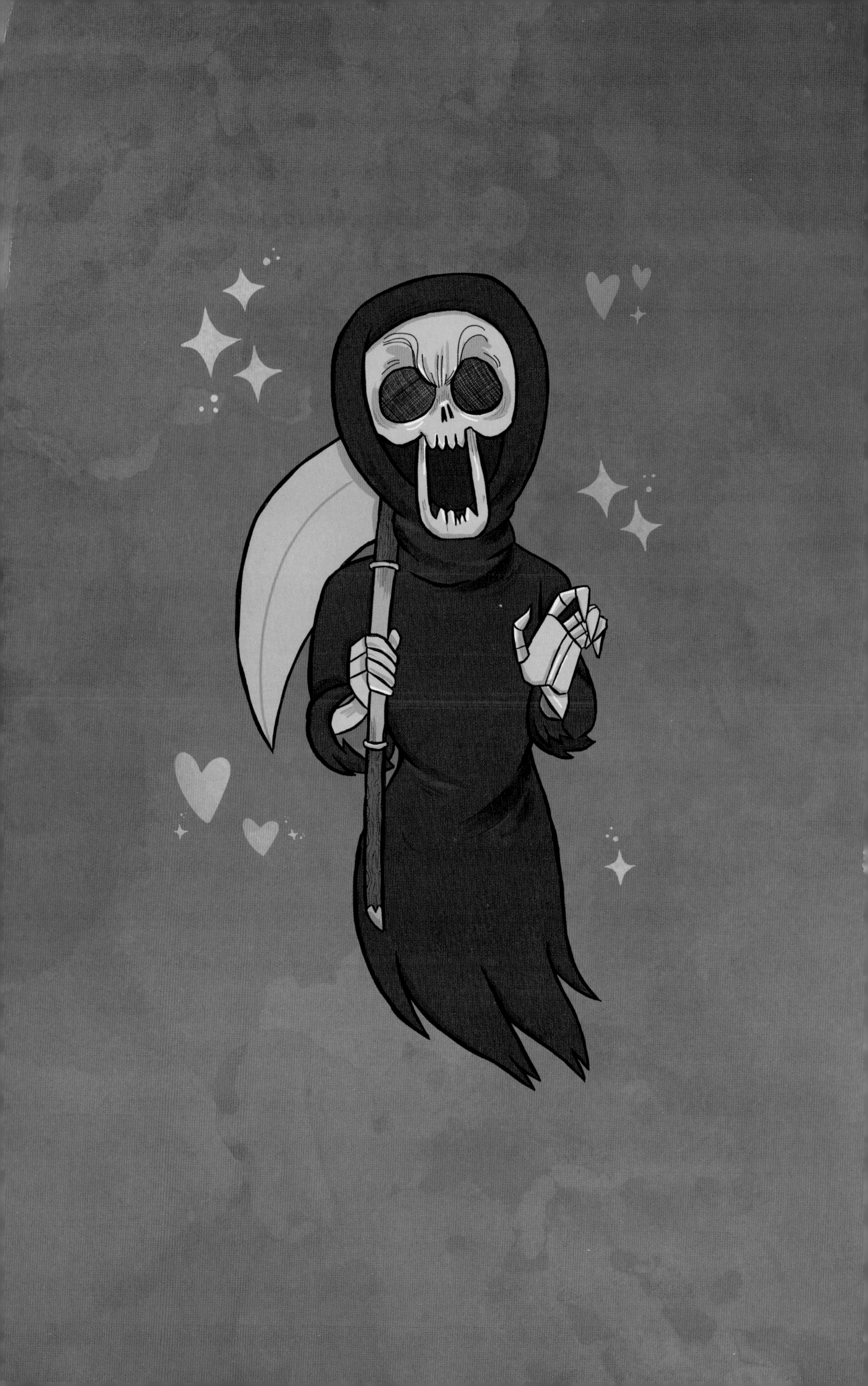

Kim Reaper

GRIM BEGINNINGS

BY SARAH GRALEY

Lettered by Crank!
Designed by Hilary Thompson
Edited by Ari Yarwood

PUBLISHED BY ONI PRESS, INC.

Joe Nozemack, founder & chief financial officer
James Lucas Jones, publisher
Charlie Chu, v.p. of creative & business development
Brad Rooks, director of operations
Rachel Reed, marketing manager
Melissa Meszaros MacFadyen, publicity manager
Troy Look, director of design & production
Hilary Thompson, graphic designer
Kate Z. Stone, junior graphic designer
Angie Knowles, digital prepress lead
Ari Yarwood, executive editor
Robin Herrera, senior editor
Desiree Wilson, associate editor
Alissa Sallah, administrative assistant
Jung Lee, logistics associate

*Originally published as issues 1-4 of
the Oni Press comic series* Kim Reaper.

ONIPRESS.COM
FACEBOOK.COM/ONIPRESS
TWITTER.COM/ONIPRESS
ONIPRESS.TUMBLR.COM
INSTAGRAM.COM/ONIPRESS

SARAHGRALEY.COM
TWITTER.COM/SARAHGRALEYART

First Edition: February 2018
ISBN: 978-1-62010-455-2
eISBN: 978-1-62010-456-9
Convention Exclusive ISBN: 978-1-62010-528-3

2 3 4 5 6 7 8 9 10

Library of Congress Control Number: 2017946413

Printed in China.

CHAPTER ONE

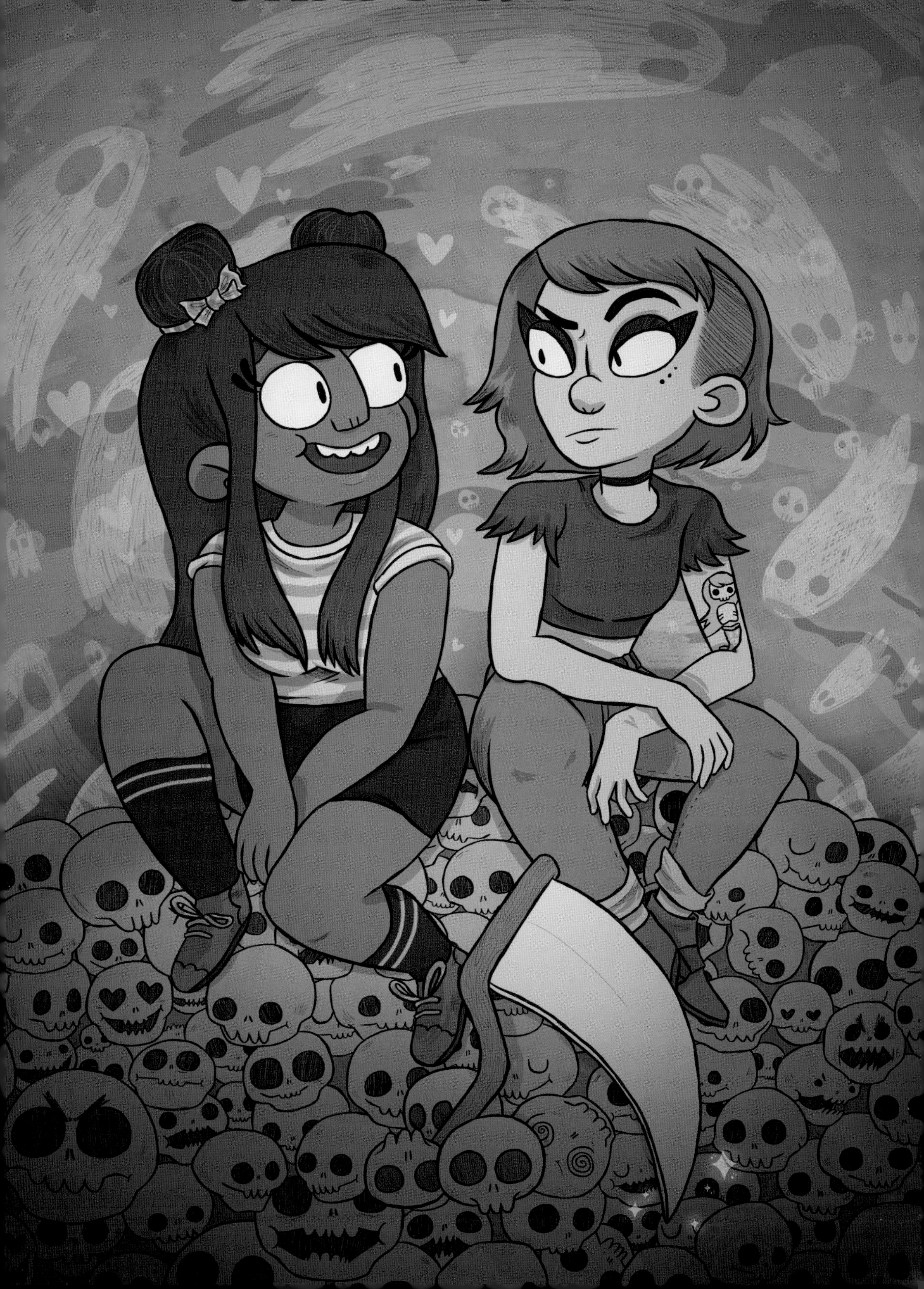

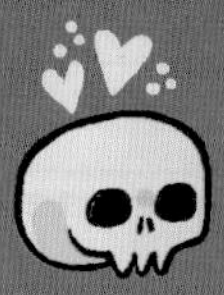

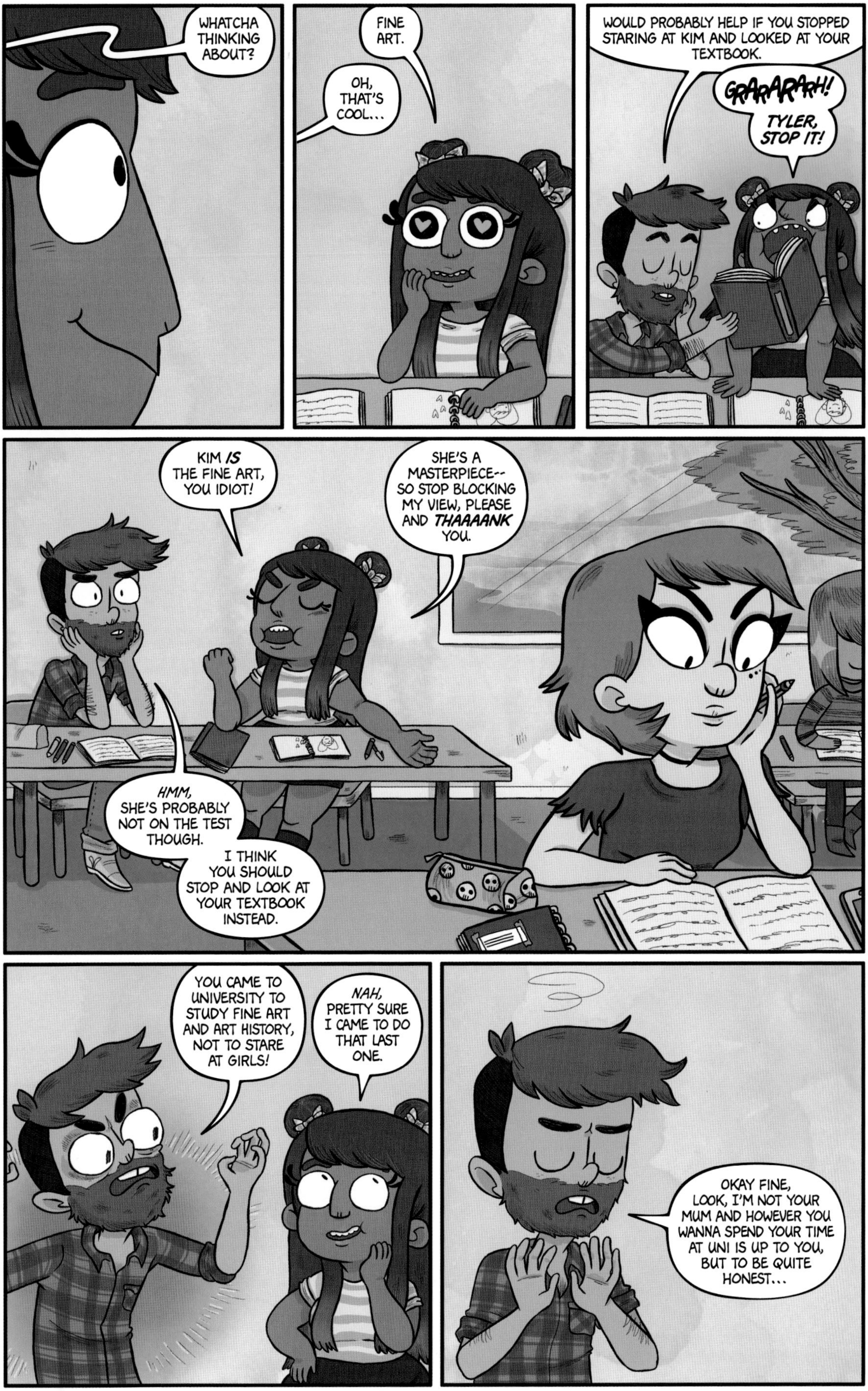
WHATCHA THINKING ABOUT?
FINE ART.
OH, THAT'S COOL...
WOULD PROBABLY HELP IF YOU STOPPED STARING AT KIM AND LOOKED AT YOUR TEXTBOOK.
GRARARARH!
TYLER, STOP IT!
KIM *IS* THE FINE ART, YOU IDIOT!
SHE'S A MASTERPIECE-- SO STOP BLOCKING MY VIEW, PLEASE AND *THAAAANK* YOU.
HMM, SHE'S PROBABLY NOT ON THE TEST THOUGH.
I THINK YOU SHOULD STOP AND LOOK AT YOUR TEXTBOOK INSTEAD.
YOU CAME TO UNIVERSITY TO STUDY FINE ART AND ART HISTORY, NOT TO STARE AT GIRLS!
NAH, PRETTY SURE I CAME TO DO THAT LAST ONE.
OKAY FINE, LOOK, I'M NOT YOUR MUM AND HOWEVER YOU WANNA SPEND YOUR TIME AT UNI IS UP TO YOU, BUT TO BE QUITE HONEST...

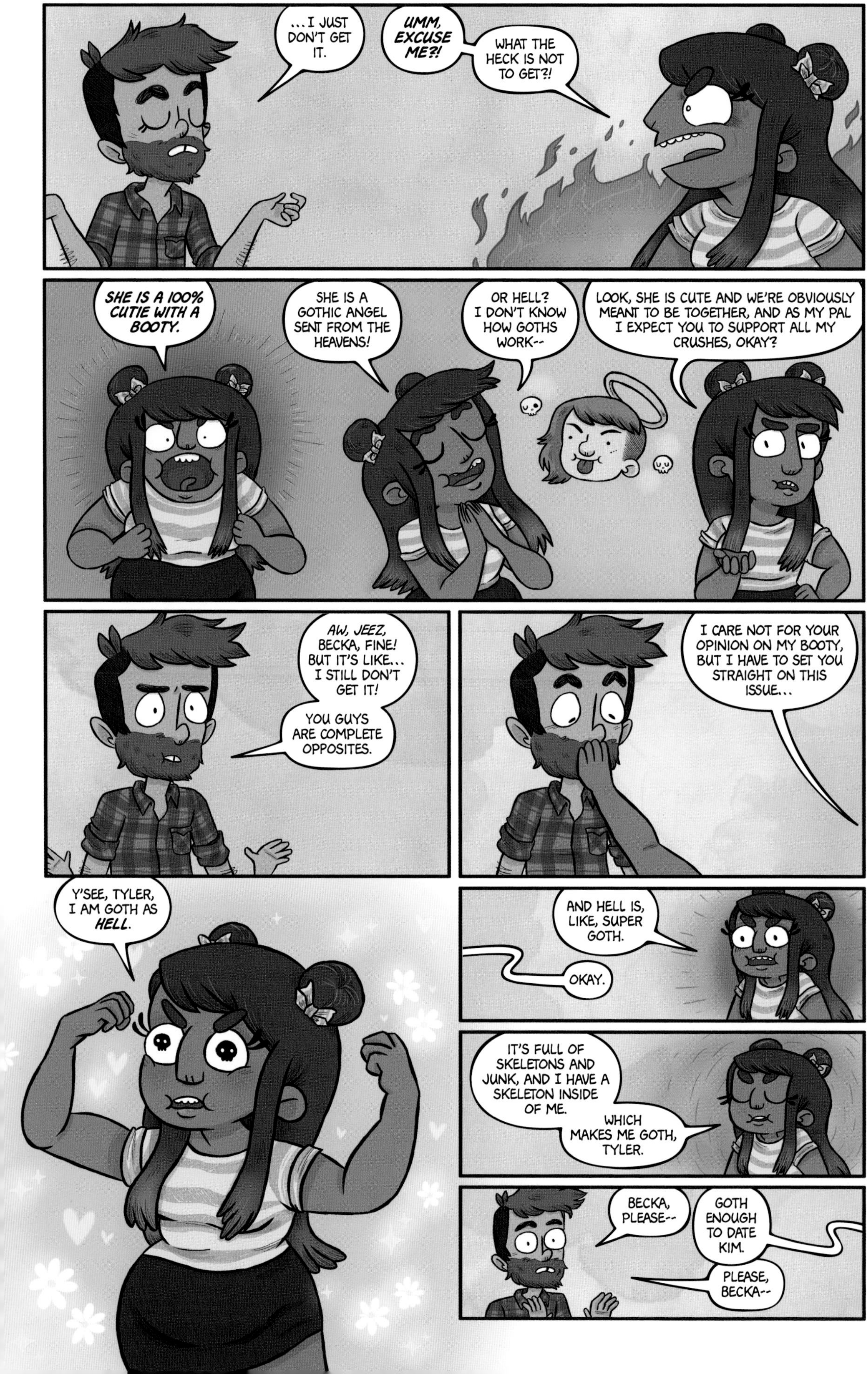
...I JUST DON'T GET IT.
UMM, EXCUSE ME?!
WHAT THE HECK IS NOT TO GET?!
SHE IS A 100% CUTIE WITH A BOOTY.
SHE IS A GOTHIC ANGEL SENT FROM THE HEAVENS!
OR HELL? I DON'T KNOW HOW GOTHS WORK--
LOOK, SHE IS CUTE AND WE'RE OBVIOUSLY MEANT TO BE TOGETHER, AND AS MY PAL I EXPECT YOU TO SUPPORT ALL MY CRUSHES, OKAY?
AW, JEEZ, BECKA, FINE! BUT IT'S LIKE... I STILL DON'T GET IT!
YOU GUYS ARE COMPLETE OPPOSITES.
I CARE NOT FOR YOUR OPINION ON MY BOOTY, BUT I HAVE TO SET YOU STRAIGHT ON THIS ISSUE...
Y'SEE, TYLER, I AM GOTH AS HELL.
AND HELL IS, LIKE, SUPER GOTH.
OKAY.
IT'S FULL OF SKELETONS AND JUNK, AND I HAVE A SKELETON INSIDE OF ME.
WHICH MAKES ME GOTH, TYLER.
BECKA, PLEASE--
GOTH ENOUGH TO DATE KIM.
PLEASE, BECKA--

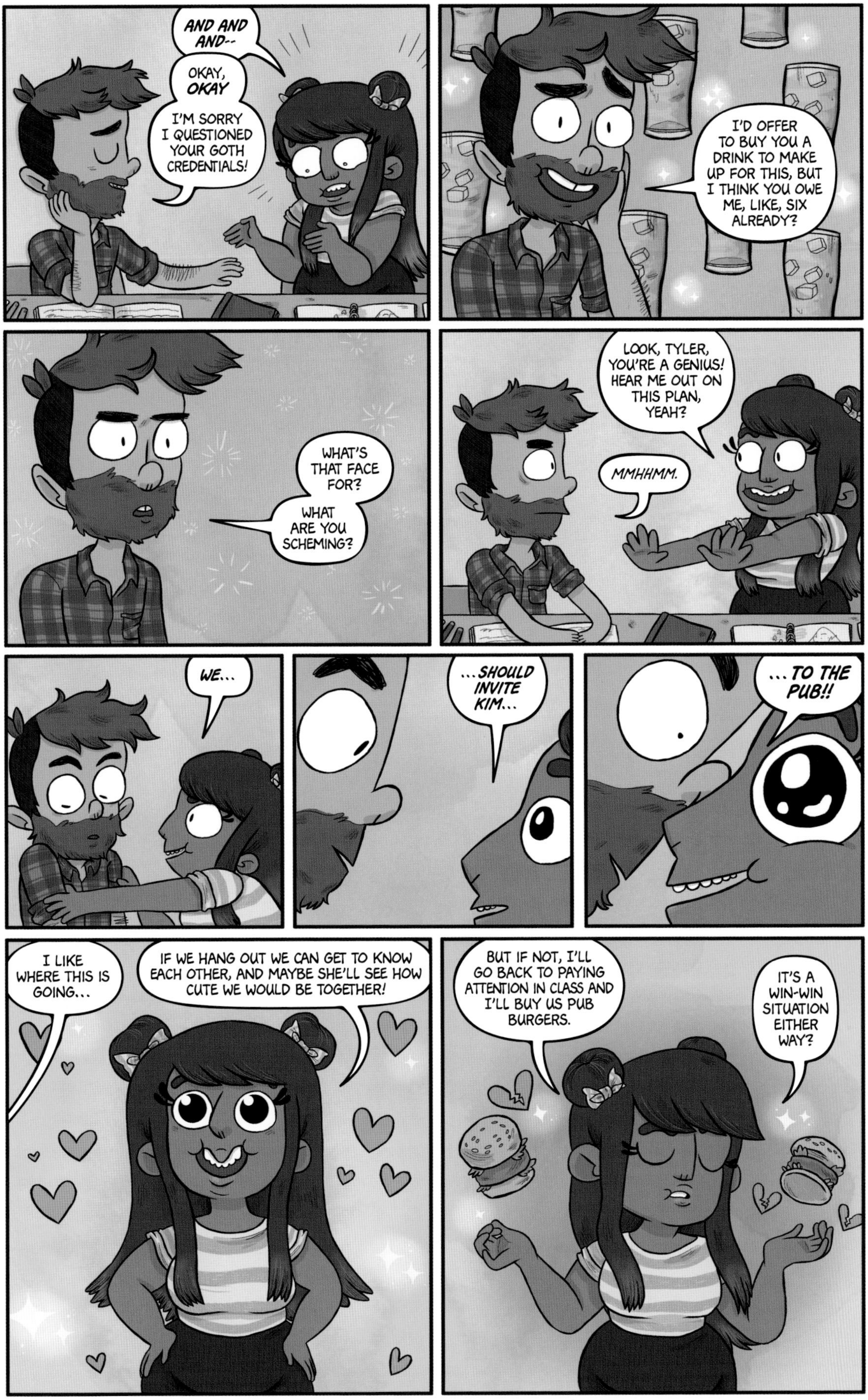
AND AND AND--
OKAY, OKAY
I'M SORRY I QUESTIONED YOUR GOTH CREDENTIALS!
I'D OFFER TO BUY YOU A DRINK TO MAKE UP FOR THIS, BUT I THINK YOU OWE ME, LIKE, SIX ALREADY?
WHAT'S THAT FACE FOR?
WHAT ARE YOU SCHEMING?
LOOK, TYLER, YOU'RE A GENIUS! HEAR ME OUT ON THIS PLAN, YEAH?
MMHHMM.
WE...
...SHOULD INVITE KIM...
...TO THE PUB!!
I LIKE WHERE THIS IS GOING...
IF WE HANG OUT WE CAN GET TO KNOW EACH OTHER, AND MAYBE SHE'LL SEE HOW CUTE WE WOULD BE TOGETHER!
BUT IF NOT, I'LL GO BACK TO PAYING ATTENTION IN CLASS AND I'LL BUY US PUB BURGERS.
IT'S A WIN-WIN SITUATION EITHER WAY?

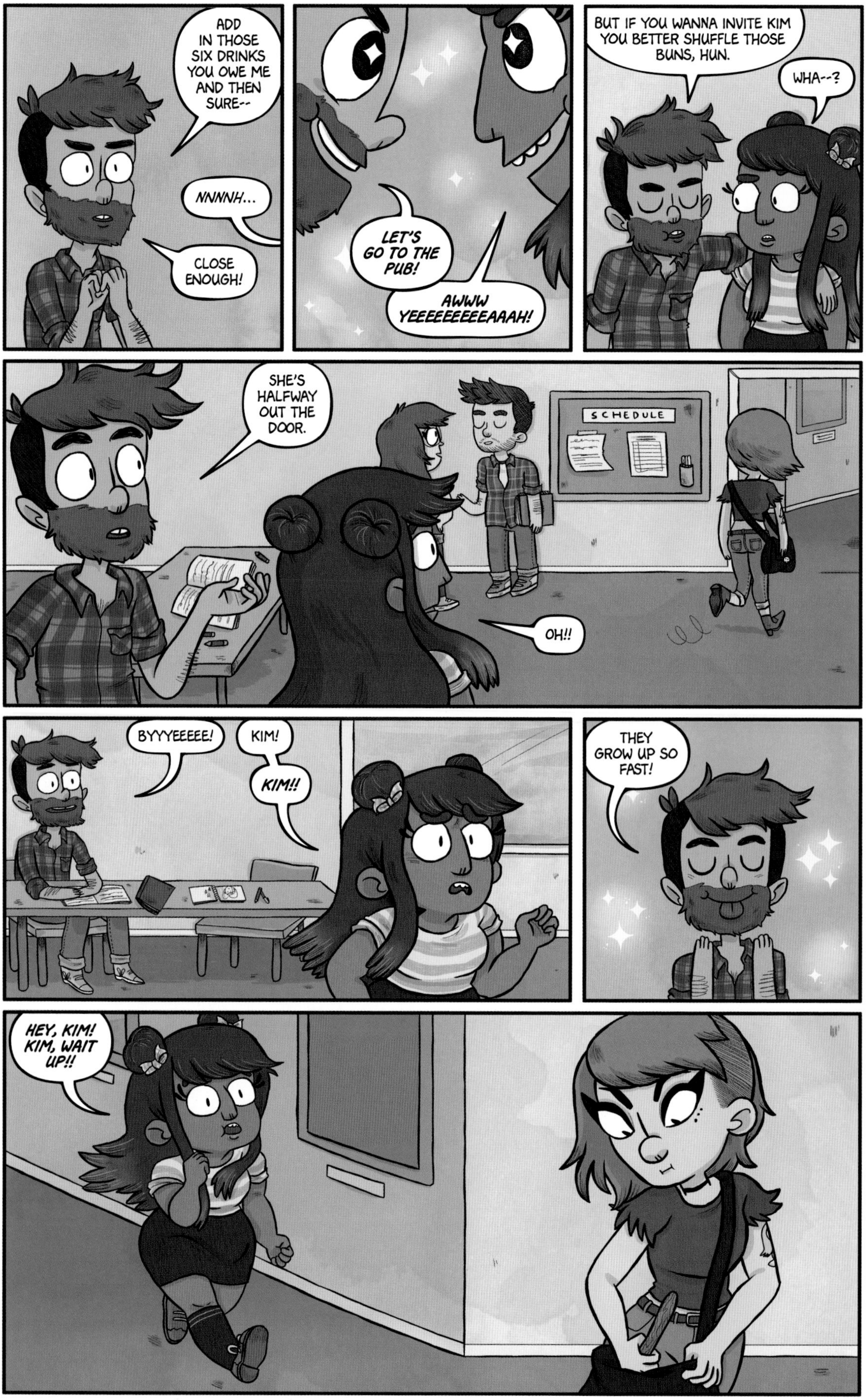
ADD IN THOSE SIX DRINKS YOU OWE ME AND THEN SURE--
NNNNH...
CLOSE ENOUGH!
LET'S GO TO THE PUB!
AWWW YEEEEEEEEEAAAH!
BUT IF YOU WANNA INVITE KIM YOU BETTER SHUFFLE THOSE BUNS, HUN.
WHA--?
SHE'S HALFWAY OUT THE DOOR.
SCHEDULE
OH!!
BYYYEEEEE!
KIM!
KIM!!
THEY GROW UP SO FAST!
HEY, KIM! KIM, WAIT UP!!

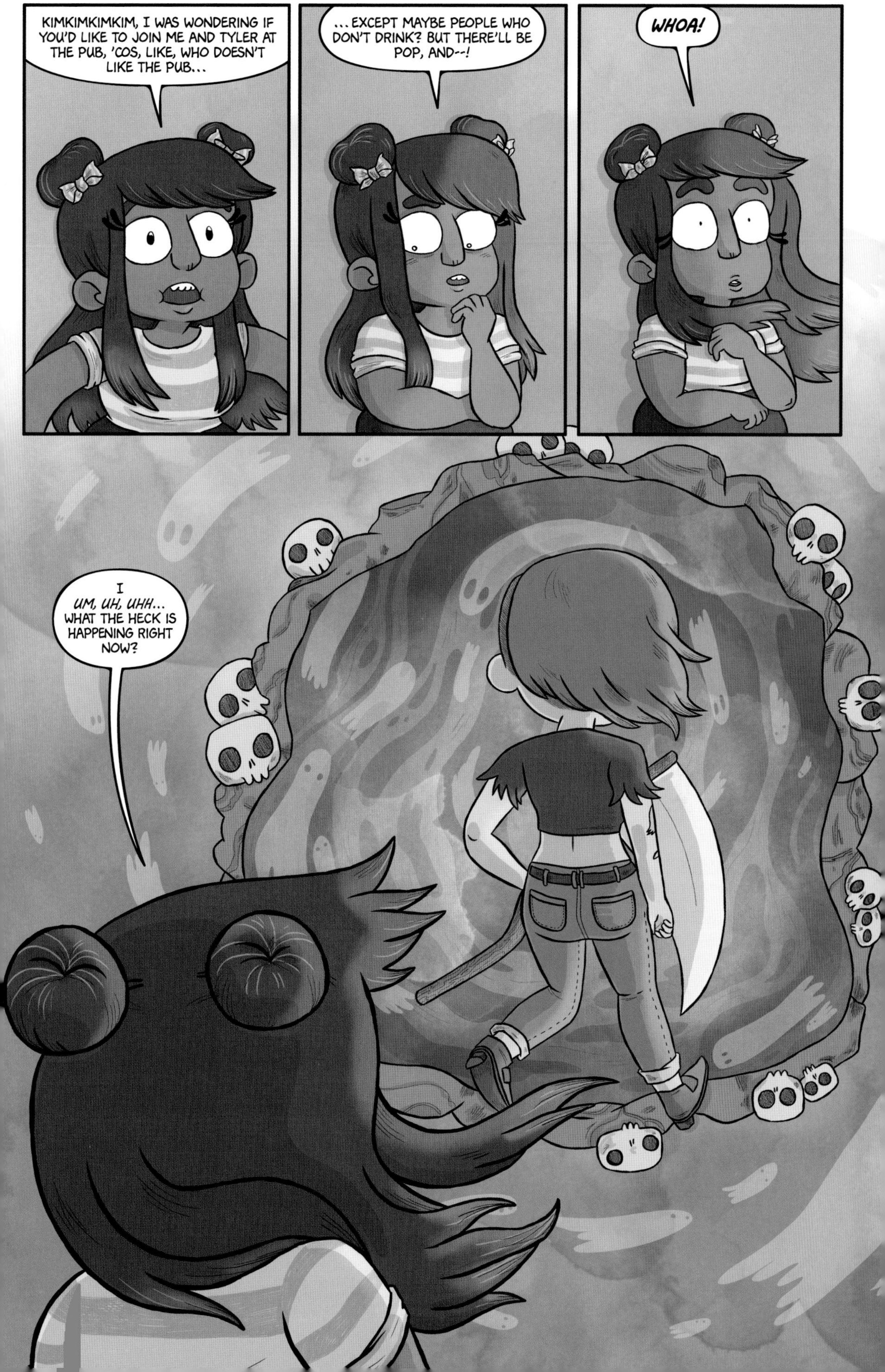
KIMKIMKIMKIM, I WAS WONDERING IF YOU'D LIKE TO JOIN ME AND TYLER AT THE PUB, 'COS, LIKE, WHO DOESN'T LIKE THE PUB...
...EXCEPT MAYBE PEOPLE WHO DON'T DRINK? BUT THERE'LL BE POP, AND--!
WHOA!
I *UM, UH, UHH...* WHAT THE HECK IS HAPPENING RIGHT NOW?

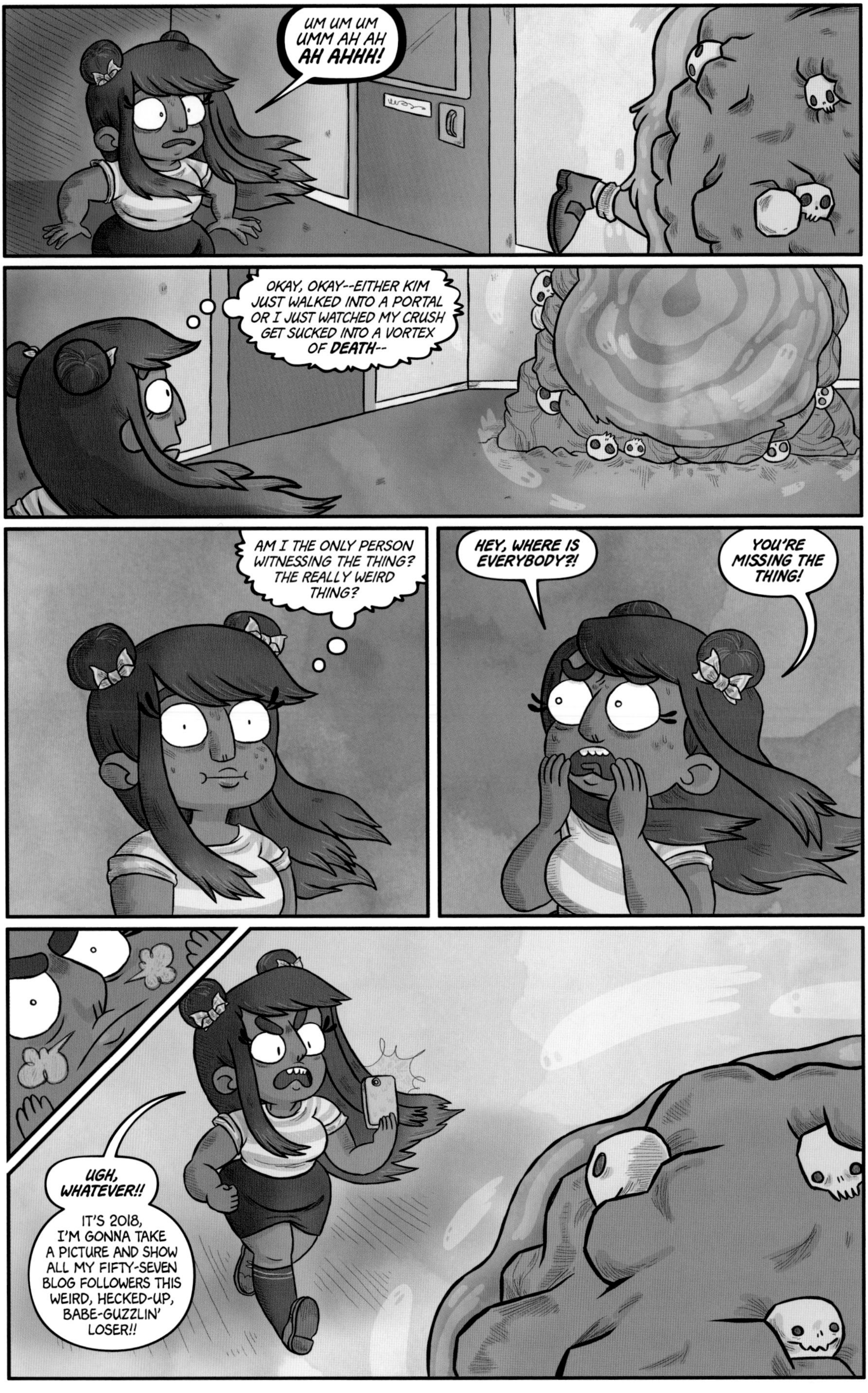
UM UM UM UMM AH AH **AH AHHH!**
OKAY, OKAY--EITHER KIM JUST WALKED INTO A PORTAL OR I JUST WATCHED MY CRUSH GET SUCKED INTO A VORTEX OF **DEATH**--
AM I THE ONLY PERSON WITNESSING THE THING? THE REALLY WEIRD THING?
HEY, WHERE IS EVERYBODY?!
YOU'RE MISSING THE THING!
UGH, WHATEVER!!
IT'S 2018, I'M GONNA TAKE A PICTURE AND SHOW ALL MY FIFTY-SEVEN BLOG FOLLOWERS THIS WEIRD, HECKED-UP, BABE-GUZZLIN' LOSER!!

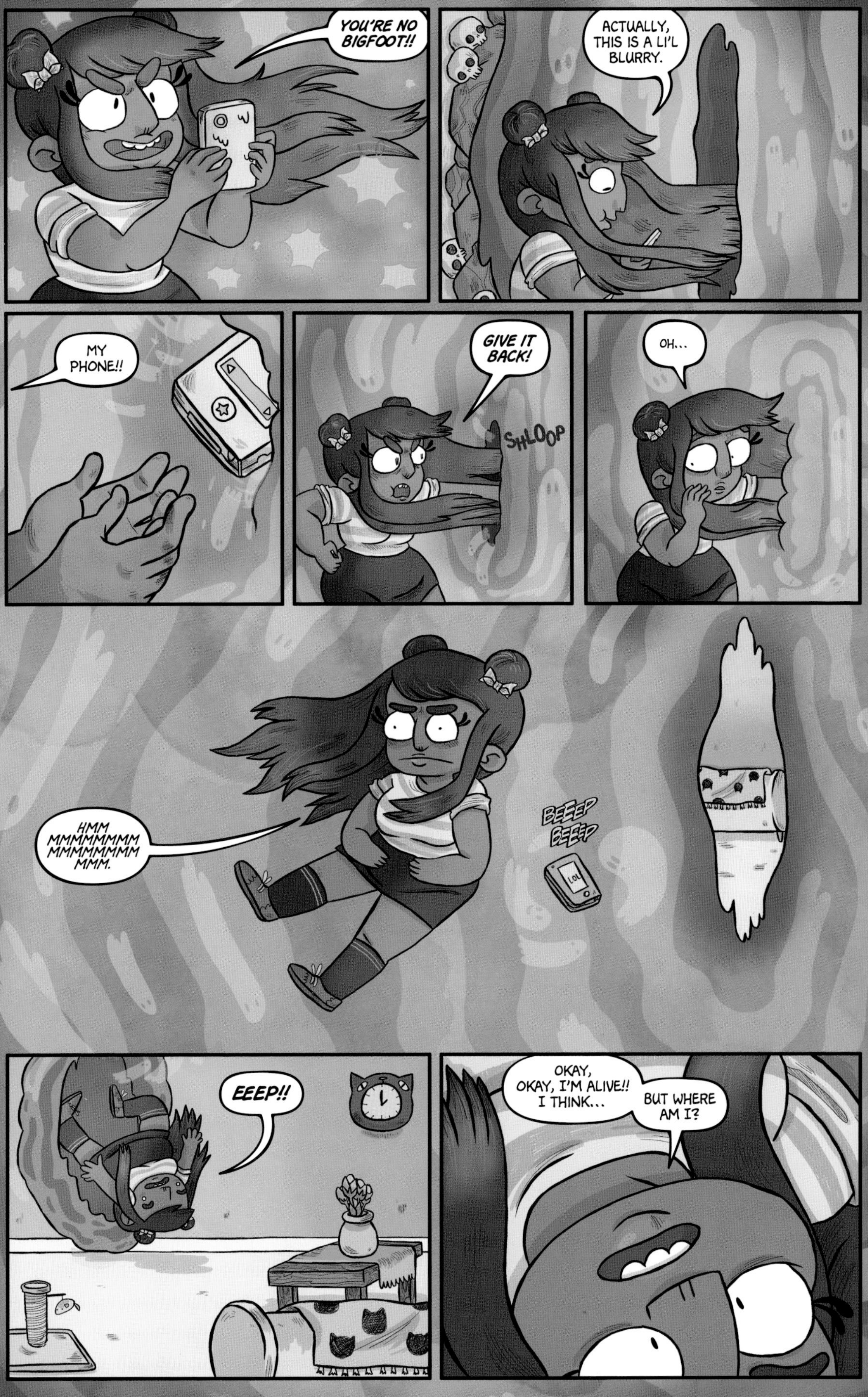
YOU'RE NO BIGFOOT!!
ACTUALLY, THIS IS A LI'L BLURRY.
MY PHONE!!
GIVE IT BACK!
SHLOOP
OH...
HMM MMMMMMMM MMMMMMMM MMM.
BEEEP BEEEP
EEEP!!
OKAY, OKAY, I'M ALIVE!! I THINK...
BUT WHERE AM I?

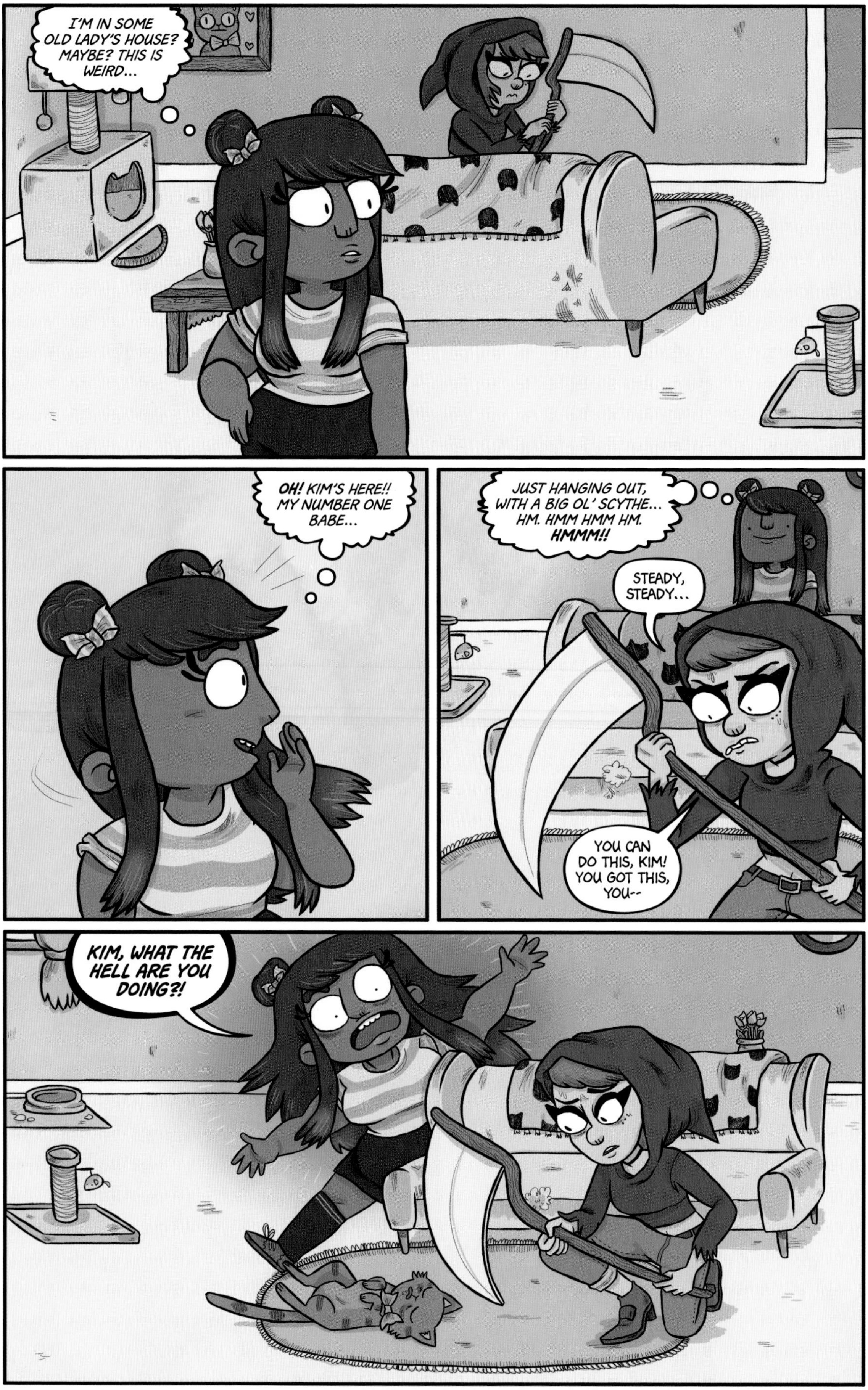
I'M IN SOME OLD LADY'S HOUSE? MAYBE? THIS IS WEIRD...
OH! KIM'S HERE!! MY NUMBER ONE BABE...
JUST HANGING OUT, WITH A BIG OL' SCYTHE... HM. HMM HMM HM. HMMM!!
STEADY, STEADY...
YOU CAN DO THIS, KIM! YOU GOT THIS, YOU--
KIM, WHAT THE HELL ARE YOU DOING?!

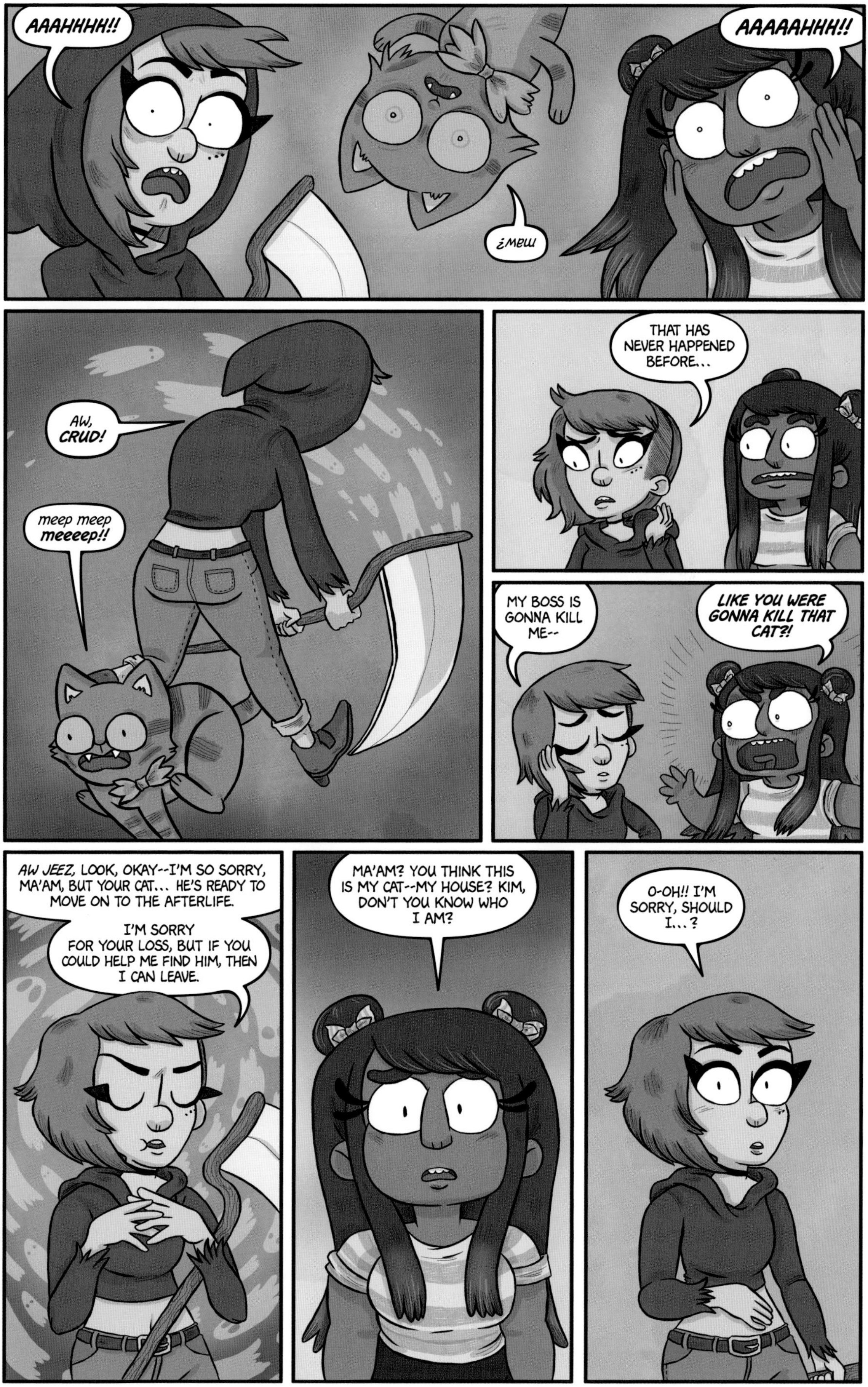

AAAHHHH!!
Mew?
AAAAAHHH!!
AW, CRUD!
meep meep meeeep!!
THAT HAS NEVER HAPPENED BEFORE...
MY BOSS IS GONNA KILL ME--
LIKE YOU WERE GONNA KILL THAT CAT?!
AW JEEZ, LOOK, OKAY--I'M SO SORRY, MA'AM, BUT YOUR CAT... HE'S READY TO MOVE ON TO THE AFTERLIFE.
I'M SORRY FOR YOUR LOSS, BUT IF YOU COULD HELP ME FIND HIM, THEN I CAN LEAVE.
MA'AM? YOU THINK THIS IS MY CAT--MY HOUSE? KIM, DON'T YOU KNOW WHO I AM?
O-OH!! I'M SORRY, SHOULD I...?

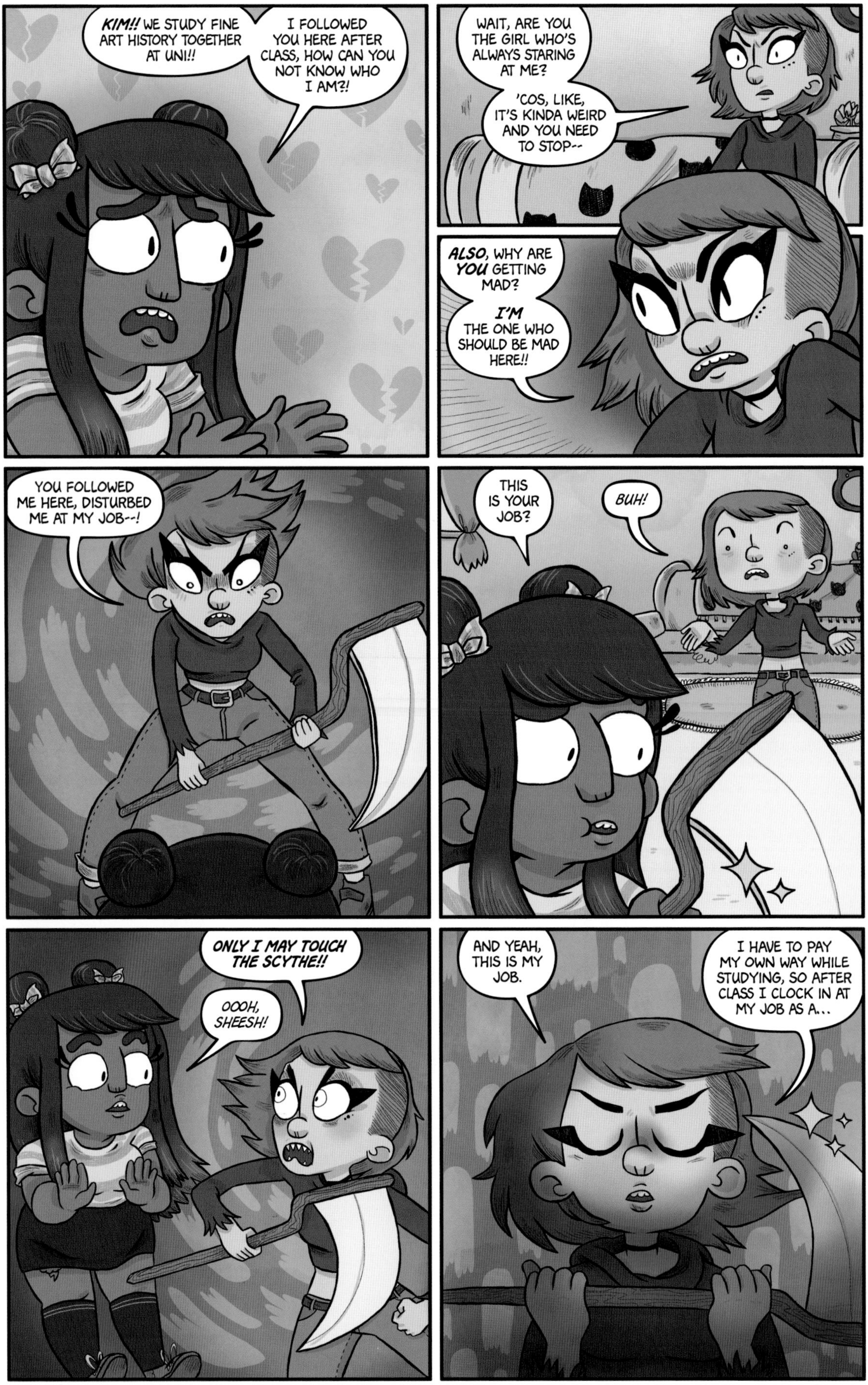
KIM!! WE STUDY FINE ART HISTORY TOGETHER AT UNI!!
I FOLLOWED YOU HERE AFTER CLASS, HOW CAN YOU NOT KNOW WHO I AM?!
WAIT, ARE YOU THE GIRL WHO'S ALWAYS STARING AT ME?
'COS, LIKE, IT'S KINDA WEIRD AND YOU NEED TO STOP--
ALSO, WHY ARE YOU GETTING MAD?
I'M THE ONE WHO SHOULD BE MAD HERE!!
YOU FOLLOWED ME HERE, DISTURBED ME AT MY JOB--!
THIS IS YOUR JOB?
BUH!
ONLY I MAY TOUCH THE SCYTHE!!
OOOH, SHEESH!
AND YEAH, THIS IS MY JOB.
I HAVE TO PAY MY OWN WAY WHILE STUDYING, SO AFTER CLASS I CLOCK IN AT MY JOB AS A...

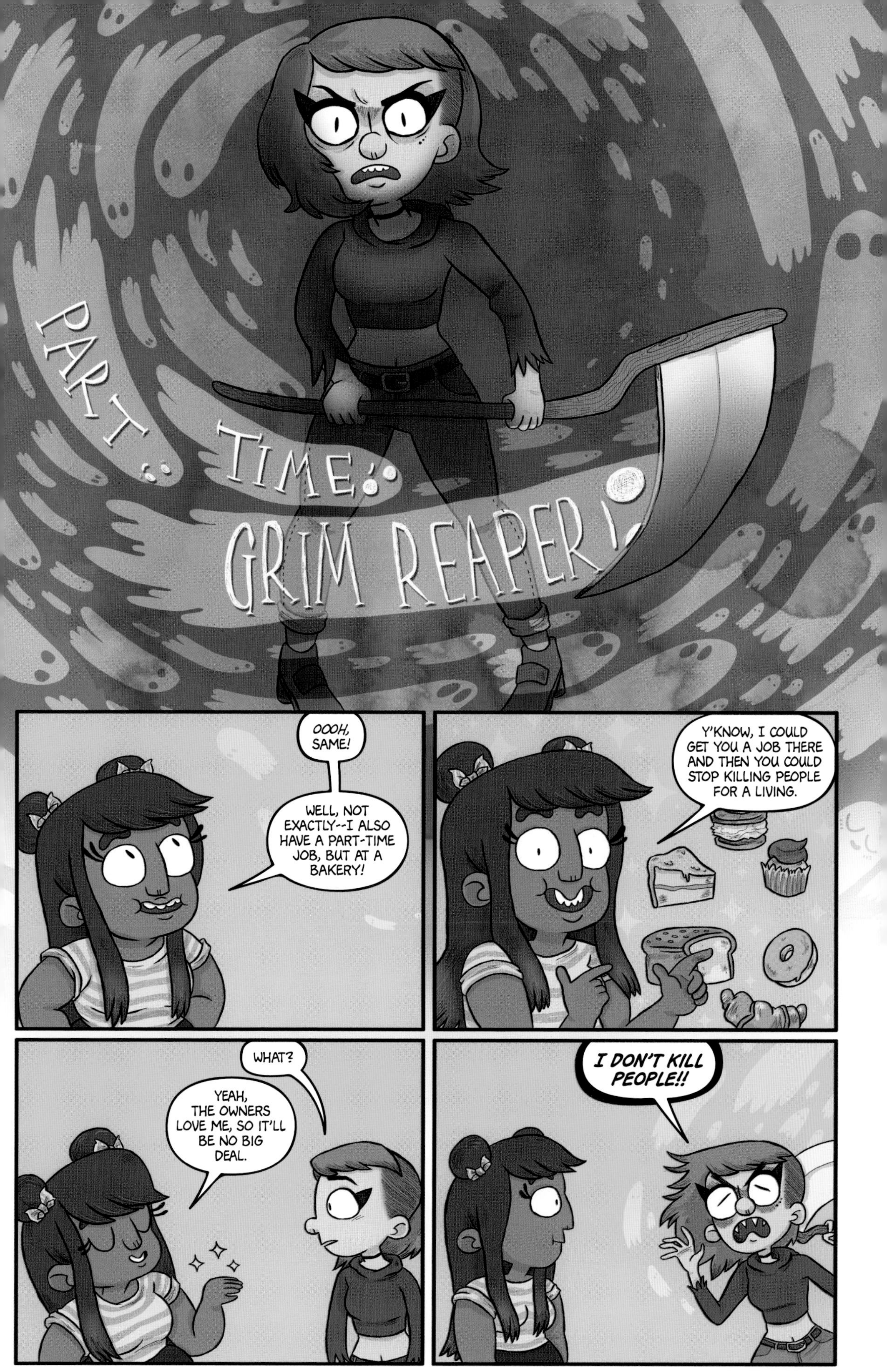
PART-TIME: GRIM REAPER!
OOOH, SAME!
WELL, NOT EXACTLY--I ALSO HAVE A PART-TIME JOB, BUT AT A BAKERY!
Y'KNOW, I COULD GET YOU A JOB THERE AND THEN YOU COULD STOP KILLING PEOPLE FOR A LIVING.
WHAT?
YEAH, THE OWNERS LOVE ME, SO IT'LL BE NO BIG DEAL.
I DON'T KILL PEOPLE!!

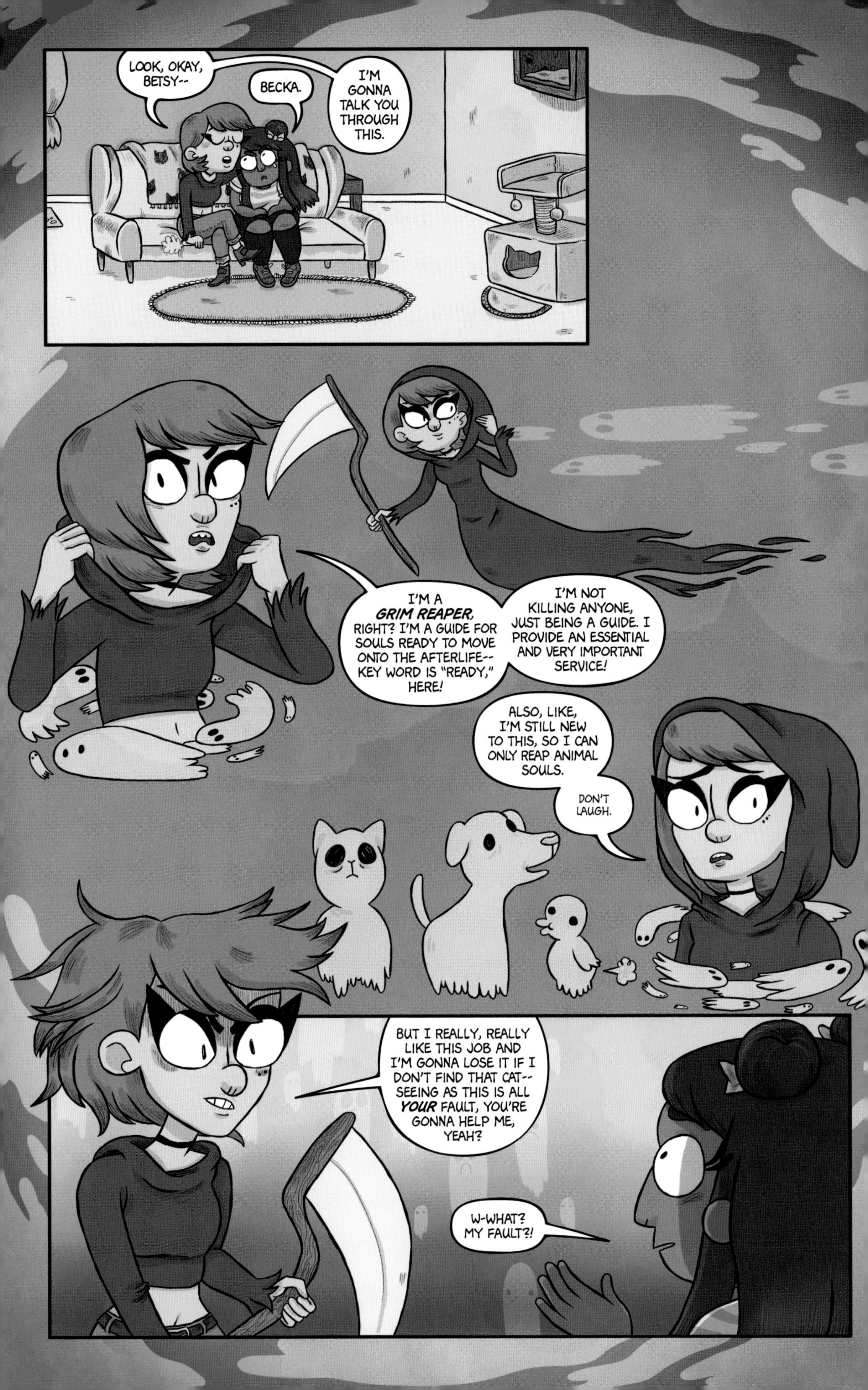
LOOK, OKAY, BETSY--
BECKA.
I'M GONNA TALK YOU THROUGH THIS.
I'M A *GRIM REAPER,* RIGHT? I'M A GUIDE FOR SOULS READY TO MOVE ONTO THE AFTERLIFE-- KEY WORD IS "READY," HERE!
I'M NOT KILLING ANYONE, JUST BEING A GUIDE. I PROVIDE AN ESSENTIAL AND VERY IMPORTANT SERVICE!
ALSO, LIKE, I'M STILL NEW TO THIS, SO I CAN ONLY REAP ANIMAL SOULS.
DON'T LAUGH.
BUT I REALLY, REALLY LIKE THIS JOB AND I'M GONNA LOSE IT IF I DON'T FIND THAT CAT-- SEEING AS THIS IS ALL *YOUR* FAULT, YOU'RE GONNA HELP ME, YEAH?
W-WHAT? MY FAULT?!

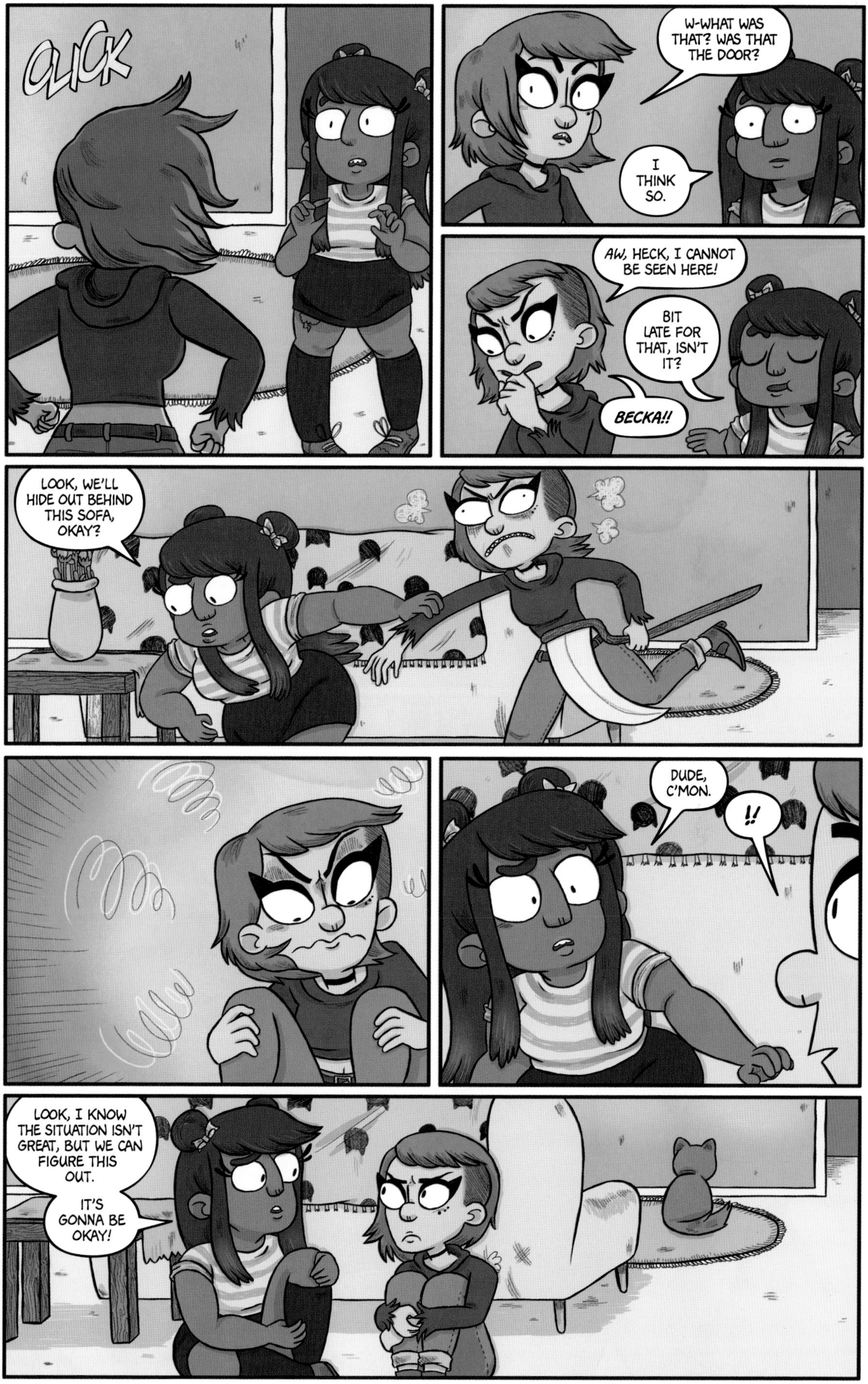
CLICK
W-WHAT WAS THAT? WAS THAT THE DOOR?
I THINK SO.
AW, HECK, I CANNOT BE SEEN HERE!
BIT LATE FOR THAT, ISN'T IT?
BECKA!!
LOOK, WE'LL HIDE OUT BEHIND THIS SOFA, OKAY?
DUDE, C'MON.
!!
LOOK, I KNOW THE SITUATION ISN'T GREAT, BUT WE CAN FIGURE THIS OUT.
IT'S GONNA BE OKAY!

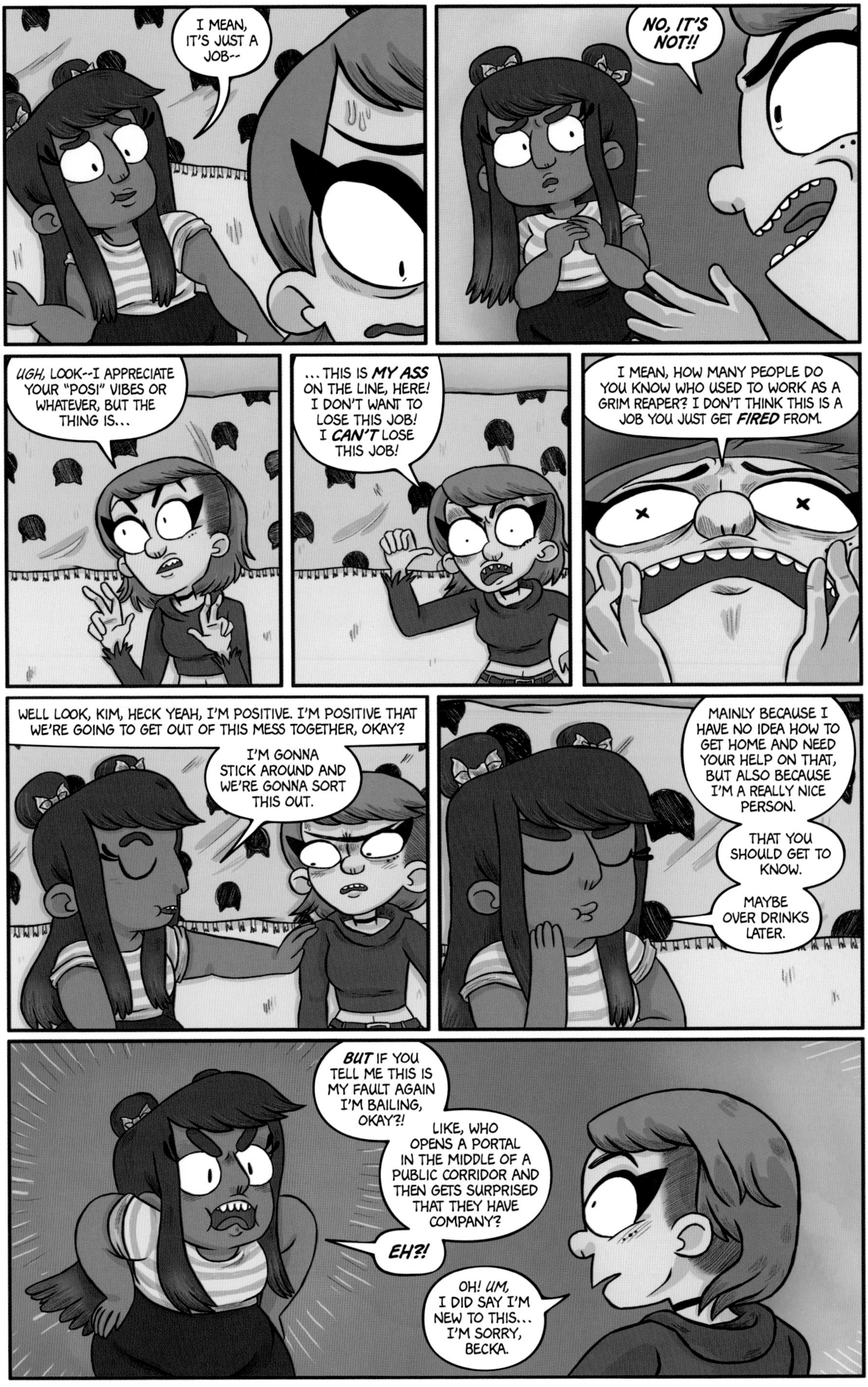
I MEAN, IT'S JUST A JOB--
NO, IT'S NOT!!
UGH, LOOK--I APPRECIATE YOUR "POSI" VIBES OR WHATEVER, BUT THE THING IS...
...THIS IS MY ASS ON THE LINE, HERE! I DON'T WANT TO LOSE THIS JOB! I CAN'T LOSE THIS JOB!
I MEAN, HOW MANY PEOPLE DO YOU KNOW WHO USED TO WORK AS A GRIM REAPER? I DON'T THINK THIS IS A JOB YOU JUST GET FIRED FROM.
WELL LOOK, KIM, HECK YEAH, I'M POSITIVE. I'M POSITIVE THAT WE'RE GOING TO GET OUT OF THIS MESS TOGETHER, OKAY?
I'M GONNA STICK AROUND AND WE'RE GONNA SORT THIS OUT.
MAINLY BECAUSE I HAVE NO IDEA HOW TO GET HOME AND NEED YOUR HELP ON THAT, BUT ALSO BECAUSE I'M A REALLY NICE PERSON.
THAT YOU SHOULD GET TO KNOW.
MAYBE OVER DRINKS LATER.
BUT IF YOU TELL ME THIS IS MY FAULT AGAIN I'M BAILING, OKAY?!
LIKE, WHO OPENS A PORTAL IN THE MIDDLE OF A PUBLIC CORRIDOR AND THEN GETS SURPRISED THAT THEY HAVE COMPANY?
EH?!
OH! UM, I DID SAY I'M NEW TO THIS... I'M SORRY, BECKA.

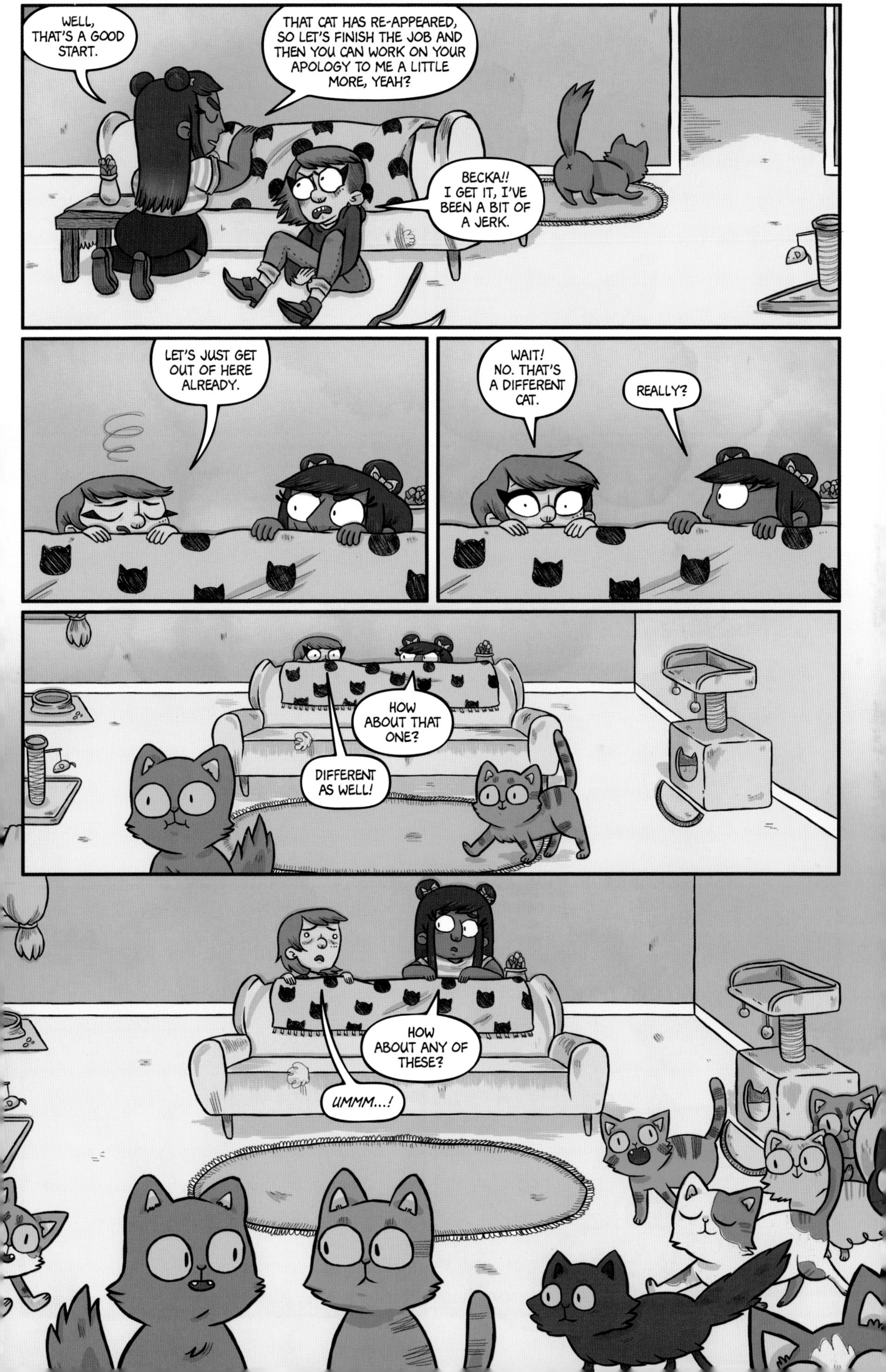
WELL, THAT'S A GOOD START.
THAT CAT HAS RE-APPEARED, SO LET'S FINISH THE JOB AND THEN YOU CAN WORK ON YOUR APOLOGY TO ME A LITTLE MORE, YEAH?
BECKA!! I GET IT, I'VE BEEN A BIT OF A JERK.
LET'S JUST GET OUT OF HERE ALREADY.
WAIT! NO. THAT'S A DIFFERENT CAT.
REALLY?
HOW ABOUT THAT ONE?
DIFFERENT AS WELL!
HOW ABOUT ANY OF THESE?
UMMM...!

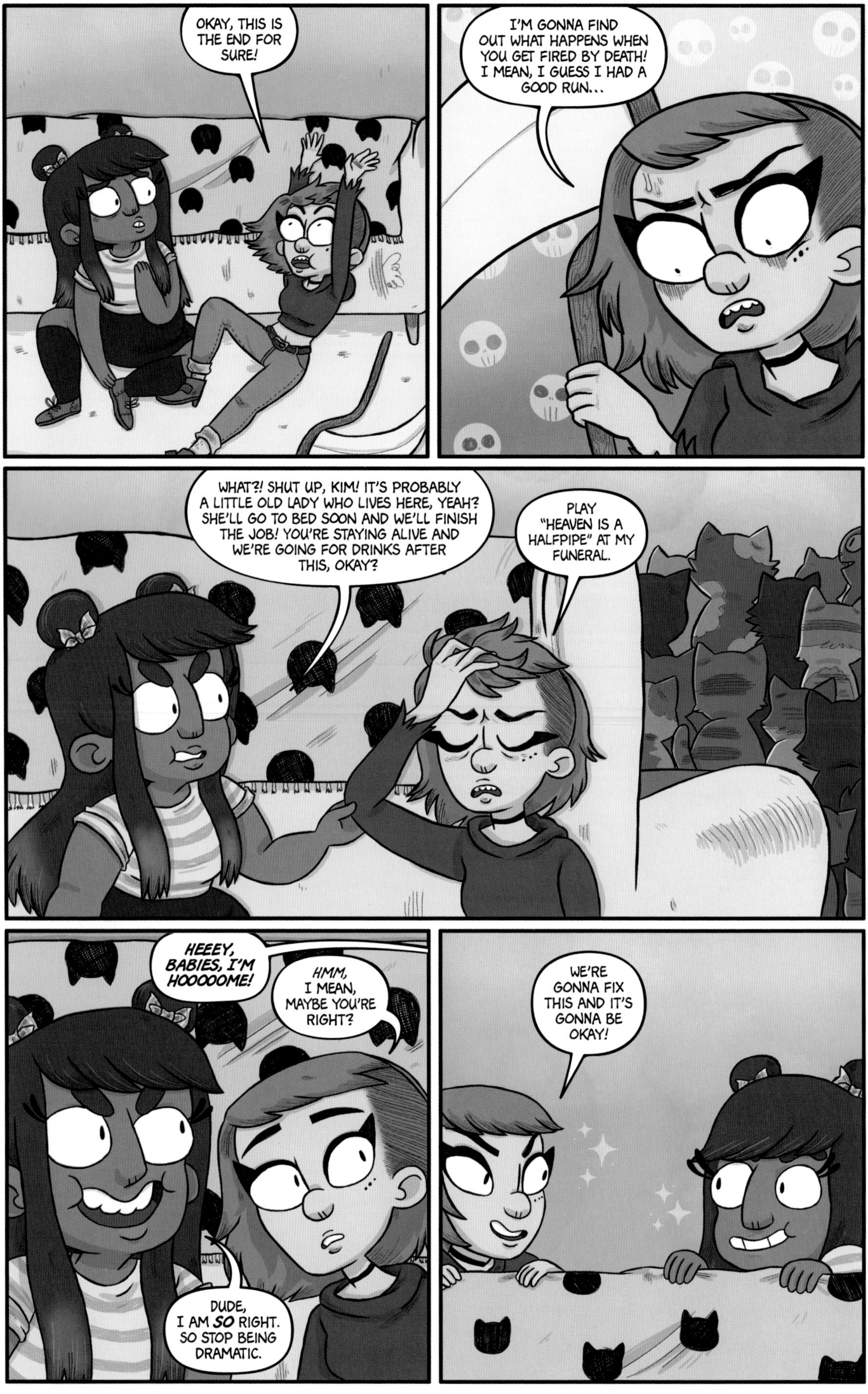
OKAY, THIS IS THE END FOR SURE!
I'M GONNA FIND OUT WHAT HAPPENS WHEN YOU GET FIRED BY DEATH! I MEAN, I GUESS I HAD A GOOD RUN...
WHAT?! SHUT UP, KIM! IT'S PROBABLY A LITTLE OLD LADY WHO LIVES HERE, YEAH? SHE'LL GO TO BED SOON AND WE'LL FINISH THE JOB! YOU'RE STAYING ALIVE AND WE'RE GOING FOR DRINKS AFTER THIS, OKAY?
PLAY "HEAVEN IS A HALFPIPE" AT MY FUNERAL.
HMM, I MEAN, MAYBE YOU'RE RIGHT?
DUDE, I AM *SO* RIGHT. SO STOP BEING DRAMATIC.
HEEEY, BABIES, I'M HOOOOOME!
WE'RE GONNA FIX THIS AND IT'S GONNA BE OKAY!

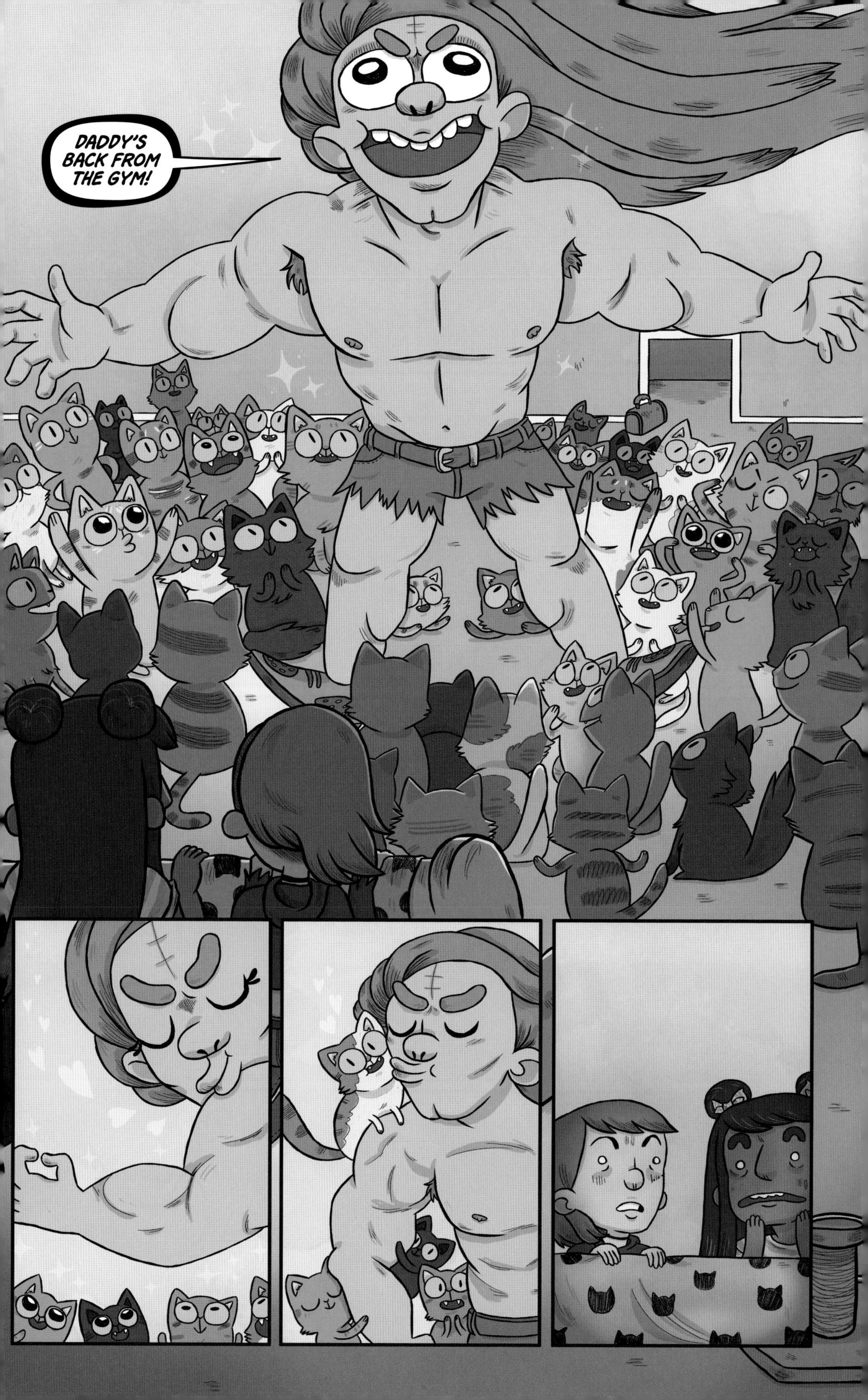
DADDY'S BACK FROM THE GYM!

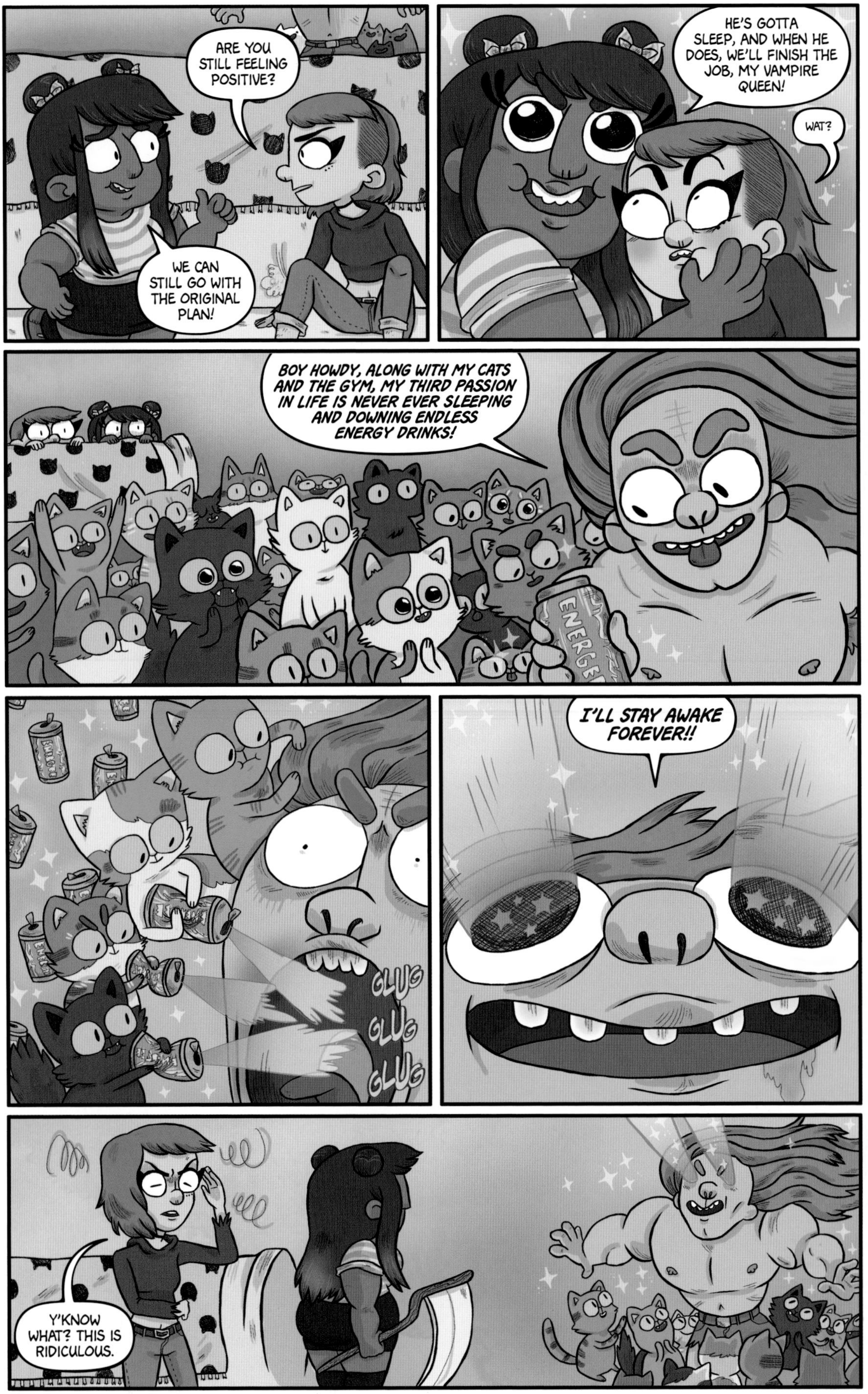
ARE YOU STILL FEELING POSITIVE?
WE CAN STILL GO WITH THE ORIGINAL PLAN!
HE'S GOTTA SLEEP, AND WHEN HE DOES, WE'LL FINISH THE JOB, MY VAMPIRE QUEEN!
WAT?
BOY HOWDY, ALONG WITH MY CATS AND THE GYM, MY THIRD PASSION IN LIFE IS NEVER EVER SLEEPING AND DOWNING ENDLESS ENERGY DRINKS!
ENERGY
GLUG
GLUG
GLUG
I'LL STAY AWAKE FOREVER!!
Y'KNOW WHAT? THIS IS RIDICULOUS.

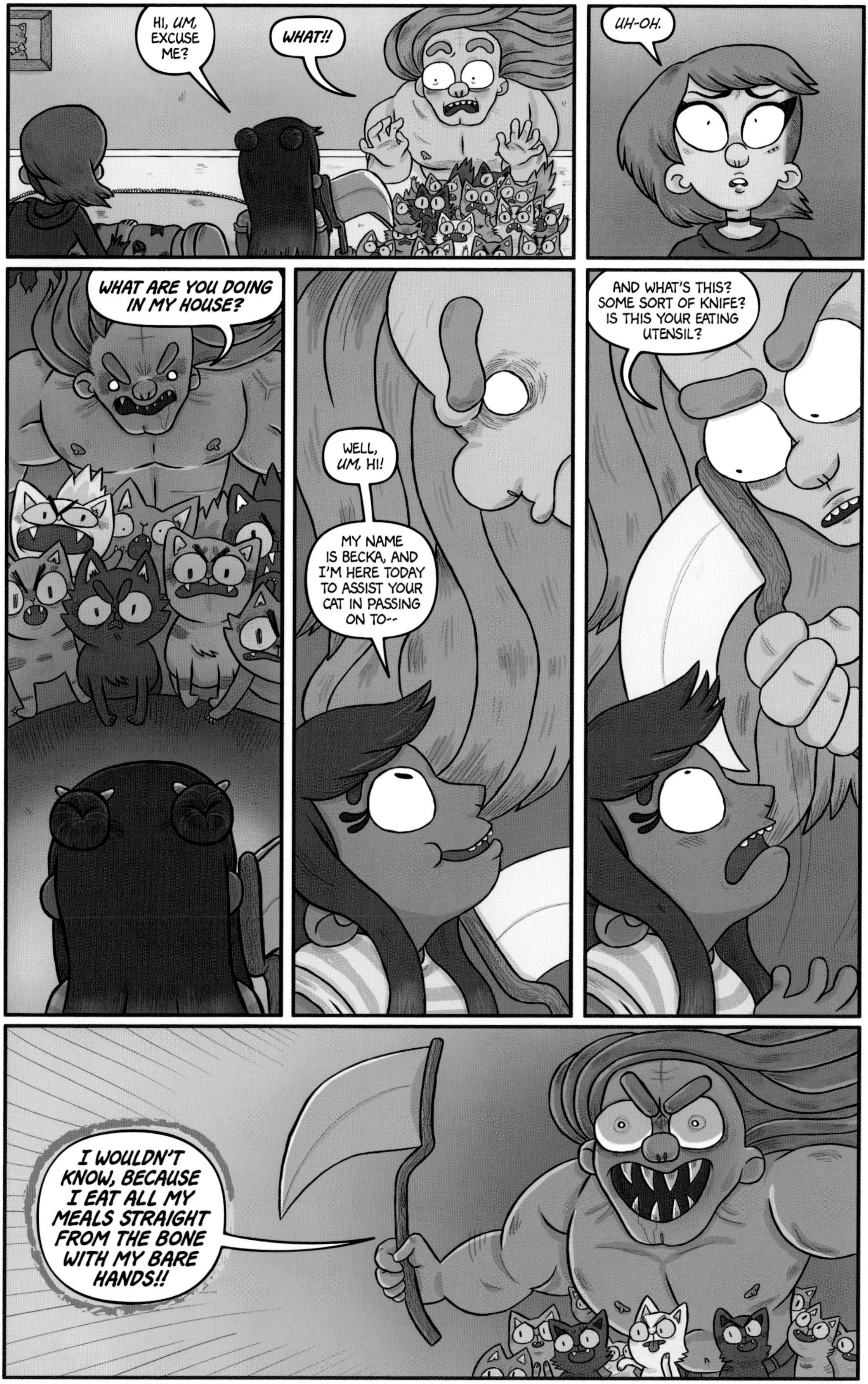
HI, UM, EXCUSE ME?
WHAT!!
UH-OH.
WHAT ARE YOU DOING IN MY HOUSE?
WELL, UM, HI!
MY NAME IS BECKA, AND I'M HERE TODAY TO ASSIST YOUR CAT IN PASSING ON TO--
AND WHAT'S THIS? SOME SORT OF KNIFE? IS THIS YOUR EATING UTENSIL?
I WOULDN'T KNOW, BECAUSE I EAT ALL MY MEALS STRAIGHT FROM THE BONE WITH MY BARE HANDS!!

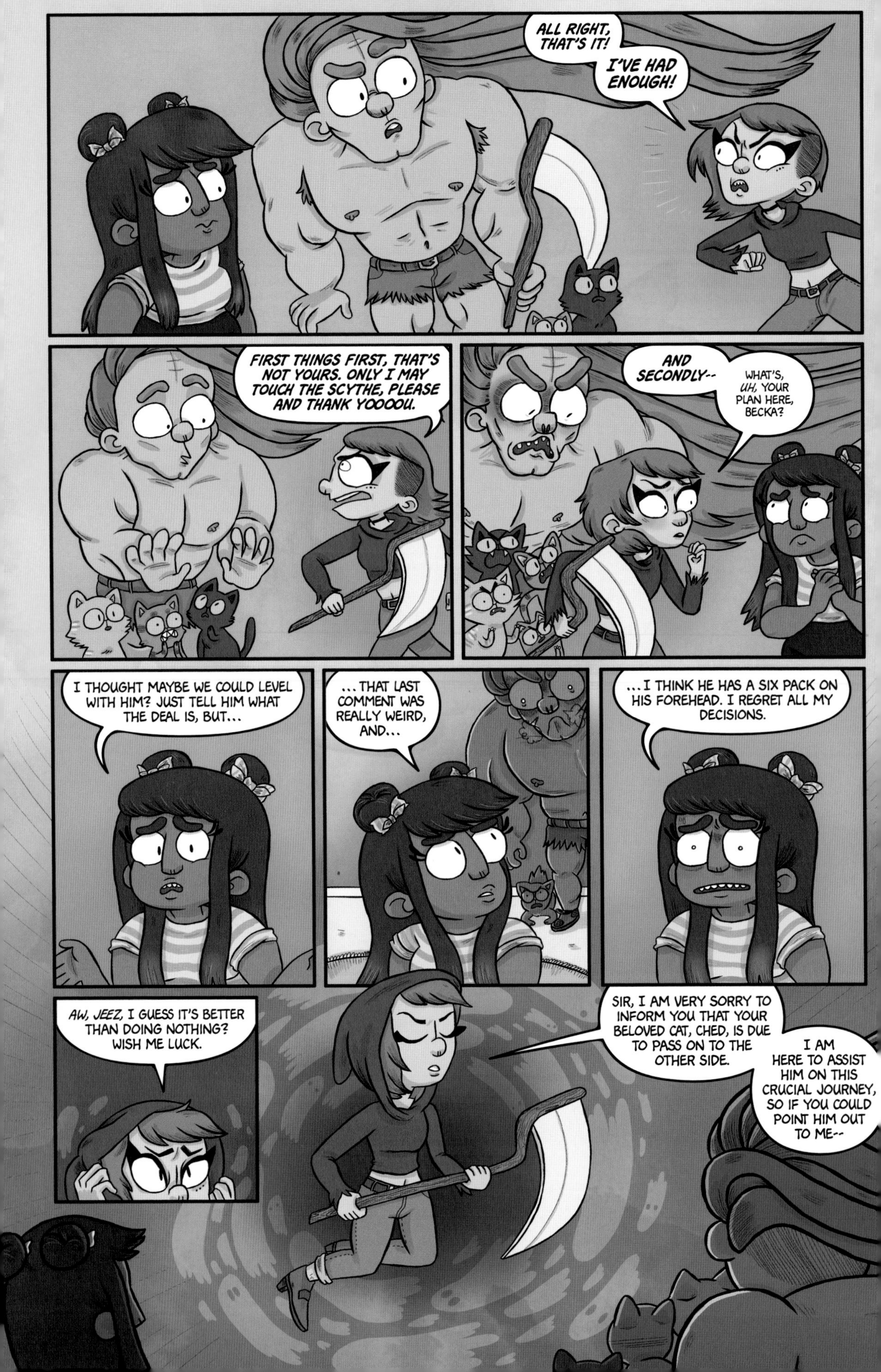
ALL RIGHT, THAT'S IT!
I'VE HAD ENOUGH!
FIRST THINGS FIRST, THAT'S NOT YOURS. ONLY I MAY TOUCH THE SCYTHE, PLEASE AND THANK YOOOOU.
AND SECONDLY--
WHAT'S, UH, YOUR PLAN HERE, BECKA?
I THOUGHT MAYBE WE COULD LEVEL WITH HIM? JUST TELL HIM WHAT THE DEAL IS, BUT...
...THAT LAST COMMENT WAS REALLY WEIRD, AND...
...I THINK HE HAS A SIX PACK ON HIS FOREHEAD. I REGRET ALL MY DECISIONS.
AW, JEEZ, I GUESS IT'S BETTER THAN DOING NOTHING? WISH ME LUCK.
SIR, I AM VERY SORRY TO INFORM YOU THAT YOUR BELOVED CAT, CHED, IS DUE TO PASS ON TO THE OTHER SIDE.
I AM HERE TO ASSIST HIM ON THIS CRUCIAL JOURNEY, SO IF YOU COULD POINT HIM OUT TO ME--

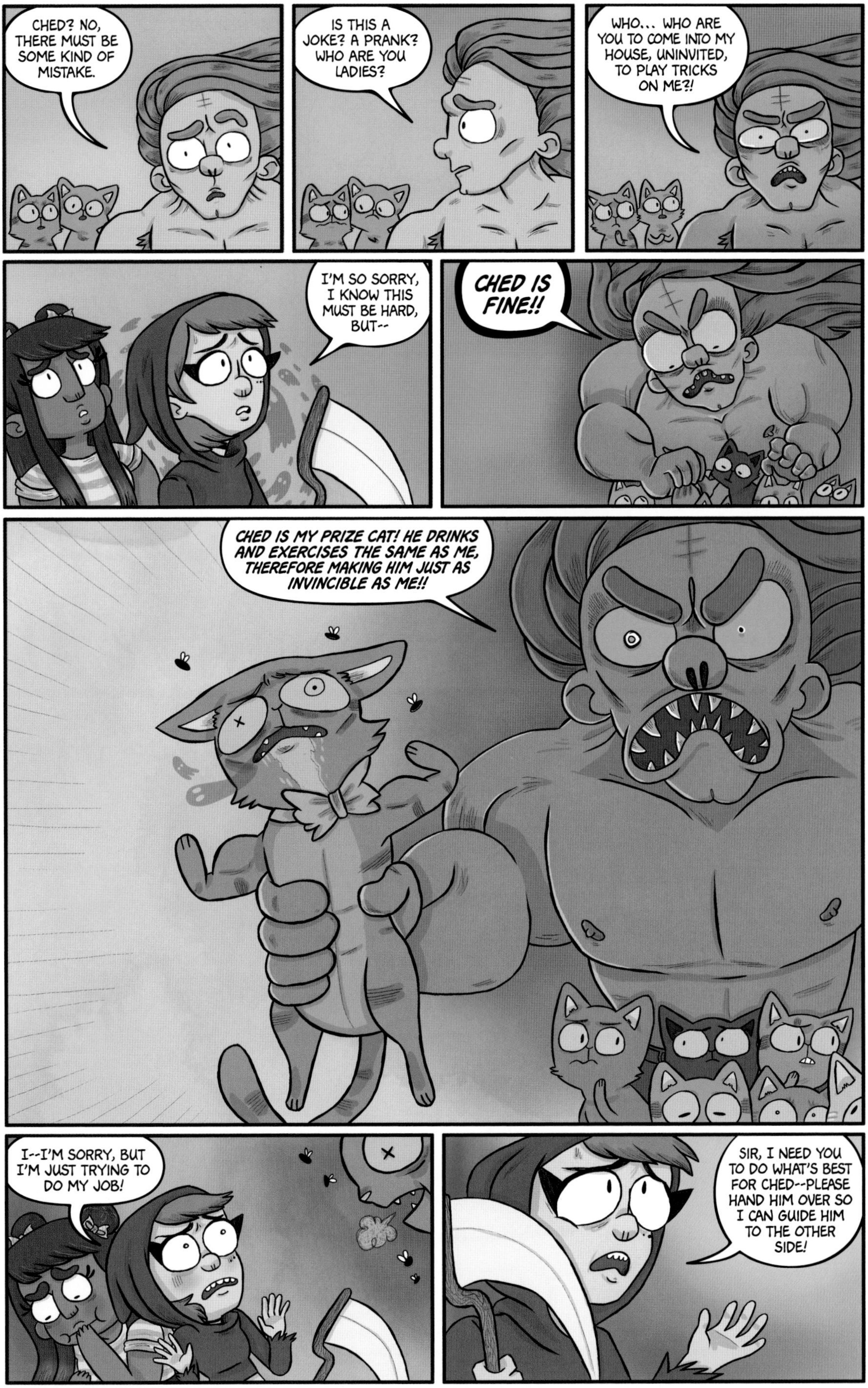
CHED? NO, THERE MUST BE SOME KIND OF MISTAKE.
IS THIS A JOKE? A PRANK? WHO ARE YOU LADIES?
WHO... WHO ARE YOU TO COME INTO MY HOUSE, UNINVITED, TO PLAY TRICKS ON ME?!
I'M SO SORRY, I KNOW THIS MUST BE HARD, BUT--
CHED IS FINE!!
CHED IS MY PRIZE CAT! HE DRINKS AND EXERCISES THE SAME AS ME, THEREFORE MAKING HIM JUST AS INVINCIBLE AS ME!!
I--I'M SORRY, BUT I'M JUST TRYING TO DO MY JOB!
SIR, I NEED YOU TO DO WHAT'S BEST FOR CHED--PLEASE HAND HIM OVER SO I CAN GUIDE HIM TO THE OTHER SIDE!

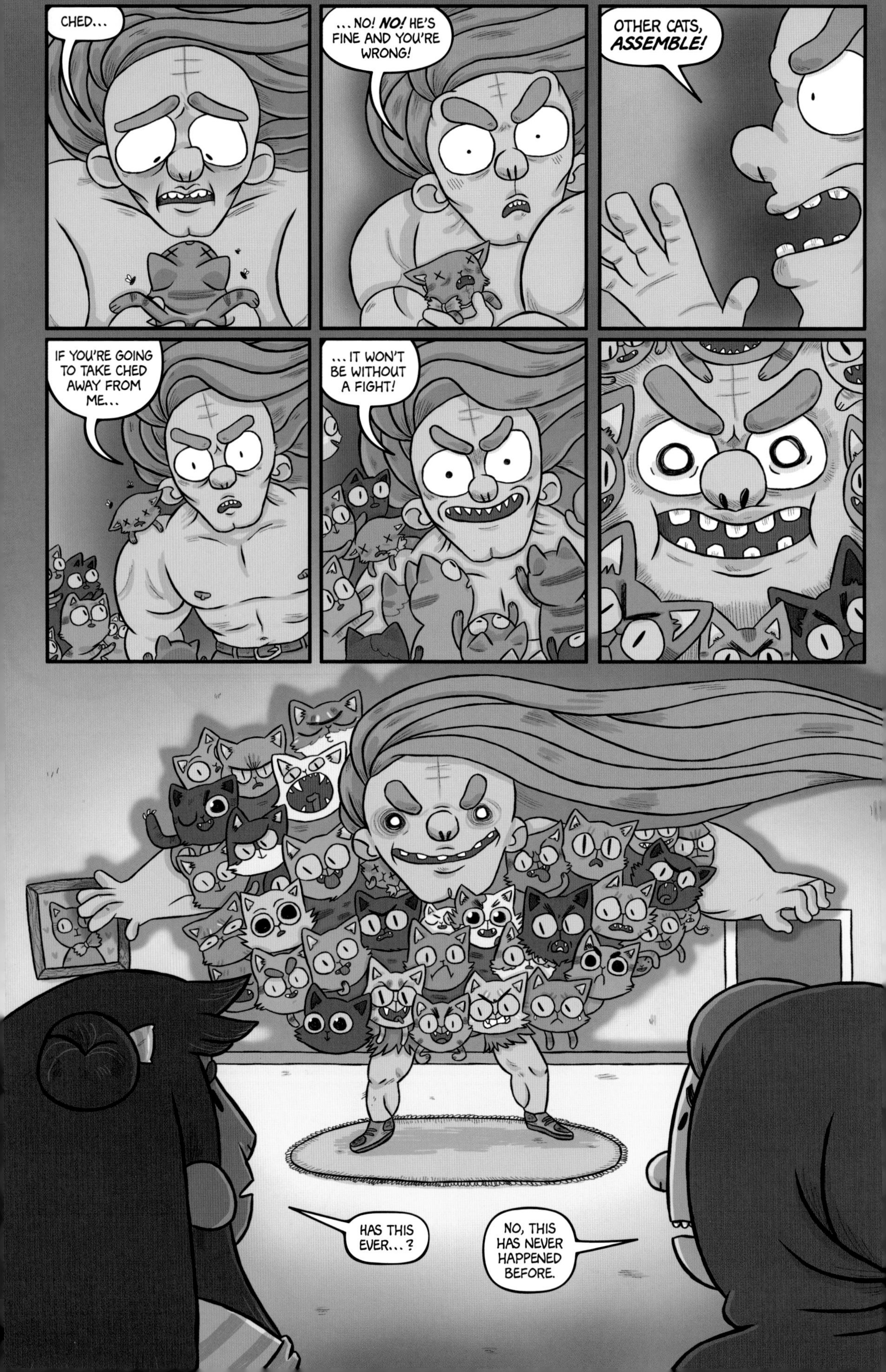
CHED...
...NO! NO! HE'S FINE AND YOU'RE WRONG!
OTHER CATS, ASSEMBLE!
IF YOU'RE GOING TO TAKE CHED AWAY FROM ME...
...IT WON'T BE WITHOUT A FIGHT!
HAS THIS EVER...?
NO, THIS HAS NEVER HAPPENED BEFORE.

CHAPTER TWO

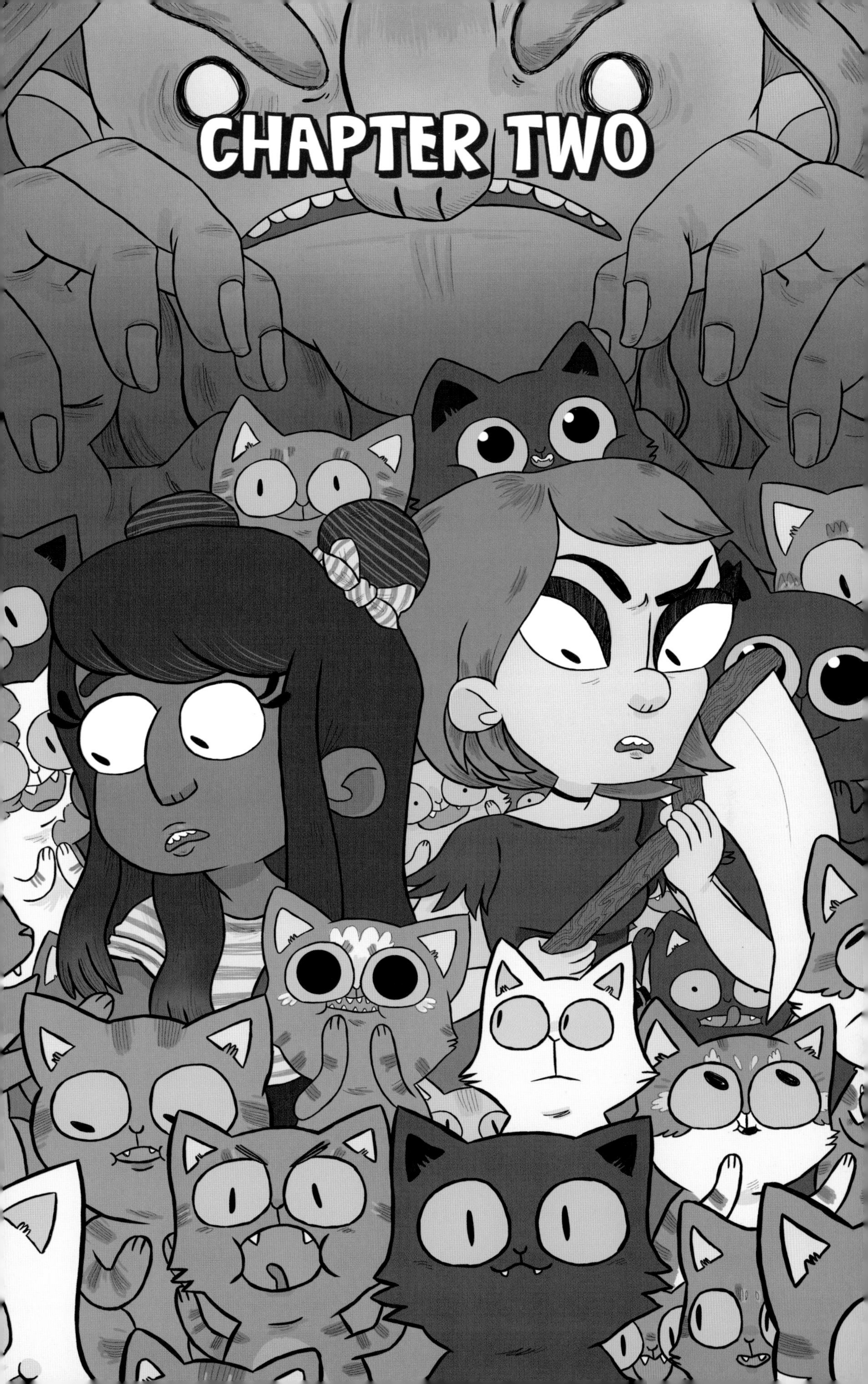

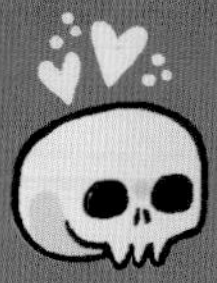

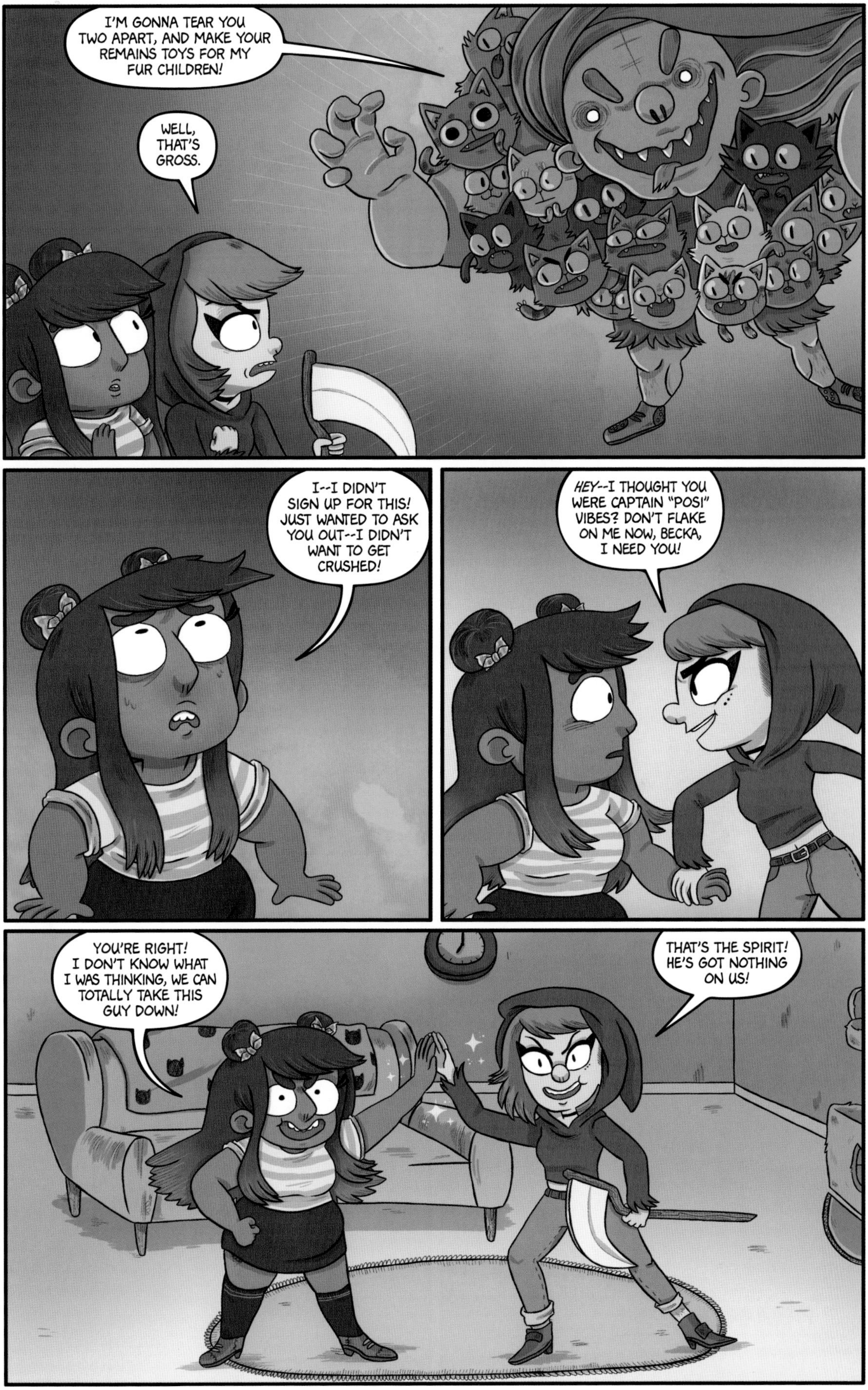
I'M GONNA TEAR YOU TWO APART, AND MAKE YOUR REMAINS TOYS FOR MY FUR CHILDREN!
WELL, THAT'S GROSS.
I--I DIDN'T SIGN UP FOR THIS! JUST WANTED TO ASK YOU OUT--I DIDN'T WANT TO GET CRUSHED!
HEY--I THOUGHT YOU WERE CAPTAIN "POSI" VIBES? DON'T FLAKE ON ME NOW, BECKA, I NEED YOU!
YOU'RE RIGHT! I DON'T KNOW WHAT I WAS THINKING, WE CAN TOTALLY TAKE THIS GUY DOWN!
THAT'S THE SPIRIT! HE'S GOT NOTHING ON US!

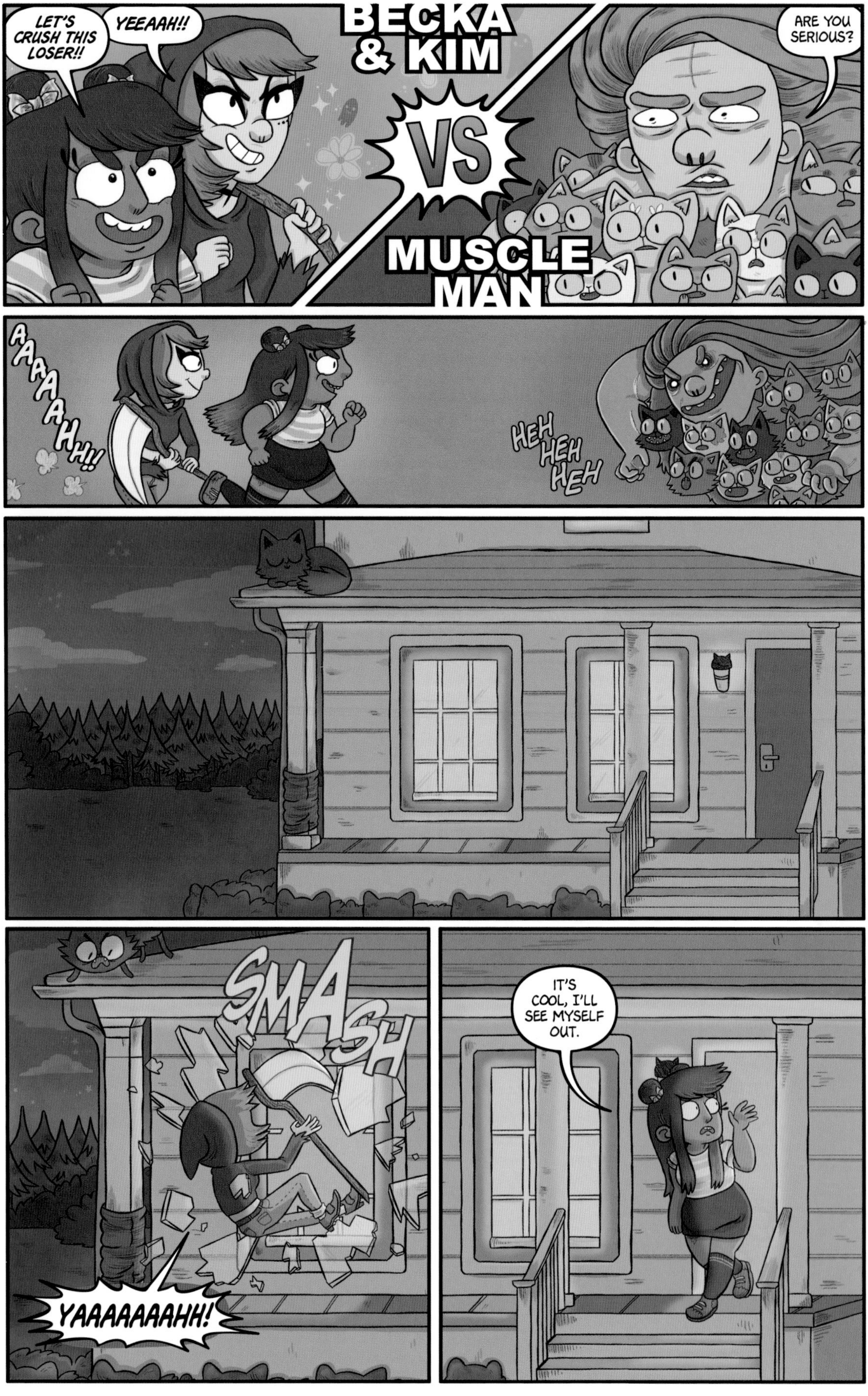
BECKA & KIM
VS
MUSCLE MAN
LET'S CRUSH THIS LOSER!!
YEEAAH!!
ARE YOU SERIOUS?
AAAAAAHH!!
HEH HEH HEH
SMASH
YAAAAAAAHH!
IT'S COOL, I'LL SEE MYSELF OUT.

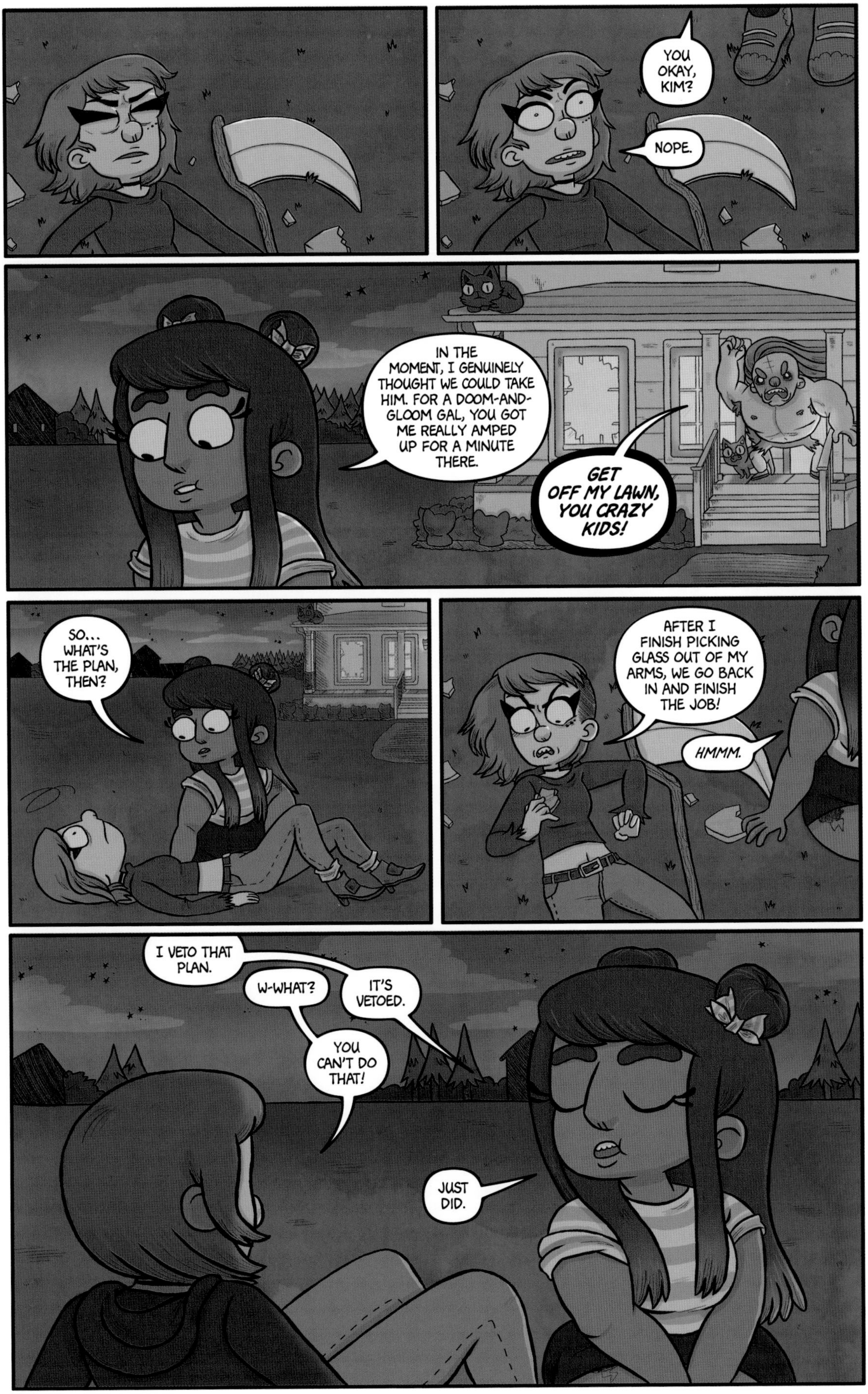
YOU OKAY, KIM?
NOPE.
IN THE MOMENT, I GENUINELY THOUGHT WE COULD TAKE HIM. FOR A DOOM-AND-GLOOM GAL, YOU GOT ME REALLY AMPED UP FOR A MINUTE THERE.
GET OFF MY LAWN, YOU CRAZY KIDS!
SO... WHAT'S THE PLAN, THEN?
AFTER I FINISH PICKING GLASS OUT OF MY ARMS, WE GO BACK IN AND FINISH THE JOB!
HMMM.
I VETO THAT PLAN.
W-WHAT?
IT'S VETOED.
YOU CAN'T DO THAT!
JUST DID.

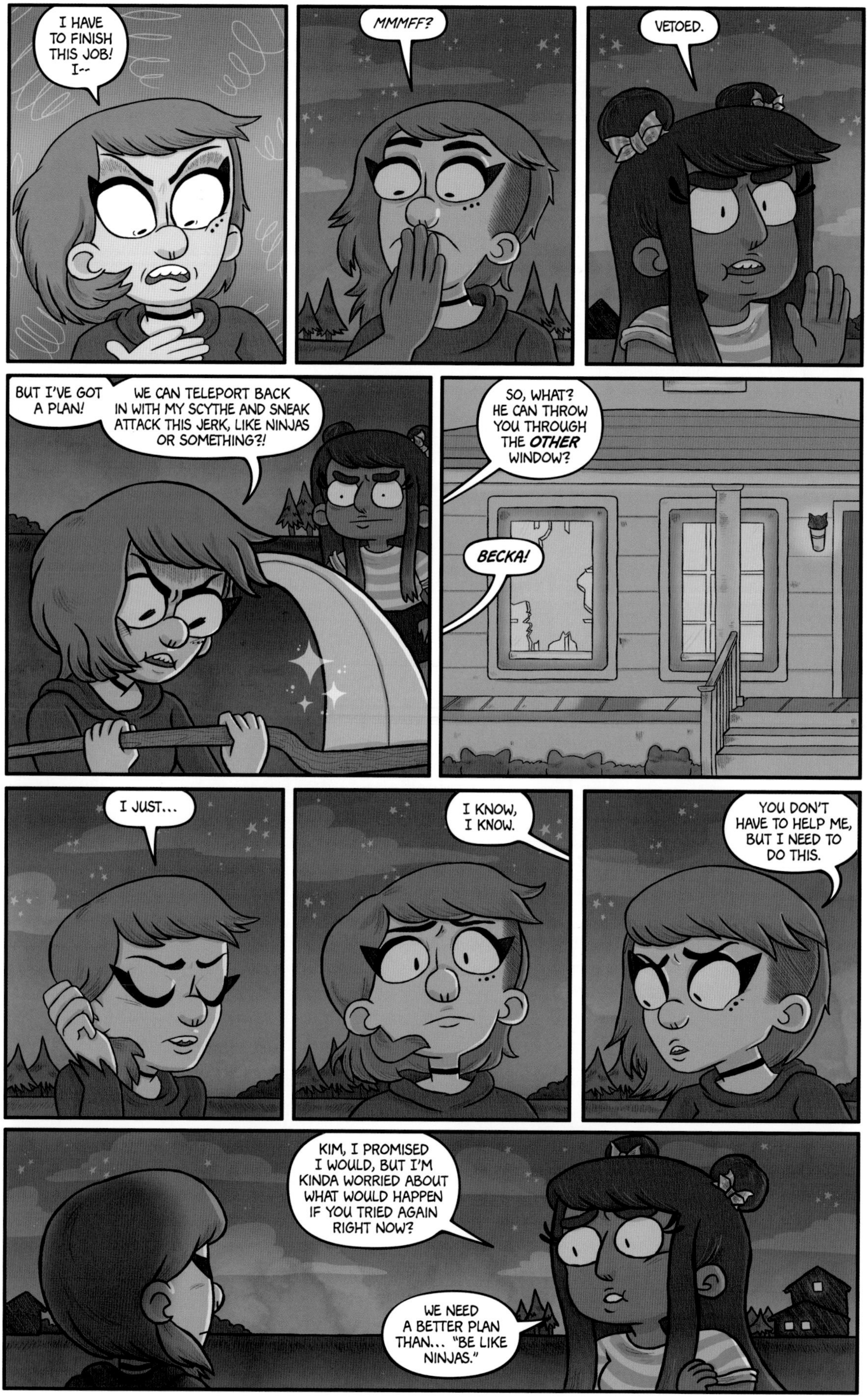

I HAVE TO FINISH THIS JOB! I--
MMMFF?
VETOED.
BUT I'VE GOT A PLAN!
WE CAN TELEPORT BACK IN WITH MY SCYTHE AND SNEAK ATTACK THIS JERK, LIKE NINJAS OR SOMETHING?!
SO, WHAT? HE CAN THROW YOU THROUGH THE OTHER WINDOW?
BECKA!
I JUST...
I KNOW, I KNOW.
YOU DON'T HAVE TO HELP ME, BUT I NEED TO DO THIS.
KIM, I PROMISED I WOULD, BUT I'M KINDA WORRIED ABOUT WHAT WOULD HAPPEN IF YOU TRIED AGAIN RIGHT NOW?
WE NEED A BETTER PLAN THAN... "BE LIKE NINJAS."

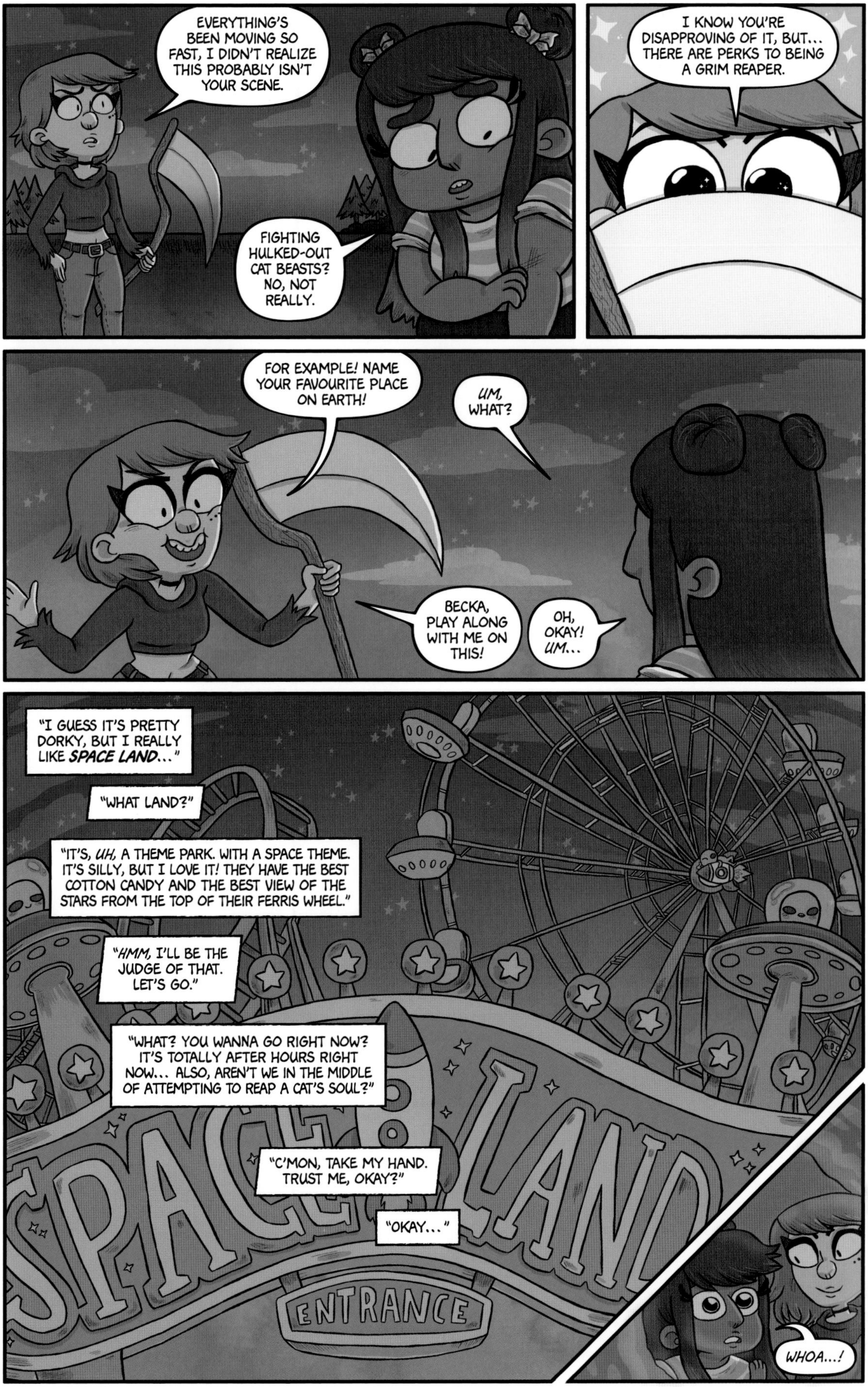
EVERYTHING'S BEEN MOVING SO FAST, I DIDN'T REALIZE THIS PROBABLY ISN'T YOUR SCENE.
FIGHTING HULKED-OUT CAT BEASTS? NO, NOT REALLY.
I KNOW YOU'RE DISAPPROVING OF IT, BUT... THERE ARE PERKS TO BEING A GRIM REAPER.
FOR EXAMPLE! NAME YOUR FAVOURITE PLACE ON EARTH!
UM, WHAT?
BECKA, PLAY ALONG WITH ME ON THIS!
OH, OKAY! UM...
"I GUESS IT'S PRETTY DORKY, BUT I REALLY LIKE SPACE LAND..."
"WHAT LAND?"
"IT'S, UH, A THEME PARK. WITH A SPACE THEME. IT'S SILLY, BUT I LOVE IT! THEY HAVE THE BEST COTTON CANDY AND THE BEST VIEW OF THE STARS FROM THE TOP OF THEIR FERRIS WHEEL."
"HMM, I'LL BE THE JUDGE OF THAT. LET'S GO."
"WHAT? YOU WANNA GO RIGHT NOW? IT'S TOTALLY AFTER HOURS RIGHT NOW... ALSO, AREN'T WE IN THE MIDDLE OF ATTEMPTING TO REAP A CAT'S SOUL?"
"C'MON, TAKE MY HAND. TRUST ME, OKAY?"
"OKAY..."
SPACE LAND
ENTRANCE
WHOA...!

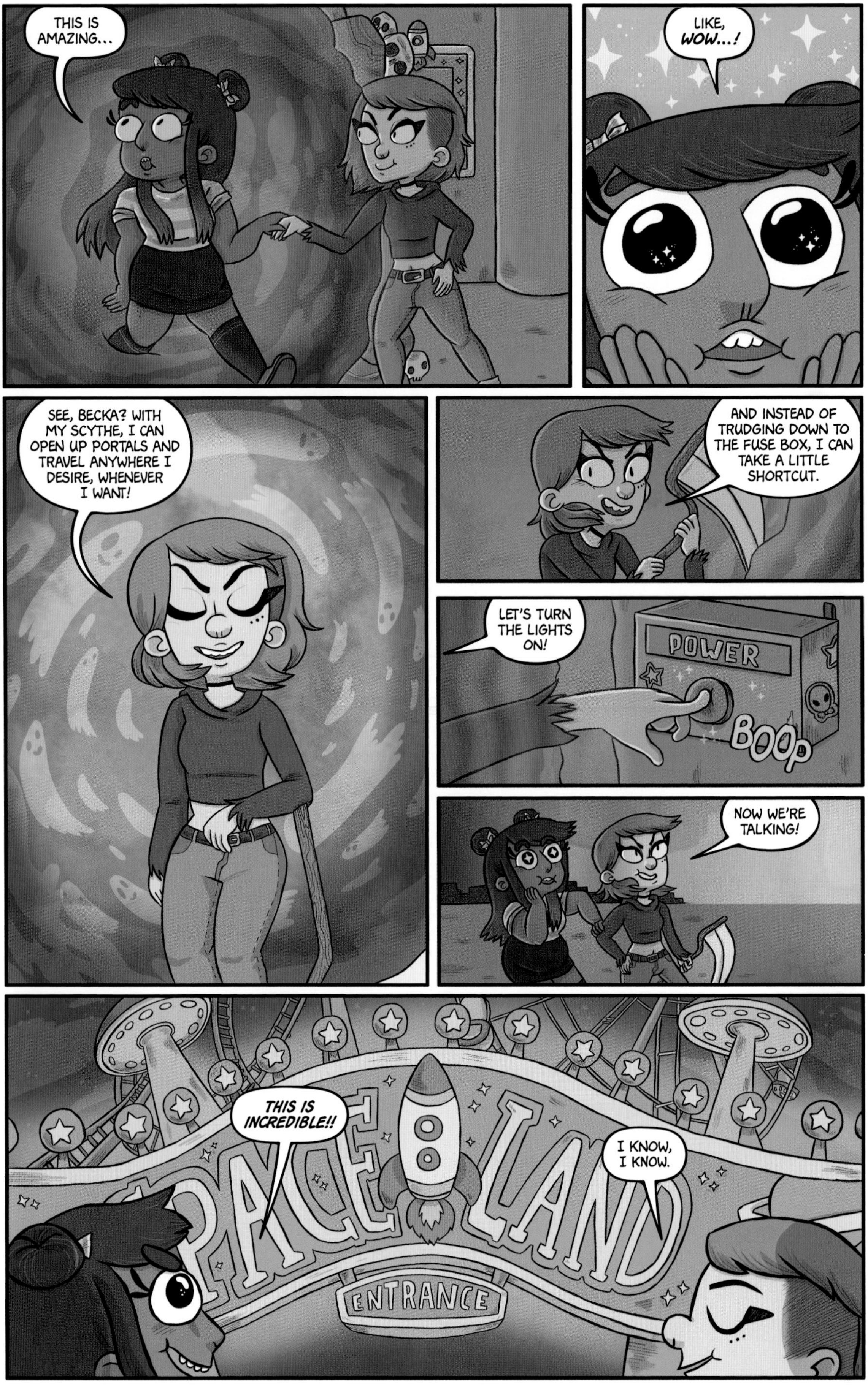
THIS IS AMAZING...
LIKE, WOW...!
SEE, BECKA? WITH MY SCYTHE, I CAN OPEN UP PORTALS AND TRAVEL ANYWHERE I DESIRE, WHENEVER I WANT!
AND INSTEAD OF TRUDGING DOWN TO THE FUSE BOX, I CAN TAKE A LITTLE SHORTCUT.
LET'S TURN THE LIGHTS ON!
POWER
BOOP
NOW WE'RE TALKING!
THIS IS INCREDIBLE!!
I KNOW, I KNOW.
ENTRANCE

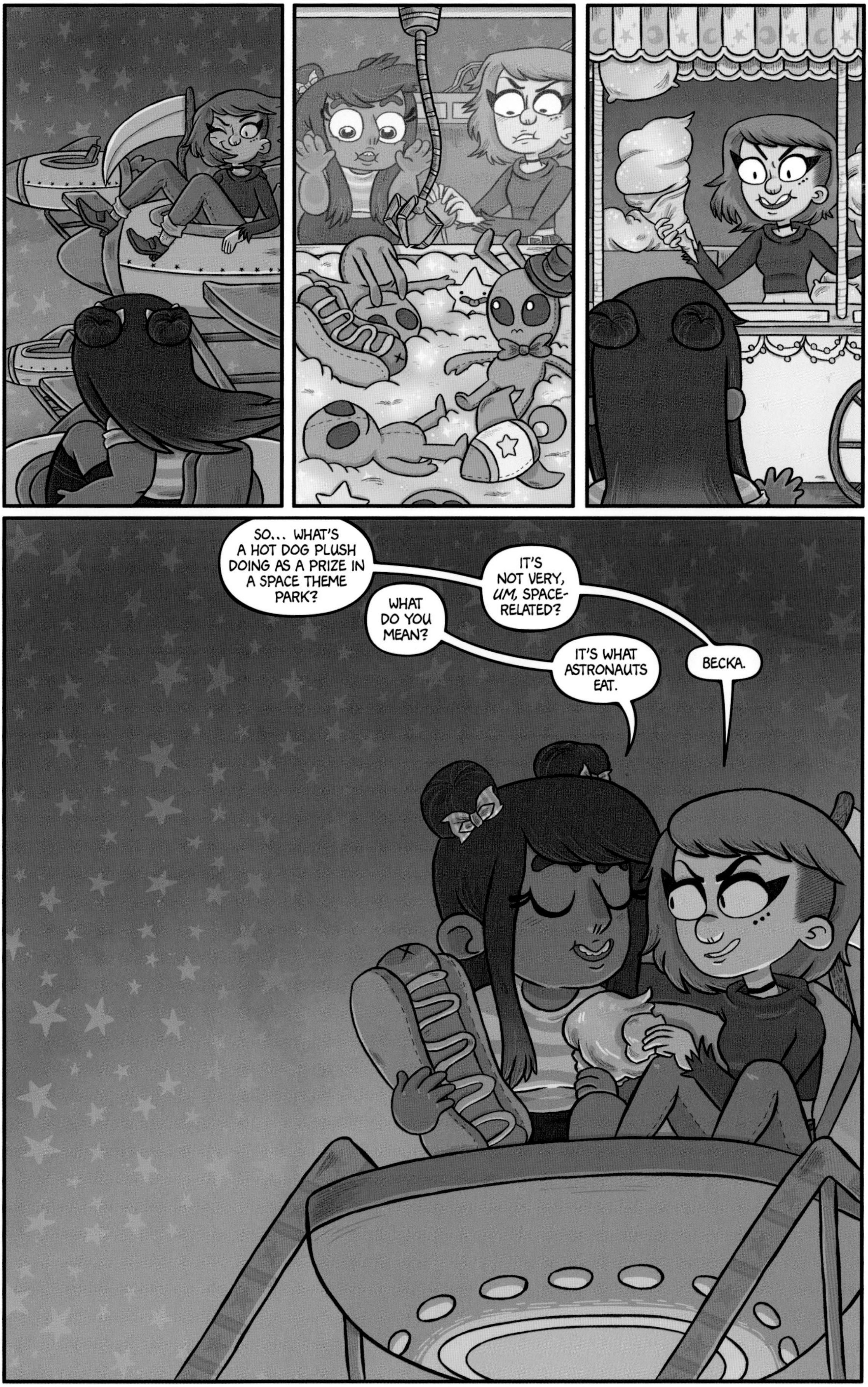
SO... WHAT'S A HOT DOG PLUSH DOING AS A PRIZE IN A SPACE THEME PARK?
WHAT DO YOU MEAN?
IT'S NOT VERY, UM, SPACE-RELATED?
IT'S WHAT ASTRONAUTS EAT.
BECKA.

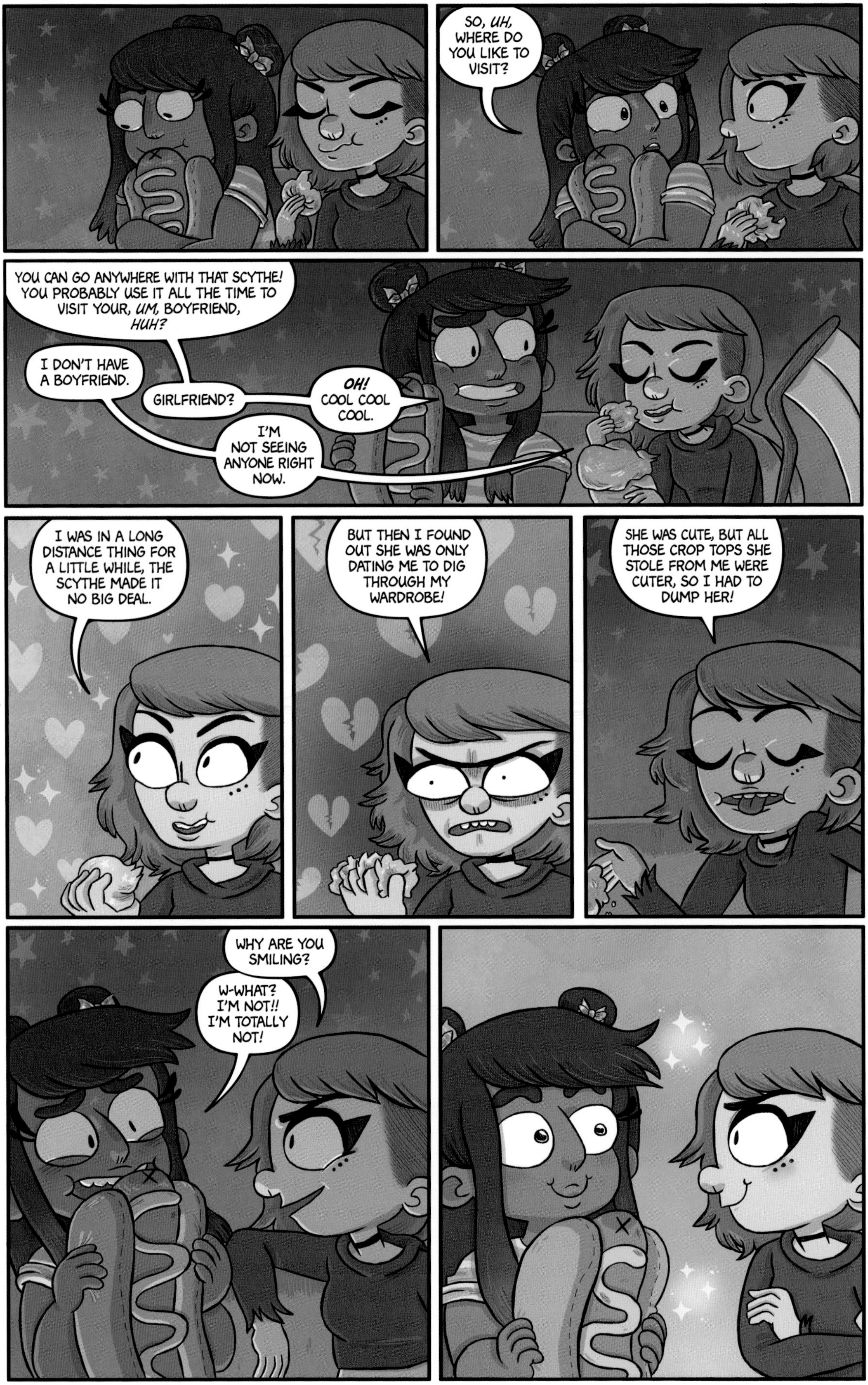

SO, UH, WHERE DO YOU LIKE TO VISIT?
YOU CAN GO ANYWHERE WITH THAT SCYTHE! YOU PROBABLY USE IT ALL THE TIME TO VISIT YOUR, UM, BOYFRIEND, HUH?
I DON'T HAVE A BOYFRIEND.
GIRLFRIEND?
OH! COOL COOL COOL.
I'M NOT SEEING ANYONE RIGHT NOW.
I WAS IN A LONG DISTANCE THING FOR A LITTLE WHILE, THE SCYTHE MADE IT NO BIG DEAL.
BUT THEN I FOUND OUT SHE WAS ONLY DATING ME TO DIG THROUGH MY WARDROBE!
SHE WAS CUTE, BUT ALL THOSE CROP TOPS SHE STOLE FROM ME WERE CUTER, SO I HAD TO DUMP HER!
WHY ARE YOU SMILING?
W-WHAT? I'M NOT!! I'M TOTALLY NOT!

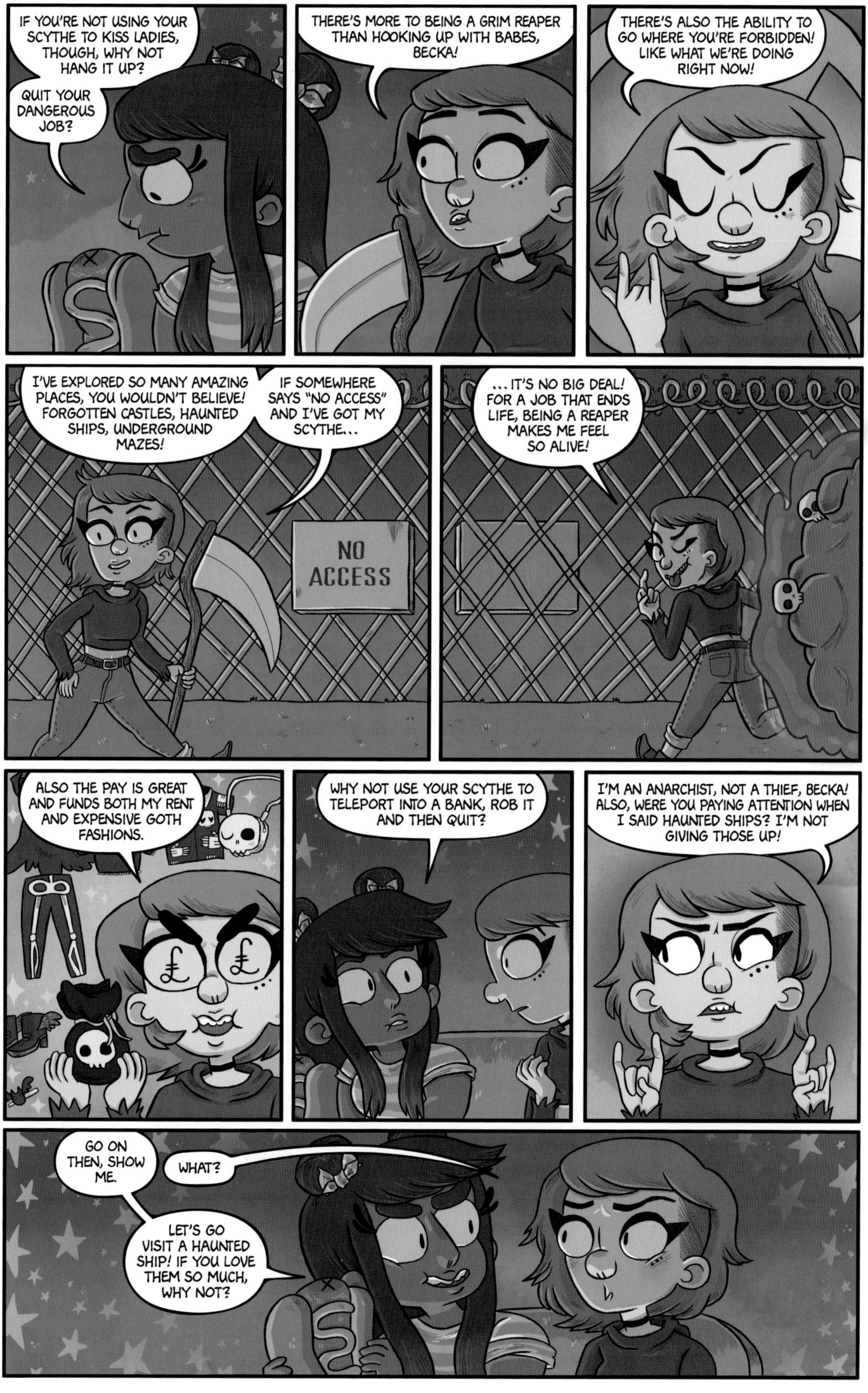
IF YOU'RE NOT USING YOUR SCYTHE TO KISS LADIES, THOUGH, WHY NOT HANG IT UP?
QUIT YOUR DANGEROUS JOB?
THERE'S MORE TO BEING A GRIM REAPER THAN HOOKING UP WITH BABES, BECKA!
THERE'S ALSO THE ABILITY TO GO WHERE YOU'RE FORBIDDEN! LIKE WHAT WE'RE DOING RIGHT NOW!
I'VE EXPLORED SO MANY AMAZING PLACES, YOU WOULDN'T BELIEVE! FORGOTTEN CASTLES, HAUNTED SHIPS, UNDERGROUND MAZES!
IF SOMEWHERE SAYS "NO ACCESS" AND I'VE GOT MY SCYTHE...
NO ACCESS
...IT'S NO BIG DEAL! FOR A JOB THAT ENDS LIFE, BEING A REAPER MAKES ME FEEL SO ALIVE!
ALSO THE PAY IS GREAT AND FUNDS BOTH MY RENT AND EXPENSIVE GOTH FASHIONS.
WHY NOT USE YOUR SCYTHE TO TELEPORT INTO A BANK, ROB IT AND THEN QUIT?
I'M AN ANARCHIST, NOT A THIEF, BECKA! ALSO, WERE YOU PAYING ATTENTION WHEN I SAID HAUNTED SHIPS? I'M NOT GIVING THOSE UP!
GO ON THEN, SHOW ME.
WHAT?
LET'S GO VISIT A HAUNTED SHIP! IF YOU LOVE THEM SO MUCH, WHY NOT?

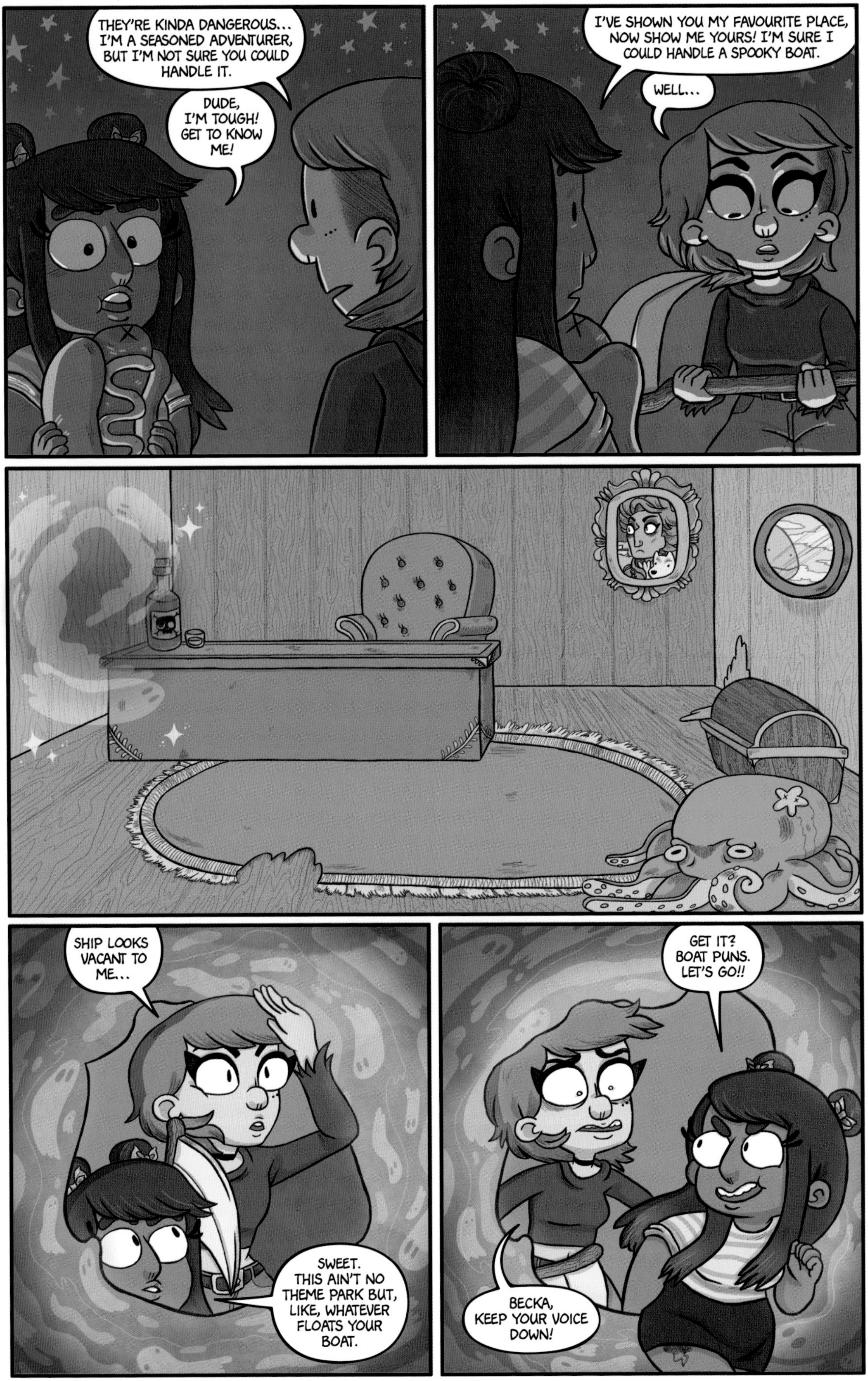
THEY'RE KINDA DANGEROUS... I'M A SEASONED ADVENTURER, BUT I'M NOT SURE YOU COULD HANDLE IT.
DUDE, I'M TOUGH! GET TO KNOW ME!
I'VE SHOWN YOU MY FAVOURITE PLACE, NOW SHOW ME YOURS! I'M SURE I COULD HANDLE A SPOOKY BOAT.
WELL...
SHIP LOOKS VACANT TO ME...
SWEET. THIS AIN'T NO THEME PARK BUT, LIKE, WHATEVER FLOATS YOUR BOAT.
GET IT? BOAT PUNS. LET'S GO!!
BECKA, KEEP YOUR VOICE DOWN!

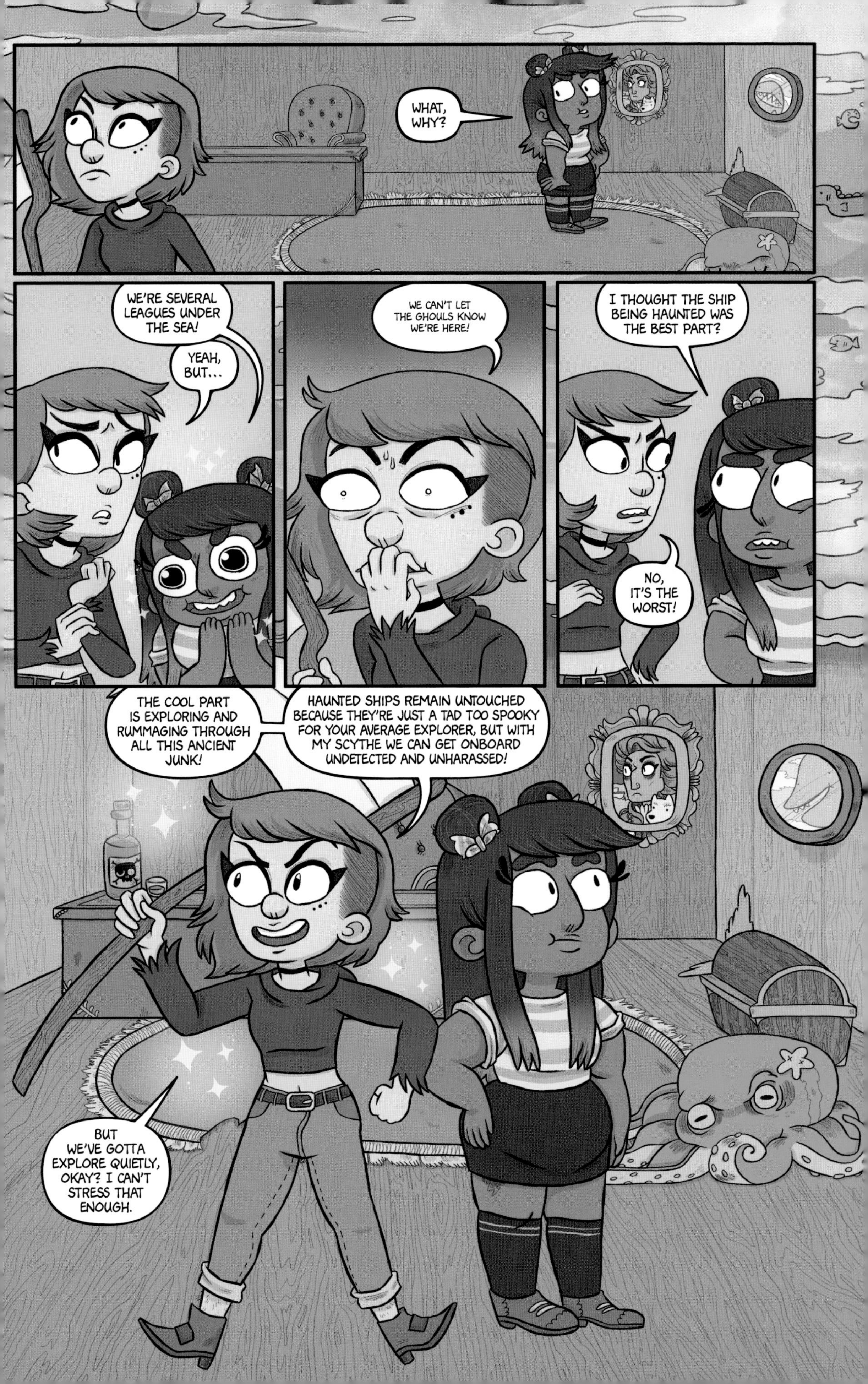
WHAT, WHY?
WE'RE SEVERAL LEAGUES UNDER THE SEA!
YEAH, BUT...
WE CAN'T LET THE GHOULS KNOW WE'RE HERE!
I THOUGHT THE SHIP BEING HAUNTED WAS THE BEST PART?
NO, IT'S THE WORST!
THE COOL PART IS EXPLORING AND RUMMAGING THROUGH ALL THIS ANCIENT JUNK!
HAUNTED SHIPS REMAIN UNTOUCHED BECAUSE THEY'RE JUST A TAD TOO SPOOKY FOR YOUR AVERAGE EXPLORER, BUT WITH MY SCYTHE WE CAN GET ONBOARD UNDETECTED AND UNHARASSED!
BUT WE'VE GOTTA EXPLORE QUIETLY, OKAY? I CAN'T STRESS THAT ENOUGH.

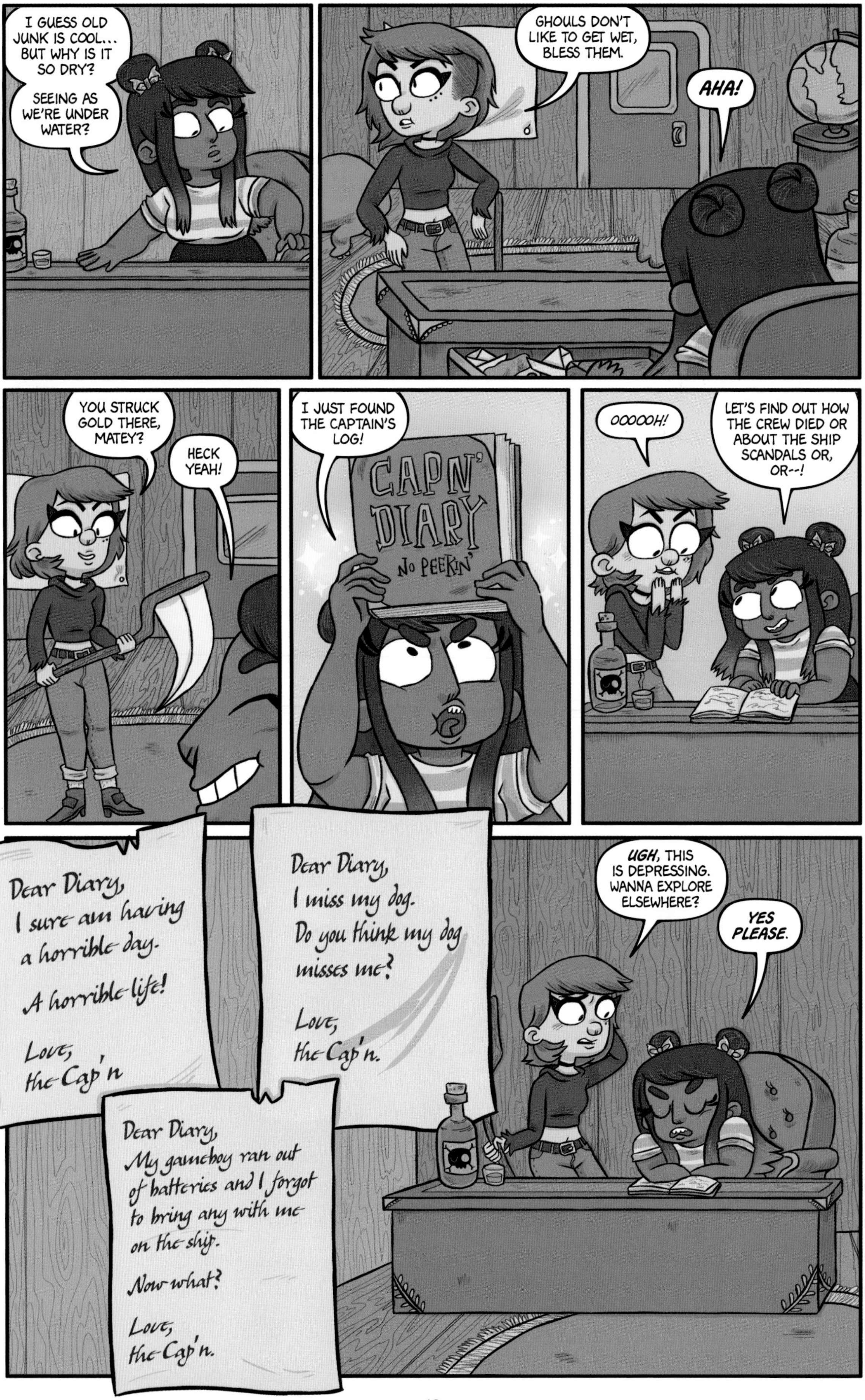
I GUESS OLD JUNK IS COOL... BUT WHY IS IT SO DRY?
SEEING AS WE'RE UNDER WATER?
GHOULS DON'T LIKE TO GET WET, BLESS THEM.
AHA!
YOU STRUCK GOLD THERE, MATEY?
HECK YEAH!
I JUST FOUND THE CAPTAIN'S LOG!
CAPN' DIARY
NO PEEKIN'
OOOOOH!
LET'S FIND OUT HOW THE CREW DIED OR ABOUT THE SHIP SCANDALS OR, OR--!
Dear Diary,
I sure am having a horrible day.
A horrible life!
Love,
the Cap'n
Dear Diary,
I miss my dog.
Do you think my dog misses me?
Love,
the Cap'n.
Dear Diary,
My gameboy ran out of batteries and I forgot to bring any with me on the ship.
Now what?
Love,
the Cap'n.
UGH, THIS IS DEPRESSING. WANNA EXPLORE ELSEWHERE?
YES PLEASE.

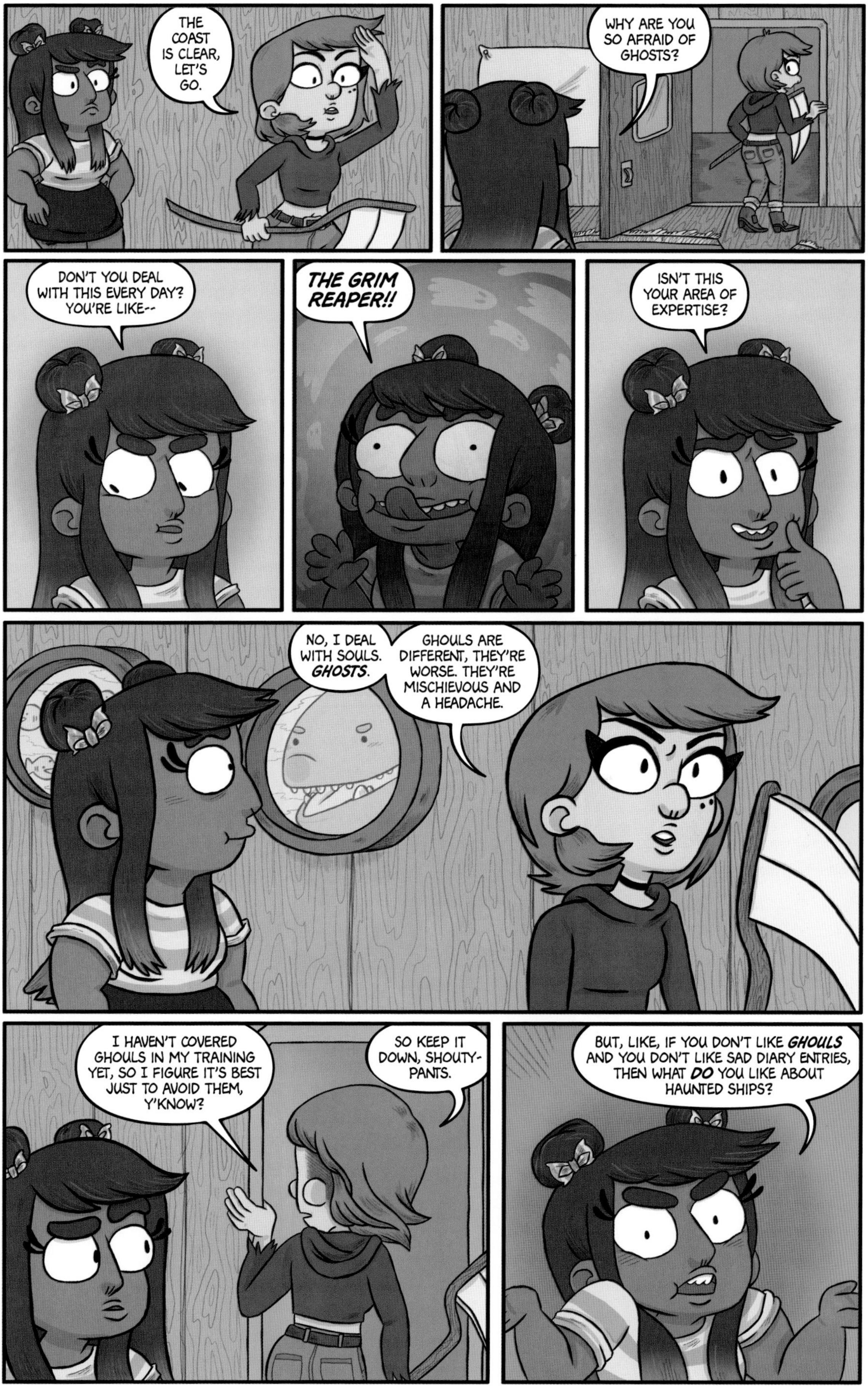
THE COAST IS CLEAR, LET'S GO.
WHY ARE YOU SO AFRAID OF GHOSTS?
DON'T YOU DEAL WITH THIS EVERY DAY? YOU'RE LIKE--
THE GRIM REAPER!!
ISN'T THIS YOUR AREA OF EXPERTISE?
NO, I DEAL WITH SOULS. GHOSTS.
GHOULS ARE DIFFERENT, THEY'RE WORSE. THEY'RE MISCHIEVOUS AND A HEADACHE.
I HAVEN'T COVERED GHOULS IN MY TRAINING YET, SO I FIGURE IT'S BEST JUST TO AVOID THEM, Y'KNOW?
SO KEEP IT DOWN, SHOUTY-PANTS.
BUT, LIKE, IF YOU DON'T LIKE GHOULS AND YOU DON'T LIKE SAD DIARY ENTRIES, THEN WHAT DO YOU LIKE ABOUT HAUNTED SHIPS?

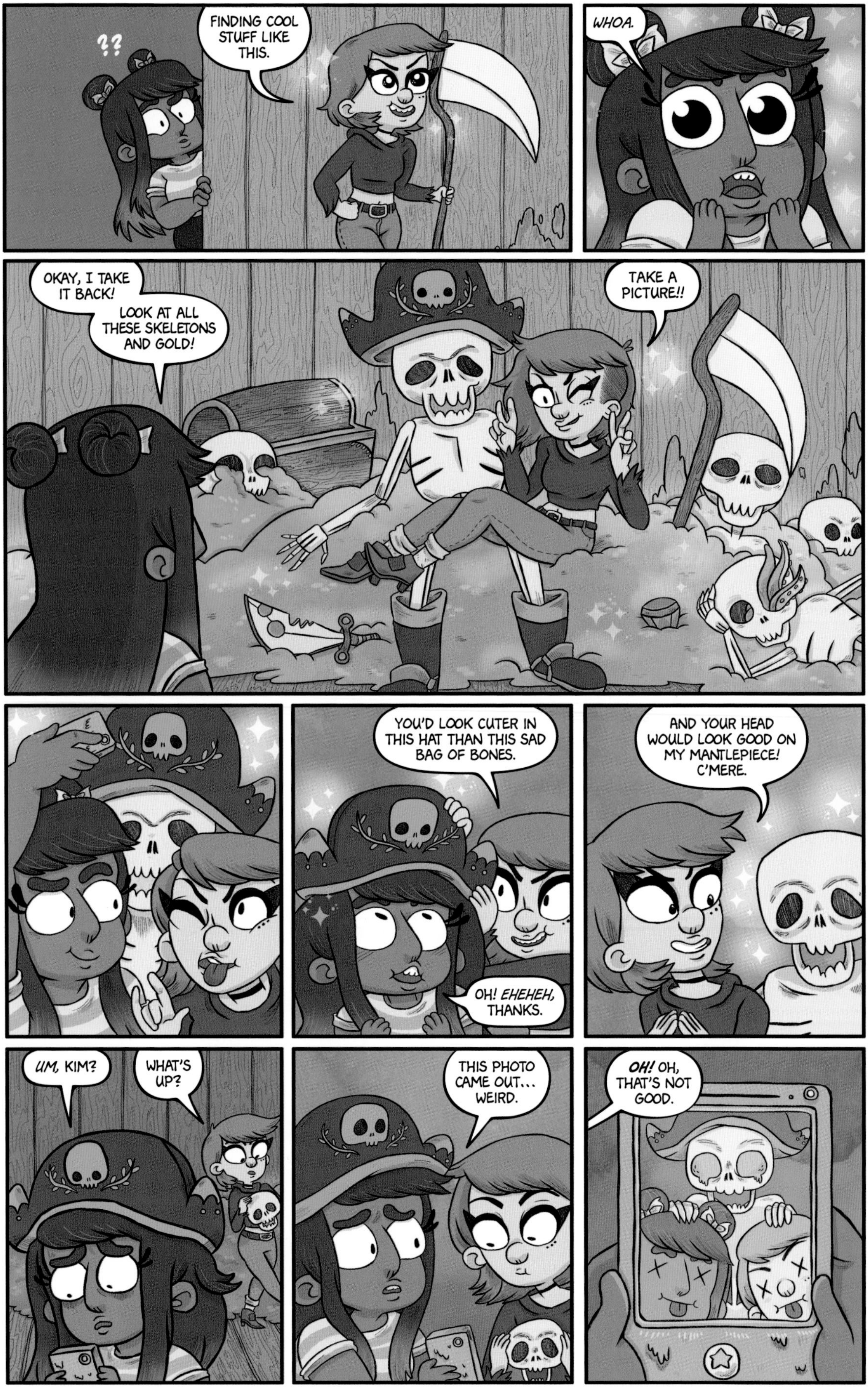
??
FINDING COOL STUFF LIKE THIS.
WHOA.
OKAY, I TAKE IT BACK!
LOOK AT ALL THESE SKELETONS AND GOLD!
TAKE A PICTURE!!
YOU'D LOOK CUTER IN THIS HAT THAN THIS SAD BAG OF BONES.
OH! EHEHEH, THANKS.
AND YOUR HEAD WOULD LOOK GOOD ON MY MANTLEPIECE! C'MERE.
UM, KIM?
WHAT'S UP?
THIS PHOTO CAME OUT... WEIRD.
OH! OH, THAT'S NOT GOOD.

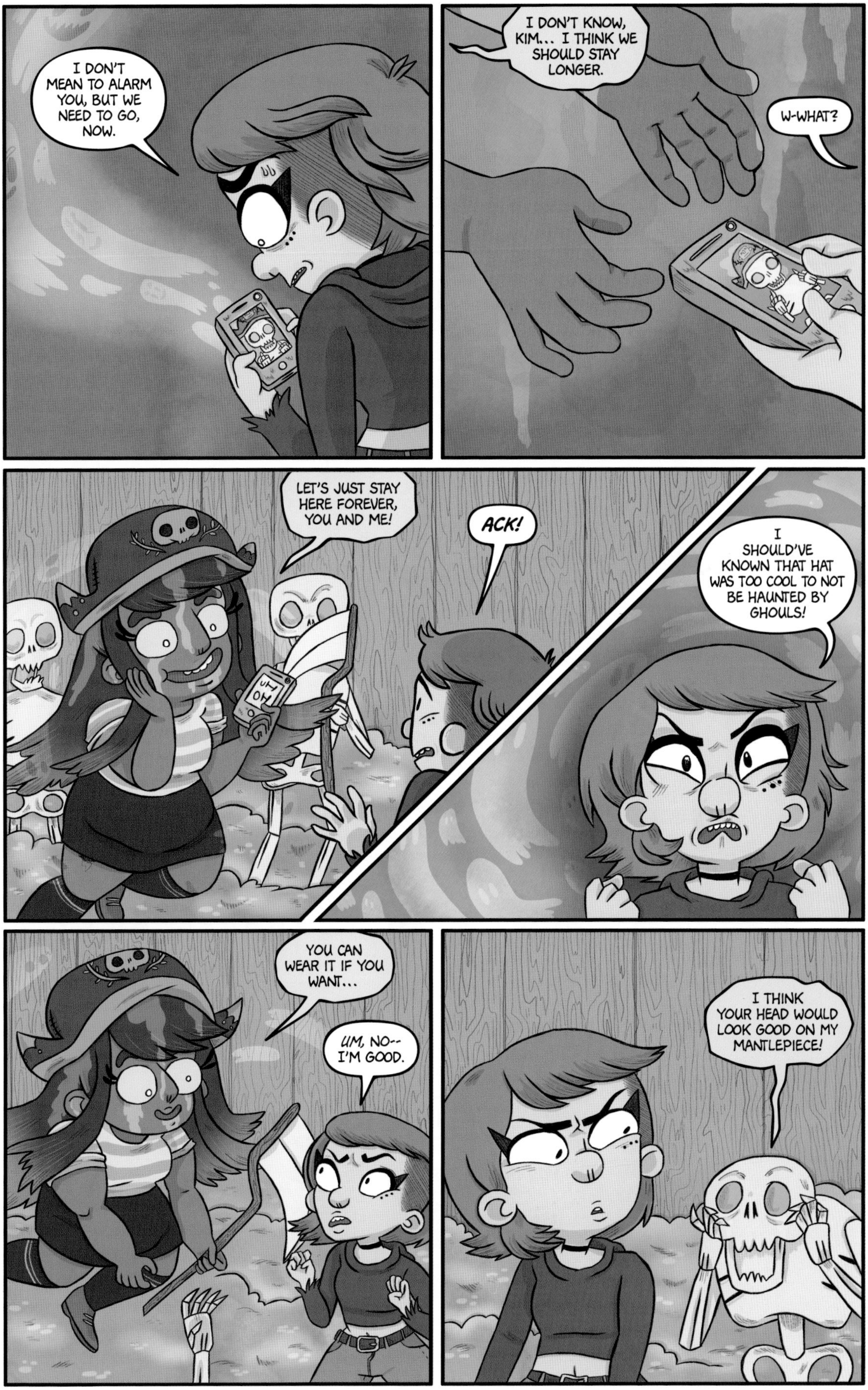
I DON'T MEAN TO ALARM YOU, BUT WE NEED TO GO, NOW.
I DON'T KNOW, KIM... I THINK WE SHOULD STAY LONGER.
W-WHAT?
LET'S JUST STAY HERE FOREVER, YOU AND ME!
UH OH
ACK!
I SHOULD'VE KNOWN THAT HAT WAS TOO COOL TO NOT BE HAUNTED BY GHOULS!
YOU CAN WEAR IT IF YOU WANT...
UM, NO-- I'M GOOD.
I THINK YOUR HEAD WOULD LOOK GOOD ON MY MANTLEPIECE!

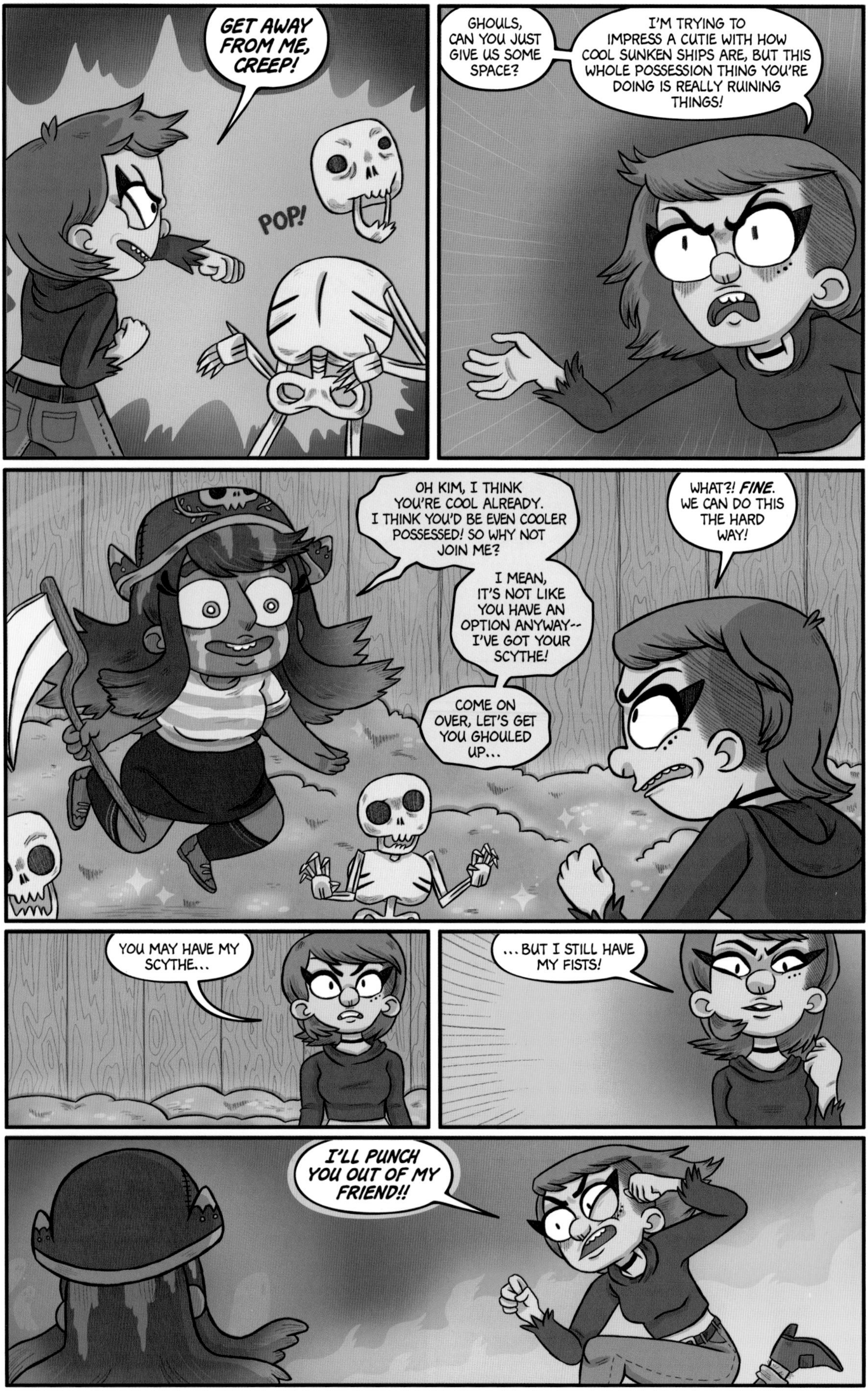
GET AWAY FROM ME, CREEP!
POP!
GHOULS, CAN YOU JUST GIVE US SOME SPACE?
I'M TRYING TO IMPRESS A CUTIE WITH HOW COOL SUNKEN SHIPS ARE, BUT THIS WHOLE POSSESSION THING YOU'RE DOING IS REALLY RUINING THINGS!
OH KIM, I THINK YOU'RE COOL ALREADY. I THINK YOU'D BE EVEN COOLER POSSESSED! SO WHY NOT JOIN ME?
I MEAN, IT'S NOT LIKE YOU HAVE AN OPTION ANYWAY-- I'VE GOT YOUR SCYTHE!
COME ON OVER, LET'S GET YOU GHOULED UP...
WHAT?! FINE. WE CAN DO THIS THE HARD WAY!
YOU MAY HAVE MY SCYTHE...
...BUT I STILL HAVE MY FISTS!
I'LL PUNCH YOU OUT OF MY FRIEND!!

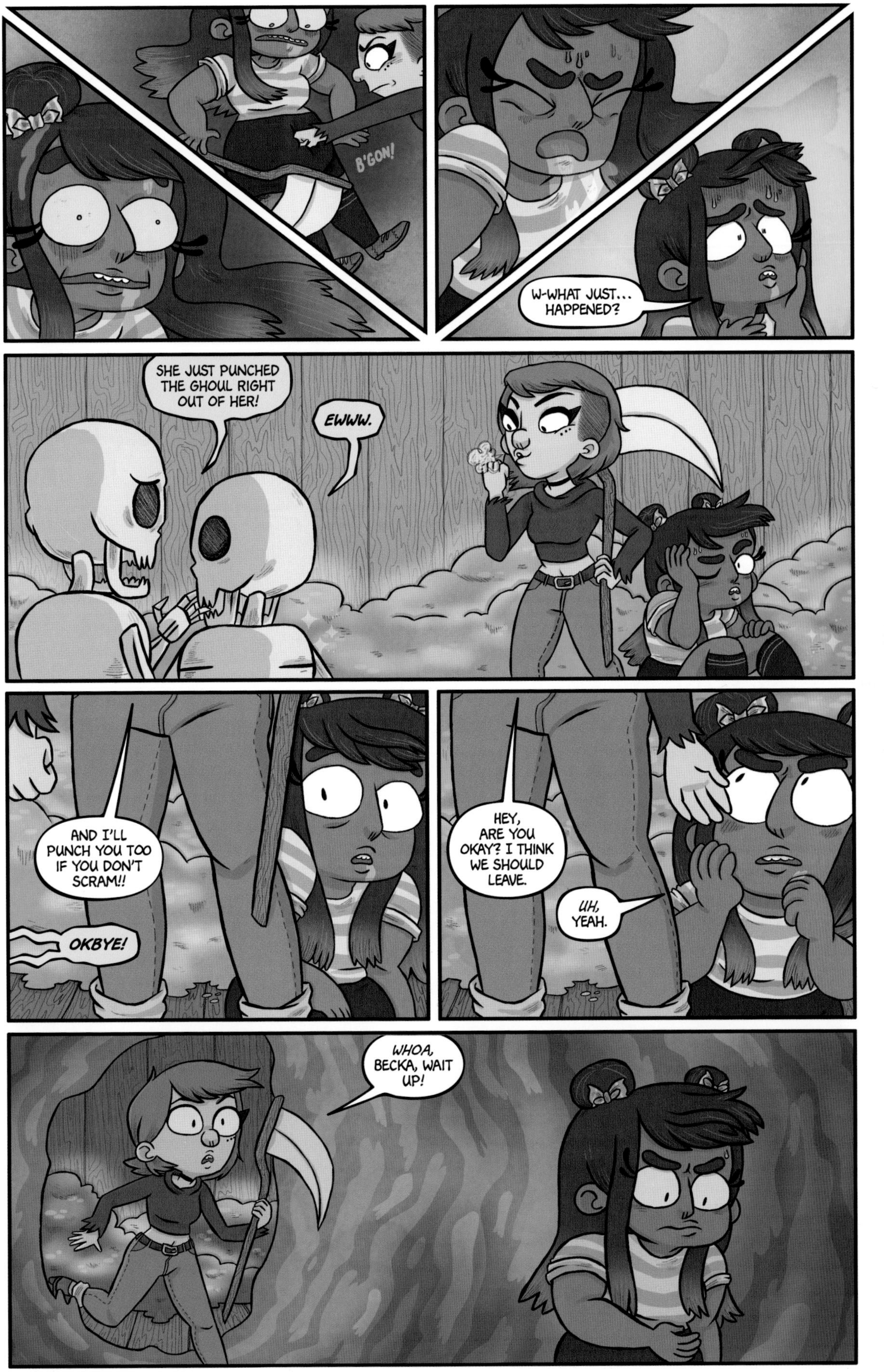
B'GON!
W-WHAT JUST... HAPPENED?
SHE JUST PUNCHED THE GHOUL RIGHT OUT OF HER!
EWWW.
AND I'LL PUNCH YOU TOO IF YOU DON'T SCRAM!!
OKBYE!
HEY, ARE YOU OKAY? I THINK WE SHOULD LEAVE.
UH, YEAH.
WHOA, BECKA, WAIT UP!

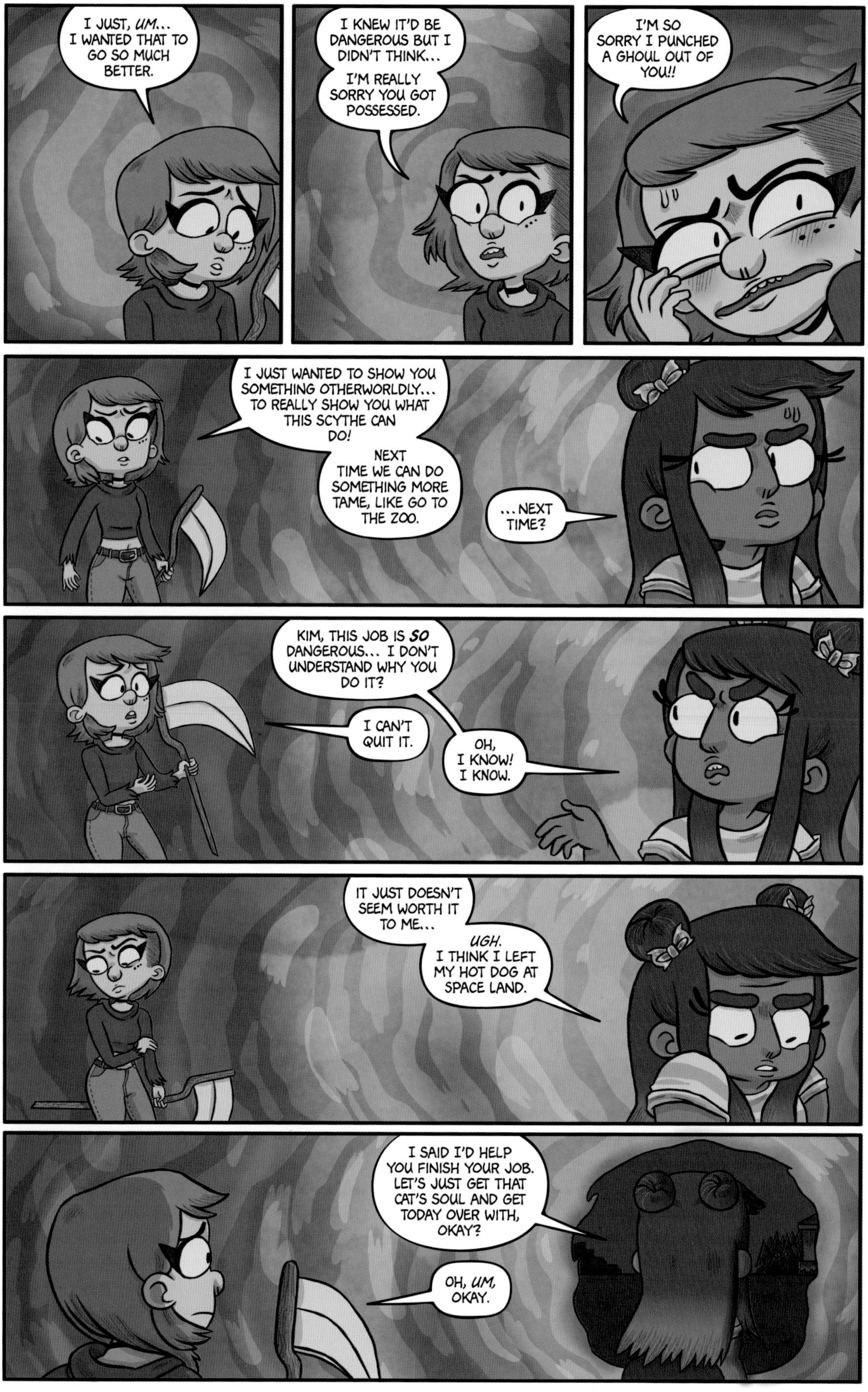
I JUST, *UM*...
I WANTED THAT TO GO SO MUCH BETTER.
I KNEW IT'D BE DANGEROUS BUT I DIDN'T THINK...
I'M REALLY SORRY YOU GOT POSSESSED.
I'M SO SORRY I PUNCHED A GHOUL OUT OF YOU!!
I JUST WANTED TO SHOW YOU SOMETHING OTHERWORLDLY... TO REALLY SHOW YOU WHAT THIS SCYTHE CAN DO!
NEXT TIME WE CAN DO SOMETHING MORE TAME, LIKE GO TO THE ZOO.
...NEXT TIME?
KIM, THIS JOB IS ***SO*** DANGEROUS... I DON'T UNDERSTAND WHY YOU DO IT?
I CAN'T QUIT IT.
OH, I KNOW! I KNOW.
IT JUST DOESN'T SEEM WORTH IT TO ME...
UGH. I THINK I LEFT MY HOT DOG AT SPACE LAND.
I SAID I'D HELP YOU FINISH YOUR JOB. LET'S JUST GET THAT CAT'S SOUL AND GET TODAY OVER WITH, OKAY?
OH, *UM*, OKAY.

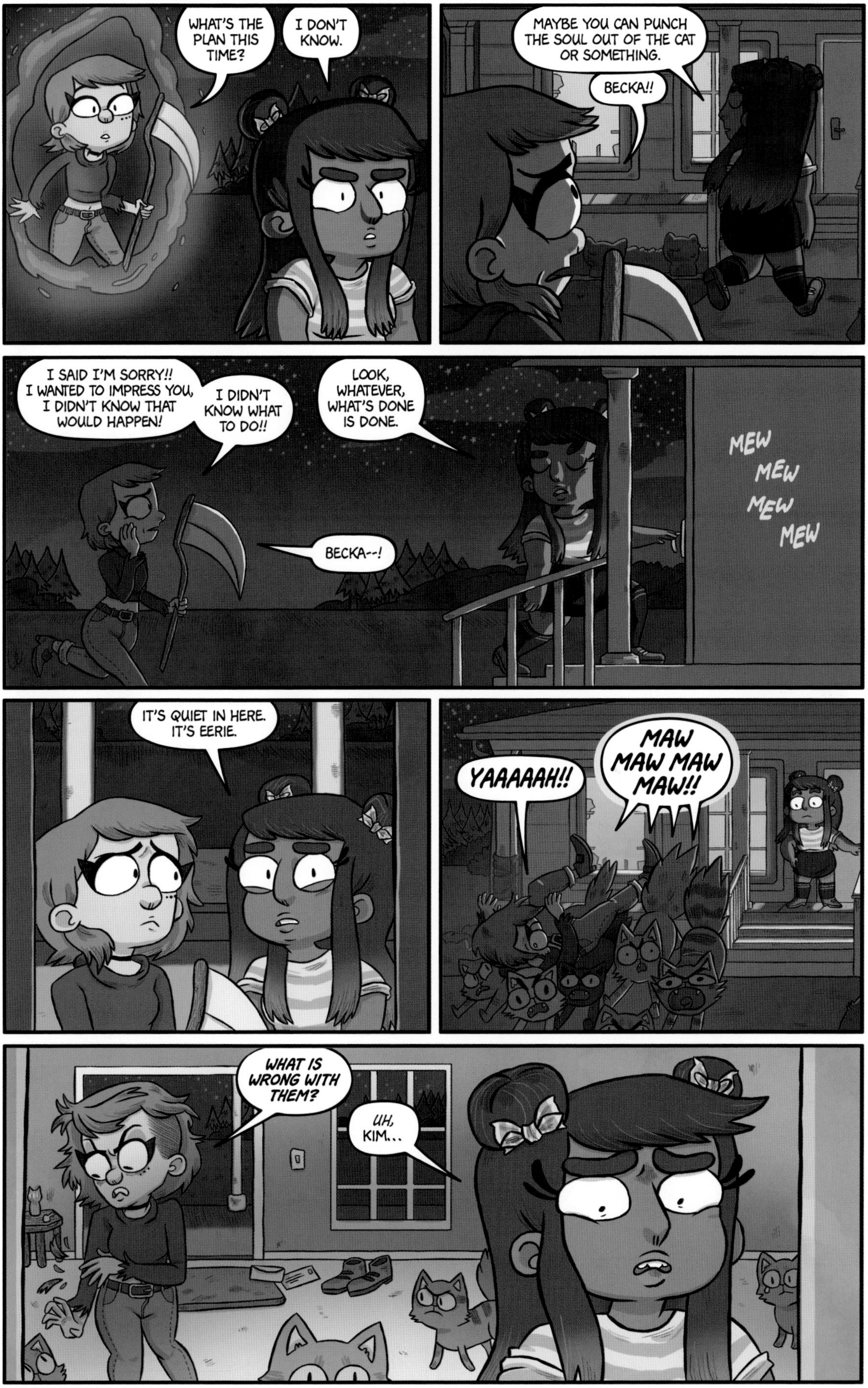
WHAT'S THE PLAN THIS TIME?
I DON'T KNOW.
MAYBE YOU CAN PUNCH THE SOUL OUT OF THE CAT OR SOMETHING.
BECKA!!
I SAID I'M SORRY!! I WANTED TO IMPRESS YOU, I DIDN'T KNOW THAT WOULD HAPPEN!
I DIDN'T KNOW WHAT TO DO!!
LOOK, WHATEVER, WHAT'S DONE IS DONE.
BECKA--!
MEW MEW MEW MEW
IT'S QUIET IN HERE. IT'S EERIE.
YAAAAAH!!
MAW MAW MAW MAW!!
WHAT IS WRONG WITH THEM?
UH, KIM...

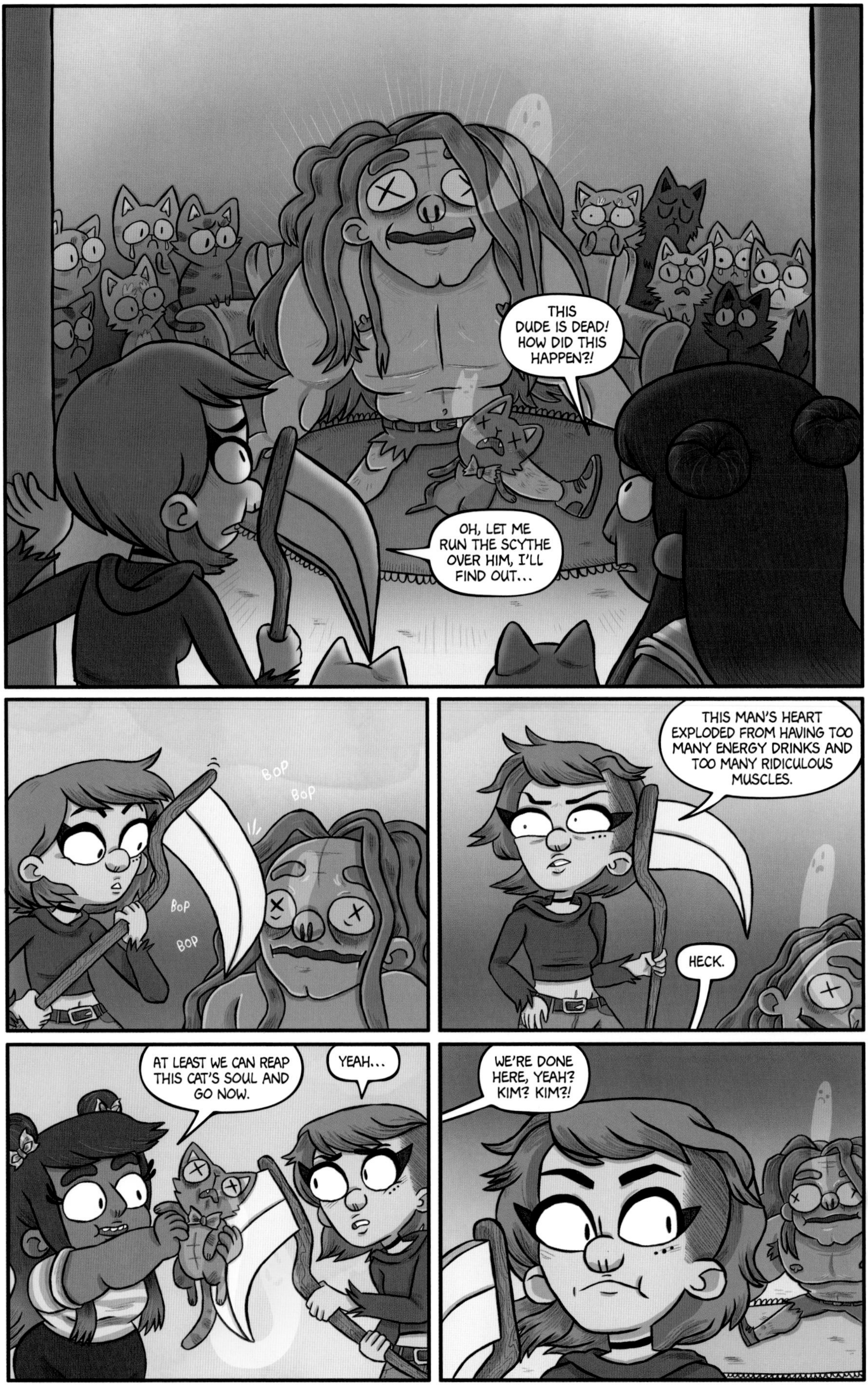
THIS DUDE IS DEAD! HOW DID THIS HAPPEN?!
OH, LET ME RUN THE SCYTHE OVER HIM, I'LL FIND OUT...
BOP
BOP
BOP
BOP
THIS MAN'S HEART EXPLODED FROM HAVING TOO MANY ENERGY DRINKS AND TOO MANY RIDICULOUS MUSCLES.
HECK.
AT LEAST WE CAN REAP THIS CAT'S SOUL AND GO NOW.
YEAH...
WE'RE DONE HERE, YEAH? KIM? KIM?!

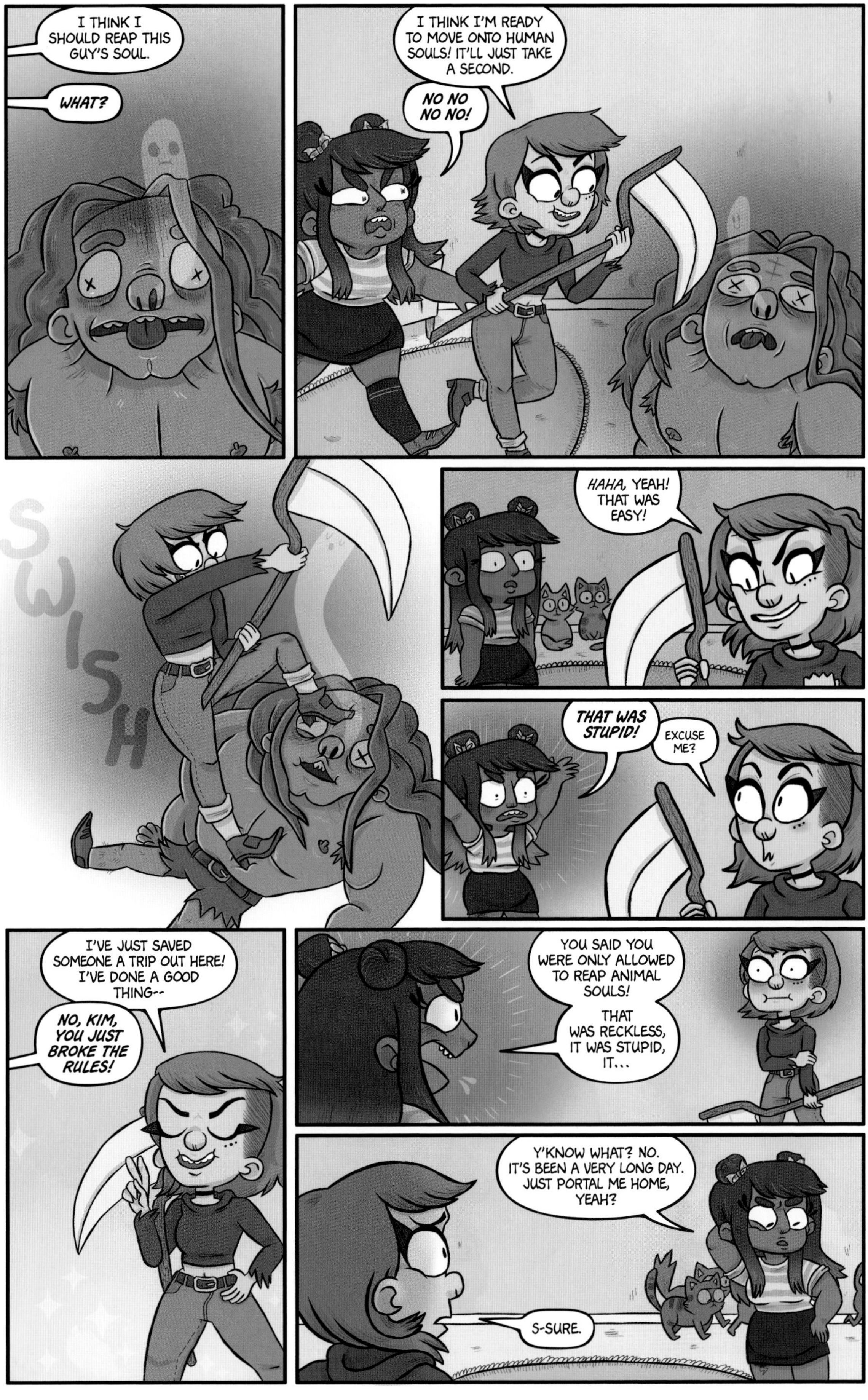
I THINK I SHOULD REAP THIS GUY'S SOUL.
WHAT?
I THINK I'M READY TO MOVE ONTO HUMAN SOULS! IT'LL JUST TAKE A SECOND.
NO NO NO NO!
SWISH
HAHA, YEAH! THAT WAS EASY!
THAT WAS STUPID!
EXCUSE ME?
I'VE JUST SAVED SOMEONE A TRIP OUT HERE! I'VE DONE A GOOD THING--
NO, KIM, YOU JUST BROKE THE RULES!
YOU SAID YOU WERE ONLY ALLOWED TO REAP ANIMAL SOULS!
THAT WAS RECKLESS, IT WAS STUPID, IT...
Y'KNOW WHAT? NO. IT'S BEEN A VERY LONG DAY. JUST PORTAL ME HOME, YEAH?
S-SURE.

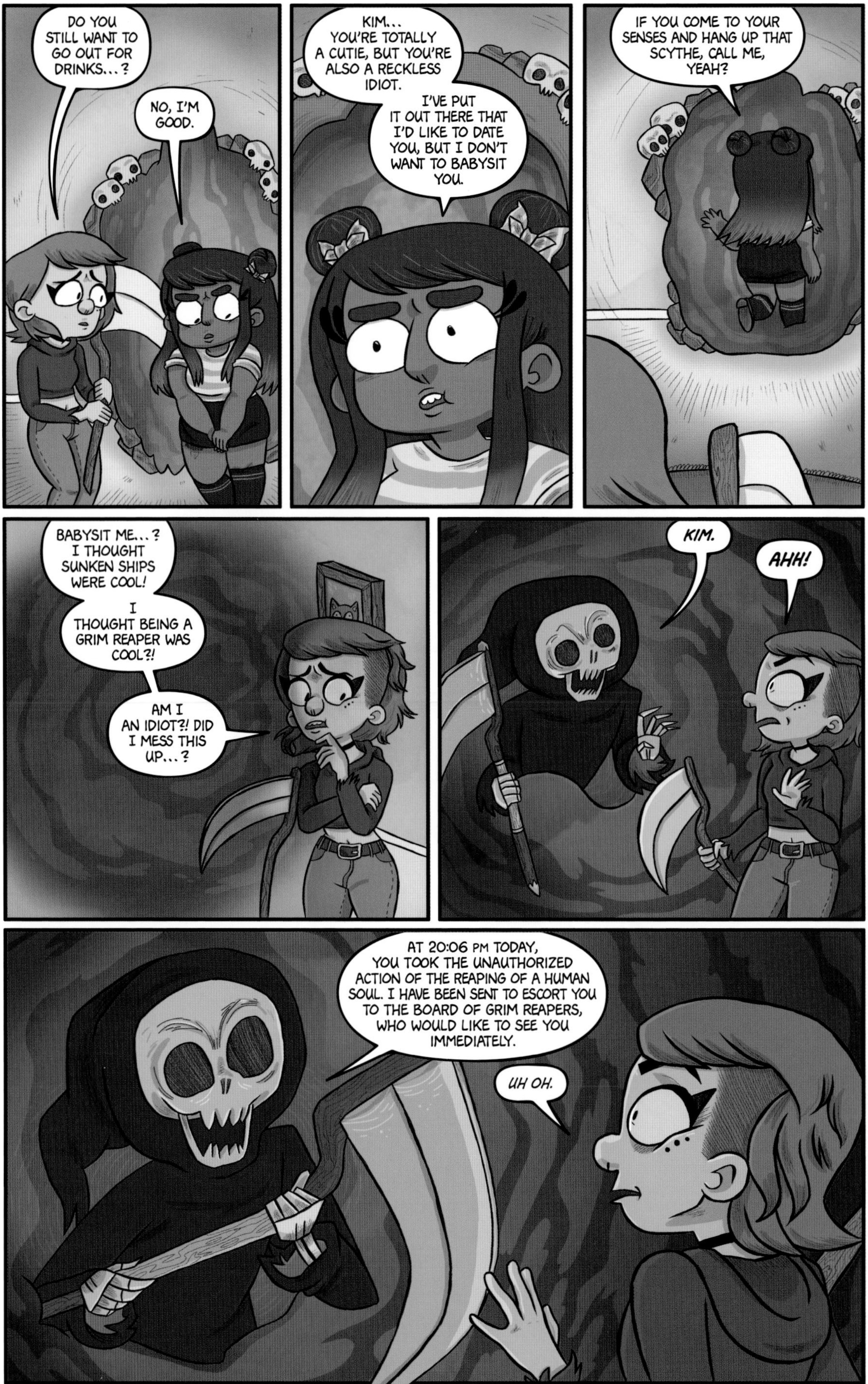
DO YOU STILL WANT TO GO OUT FOR DRINKS...?
NO, I'M GOOD.
KIM... YOU'RE TOTALLY A CUTIE, BUT YOU'RE ALSO A RECKLESS IDIOT.
I'VE PUT IT OUT THERE THAT I'D LIKE TO DATE YOU, BUT I DON'T WANT TO BABYSIT YOU.
IF YOU COME TO YOUR SENSES AND HANG UP THAT SCYTHE, CALL ME, YEAH?
BABYSIT ME...? I THOUGHT SUNKEN SHIPS WERE COOL!
I THOUGHT BEING A GRIM REAPER WAS COOL?!
AM I AN IDIOT?! DID I MESS THIS UP...?
KIM.
AHH!
AT 20:06 PM TODAY, YOU TOOK THE UNAUTHORIZED ACTION OF THE REAPING OF A HUMAN SOUL. I HAVE BEEN SENT TO ESCORT YOU TO THE BOARD OF GRIM REAPERS, WHO WOULD LIKE TO SEE YOU IMMEDIATELY.
UH OH.

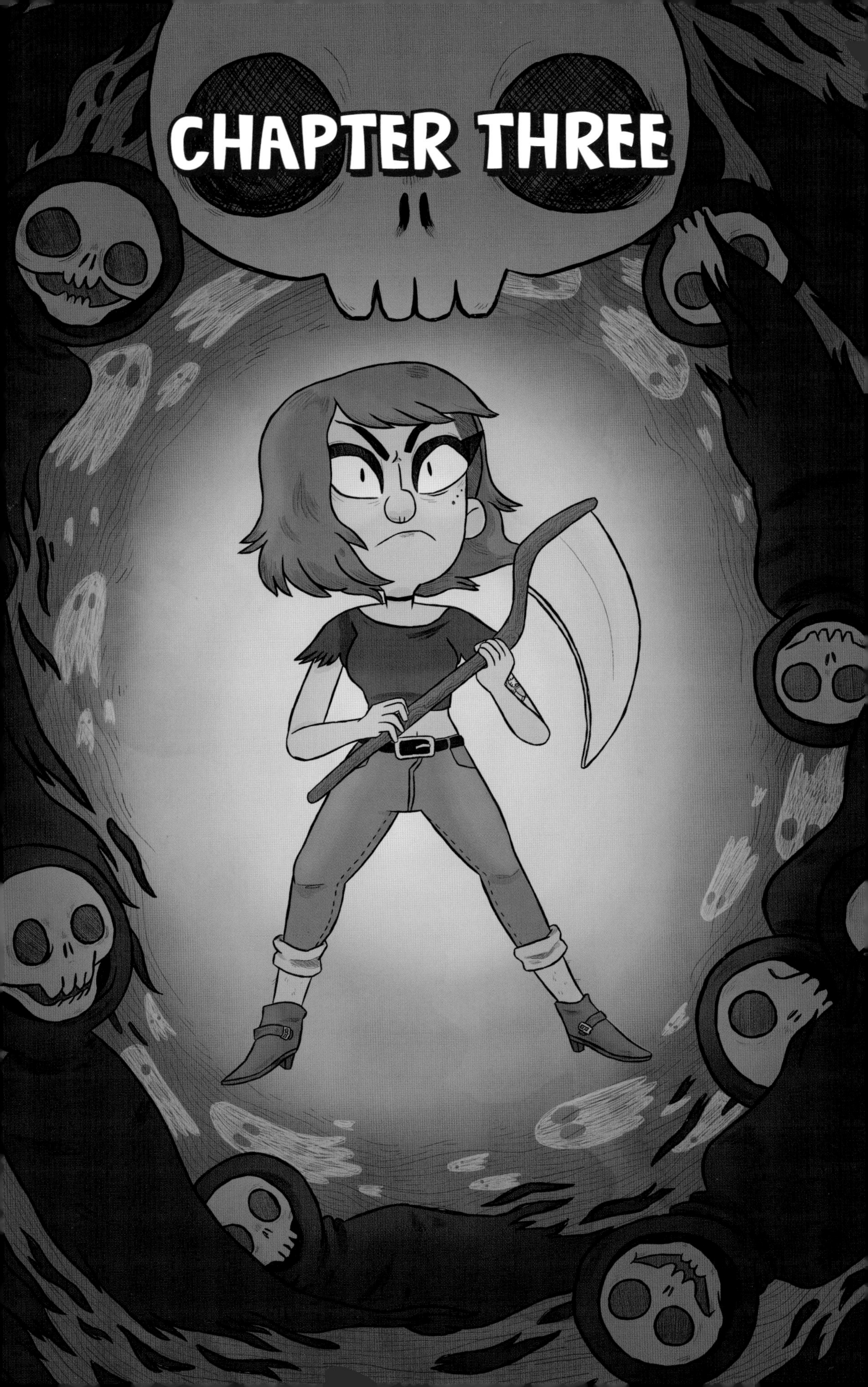
CHAPTER THREE

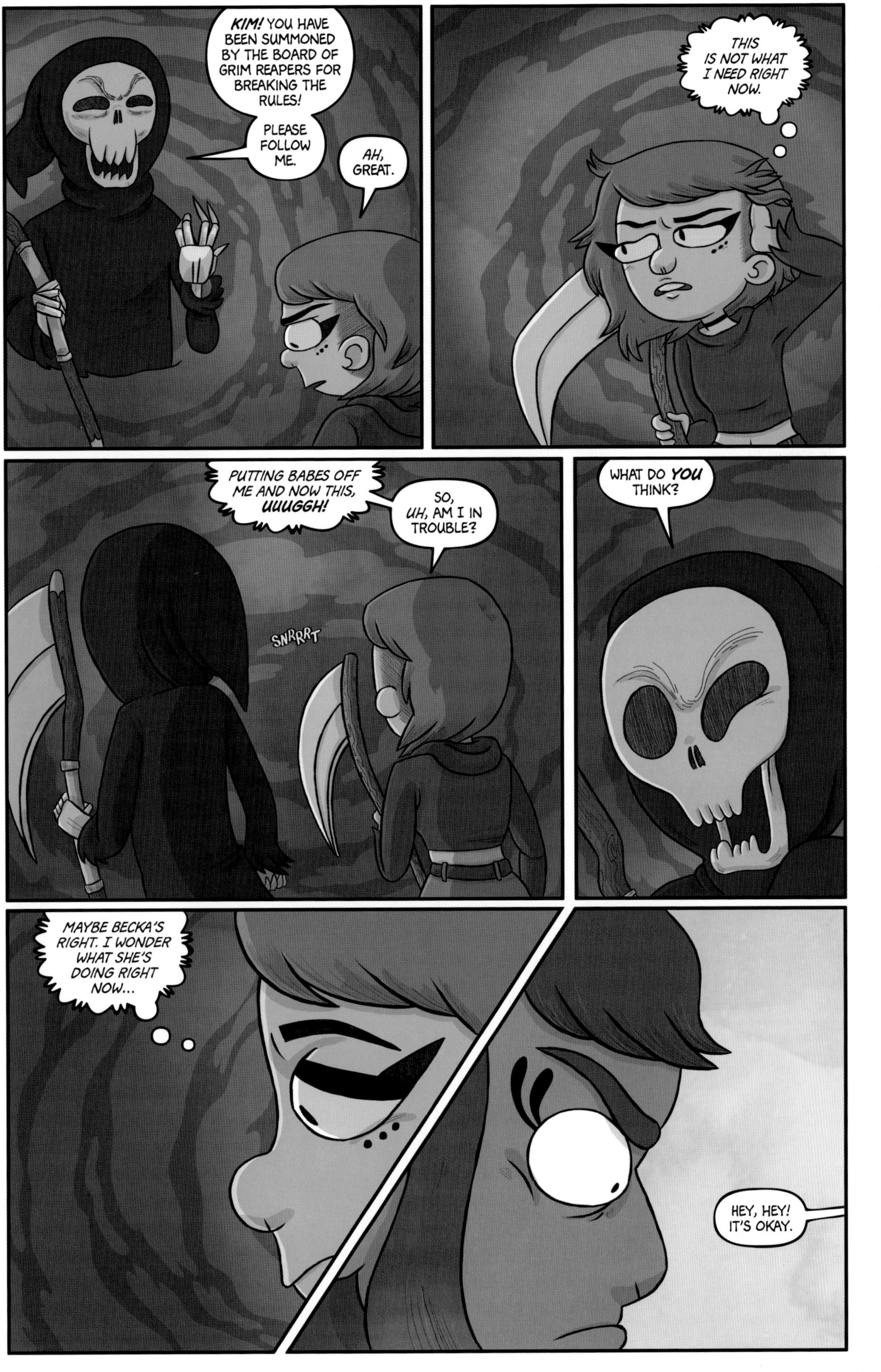
KIM! YOU HAVE BEEN SUMMONED BY THE BOARD OF GRIM REAPERS FOR BREAKING THE RULES!
PLEASE FOLLOW ME.
AH, GREAT.
THIS IS NOT WHAT I NEED RIGHT NOW.
PUTTING BABES OFF ME AND NOW THIS, UUUGGH!
SO, UH, AM I IN TROUBLE?
SNRRRT
WHAT DO YOU THINK?
MAYBE BECKA'S RIGHT. I WONDER WHAT SHE'S DOING RIGHT NOW...
HEY, HEY! IT'S OKAY.

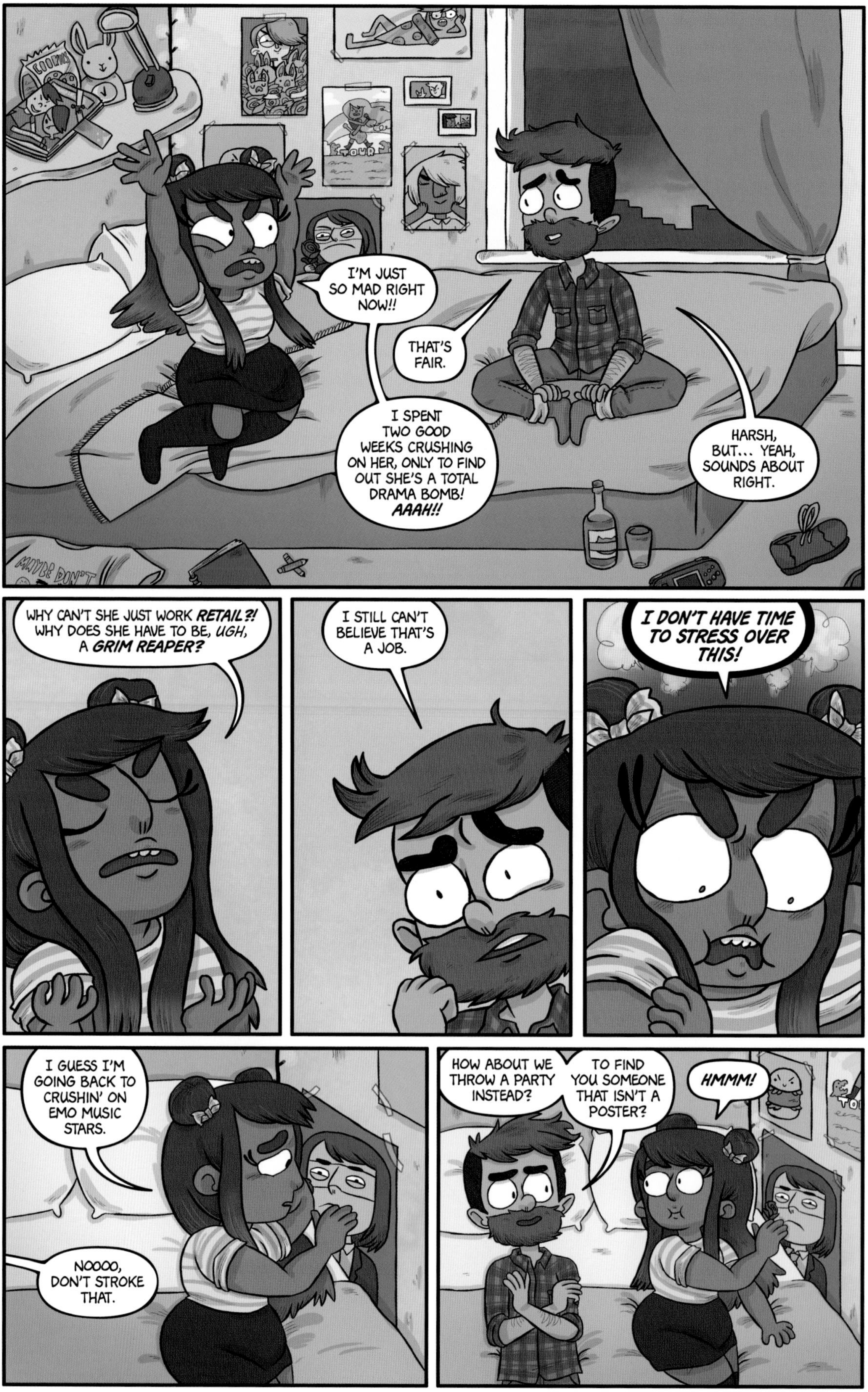
I'M JUST SO MAD RIGHT NOW!!
THAT'S FAIR.
I SPENT TWO GOOD WEEKS CRUSHING ON HER, ONLY TO FIND OUT SHE'S A TOTAL DRAMA BOMB! ***AAAH!!***
HARSH, BUT... YEAH, SOUNDS ABOUT RIGHT.
MAYBE DON'T
WHY CAN'T SHE JUST WORK ***RETAIL?!*** WHY DOES SHE HAVE TO BE, *UGH*, A ***GRIM REAPER?***
I STILL CAN'T BELIEVE THAT'S A JOB.
I DON'T HAVE TIME TO STRESS OVER THIS!
I GUESS I'M GOING BACK TO CRUSHIN' ON EMO MUSIC STARS.
NOOOO, DON'T STROKE THAT.
HOW ABOUT WE THROW A PARTY INSTEAD?
TO FIND YOU SOMEONE THAT ISN'T A POSTER?
HMMM!

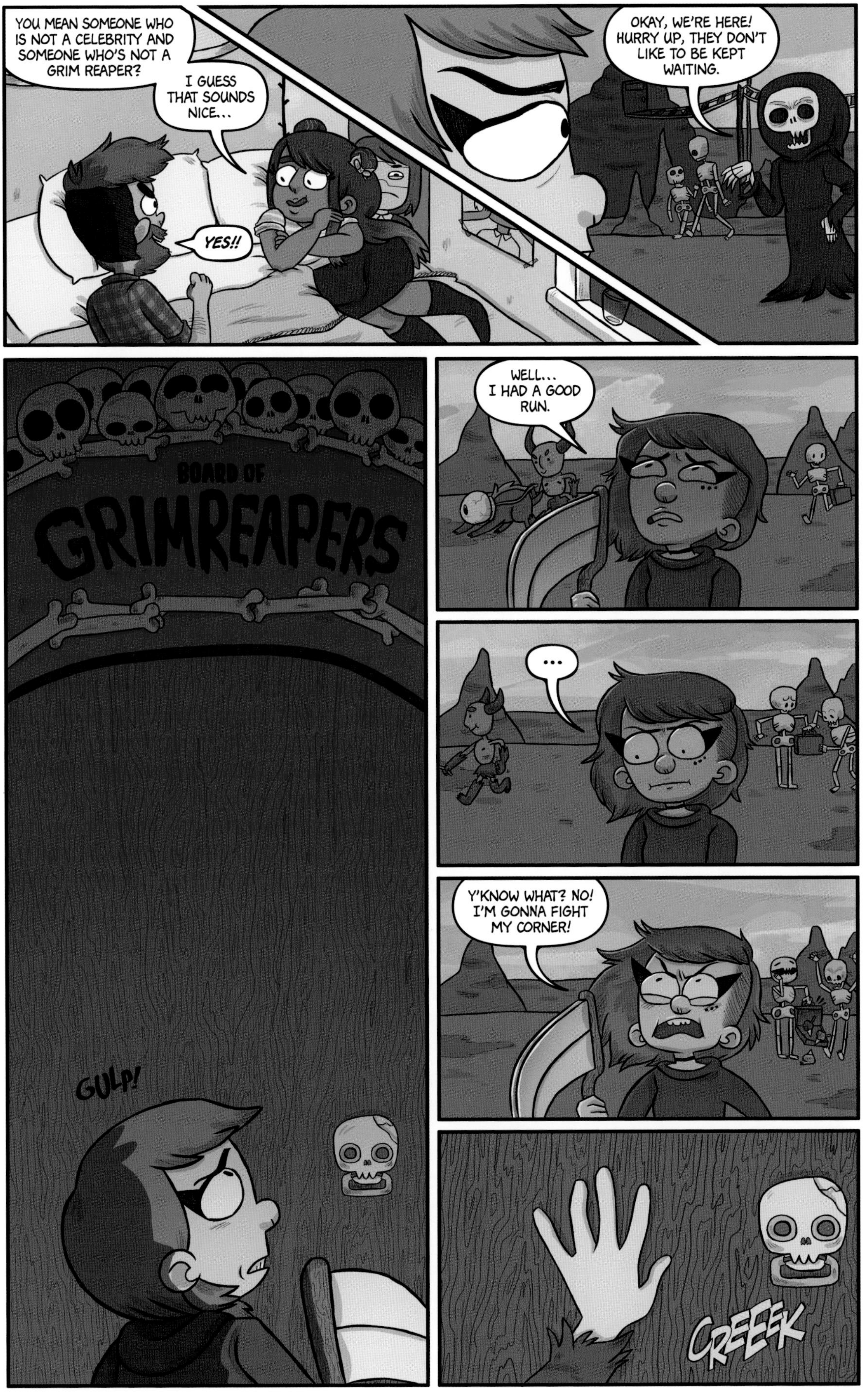
YOU MEAN SOMEONE WHO IS NOT A CELEBRITY AND SOMEONE WHO'S NOT A GRIM REAPER?
I GUESS THAT SOUNDS NICE...
YES!!
OKAY, WE'RE HERE! HURRY UP, THEY DON'T LIKE TO BE KEPT WAITING.
BOARD OF GRIMREAPERS
GULP!
WELL... I HAD A GOOD RUN.
...
Y'KNOW WHAT? NO! I'M GONNA FIGHT MY CORNER!
CREEEK

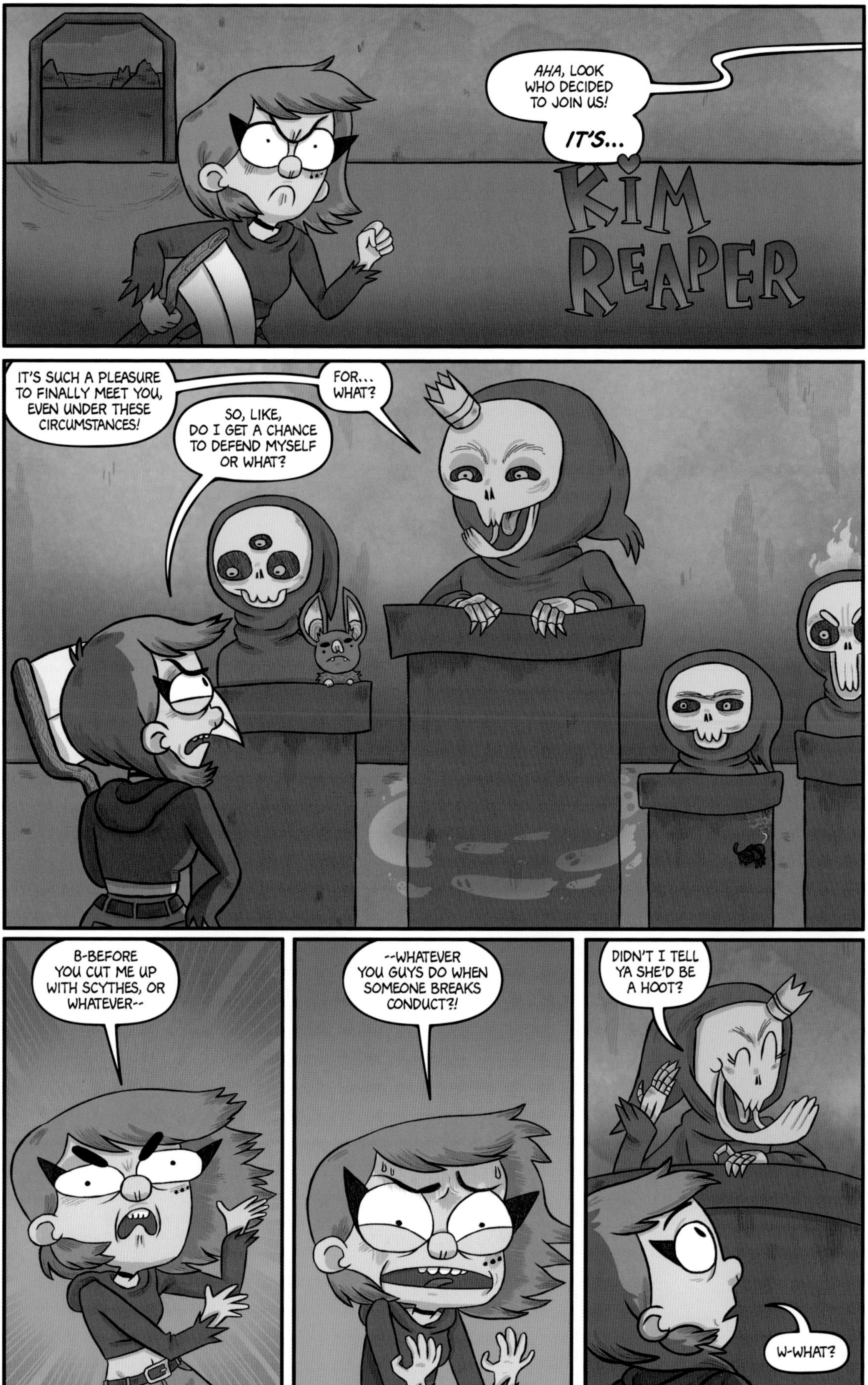

AHA, LOOK WHO DECIDED TO JOIN US!
IT'S...
KIM REAPER
IT'S SUCH A PLEASURE TO FINALLY MEET YOU, EVEN UNDER THESE CIRCUMSTANCES!
SO, LIKE, DO I GET A CHANCE TO DEFEND MYSELF OR WHAT?
FOR... WHAT?
B-BEFORE YOU CUT ME UP WITH SCYTHES, OR WHATEVER--
--WHATEVER YOU GUYS DO WHEN SOMEONE BREAKS CONDUCT?!
DIDN'T I TELL YA SHE'D BE A HOOT?
W-WHAT?

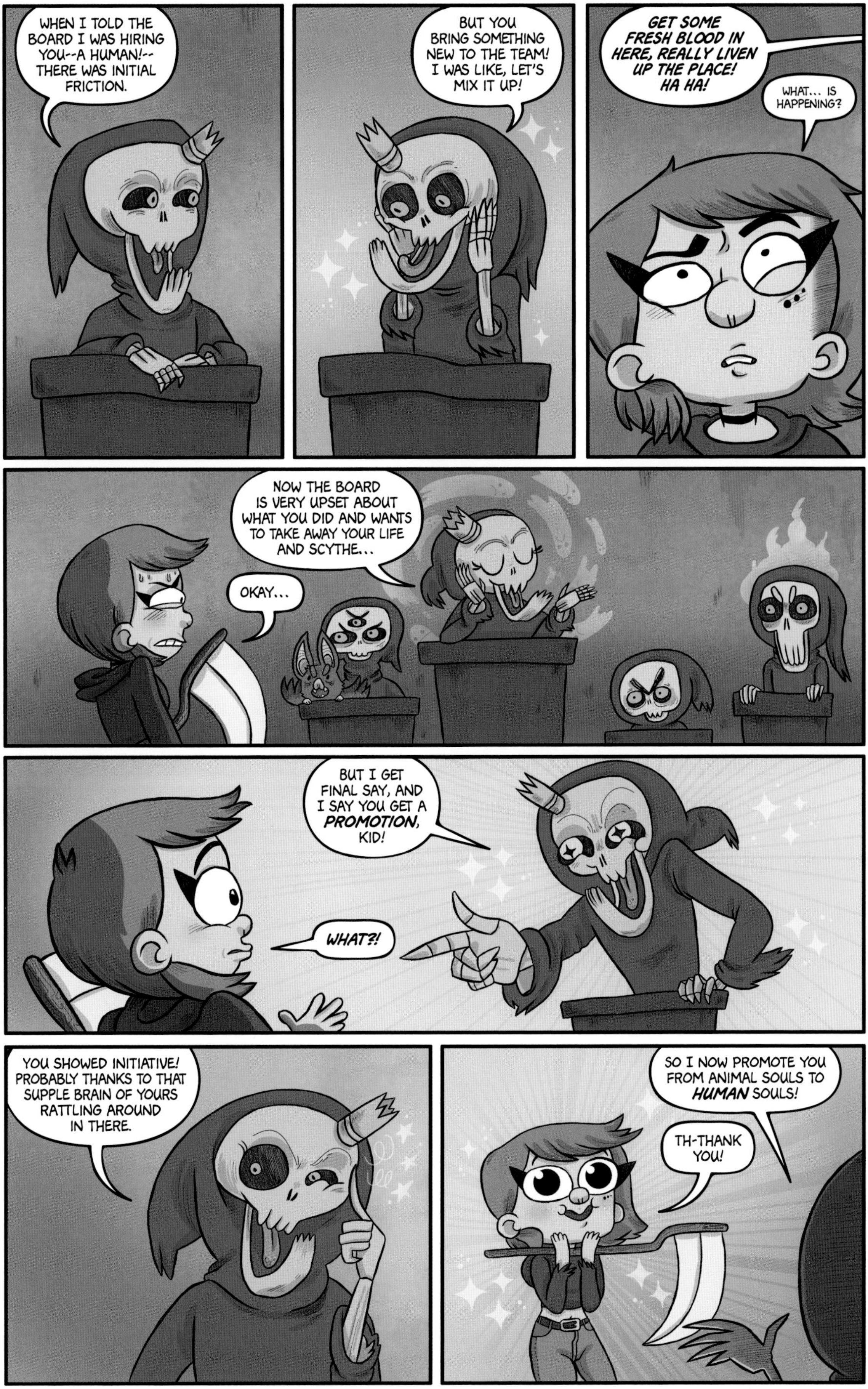
WHEN I TOLD THE BOARD I WAS HIRING YOU--A HUMAN!--THERE WAS INITIAL FRICTION.
BUT YOU BRING SOMETHING NEW TO THE TEAM! I WAS LIKE, LET'S MIX IT UP!
GET SOME FRESH BLOOD IN HERE, REALLY LIVEN UP THE PLACE! HA HA!
WHAT... IS HAPPENING?
NOW THE BOARD IS VERY UPSET ABOUT WHAT YOU DID AND WANTS TO TAKE AWAY YOUR LIFE AND SCYTHE...
OKAY...
BUT I GET FINAL SAY, AND I SAY YOU GET A PROMOTION, KID!
WHAT?!
YOU SHOWED INITIATIVE! PROBABLY THANKS TO THAT SUPPLE BRAIN OF YOURS RATTLING AROUND IN THERE.
SO I NOW PROMOTE YOU FROM ANIMAL SOULS TO HUMAN SOULS!
TH-THANK YOU!

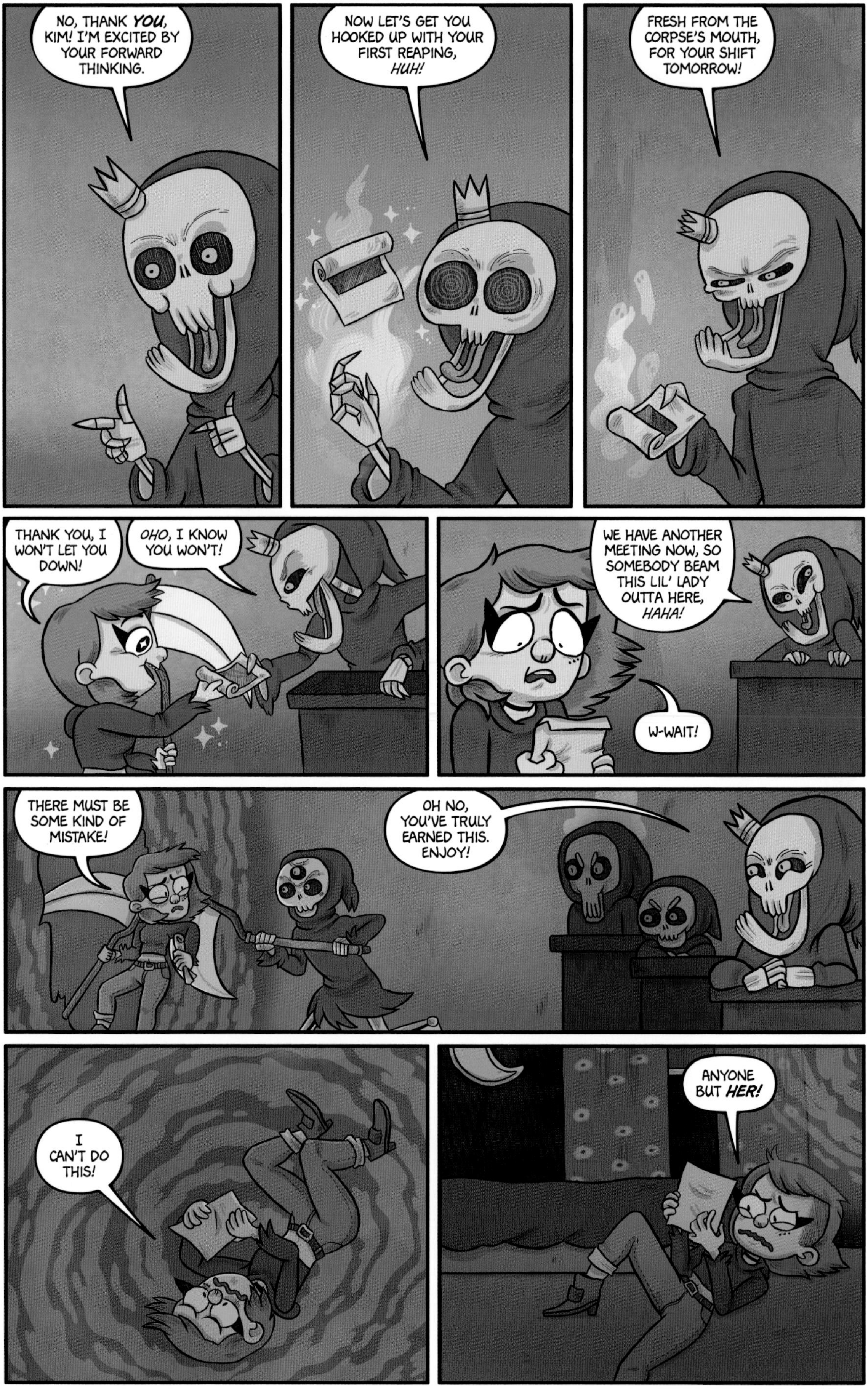

NO, THANK YOU, KIM! I'M EXCITED BY YOUR FORWARD THINKING.
NOW LET'S GET YOU HOOKED UP WITH YOUR FIRST REAPING, HUH!
FRESH FROM THE CORPSE'S MOUTH, FOR YOUR SHIFT TOMORROW!
THANK YOU, I WON'T LET YOU DOWN!
OHO, I KNOW YOU WON'T!
WE HAVE ANOTHER MEETING NOW, SO SOMEBODY BEAM THIS LIL' LADY OUTTA HERE, HAHA!
W-WAIT!
THERE MUST BE SOME KIND OF MISTAKE!
OH NO, YOU'VE TRULY EARNED THIS. ENJOY!
I CAN'T DO THIS!
ANYONE BUT HER!

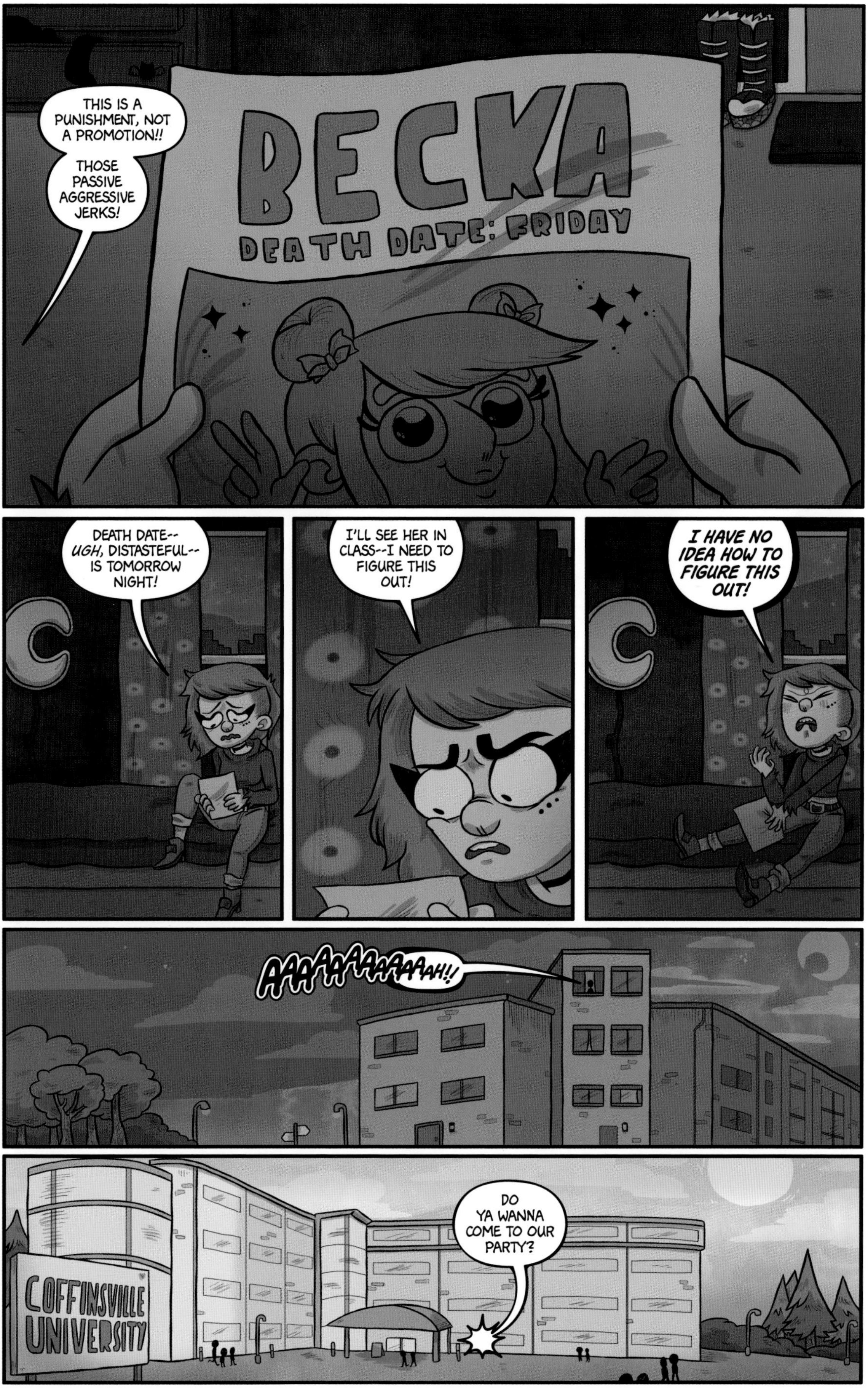
THIS IS A PUNISHMENT, NOT A PROMOTION!!
THOSE PASSIVE AGGRESSIVE JERKS!
BECKA
DEATH DATE: FRIDAY
DEATH DATE-- *UGH,* DISTASTEFUL-- IS TOMORROW NIGHT!
I'LL SEE HER IN CLASS--I NEED TO FIGURE THIS OUT!
I HAVE NO IDEA HOW TO FIGURE THIS OUT!
AAAAAAAAAAAAH!!
COFFINSVILLE UNIVERSITY
DO YA WANNA COME TO OUR PARTY?

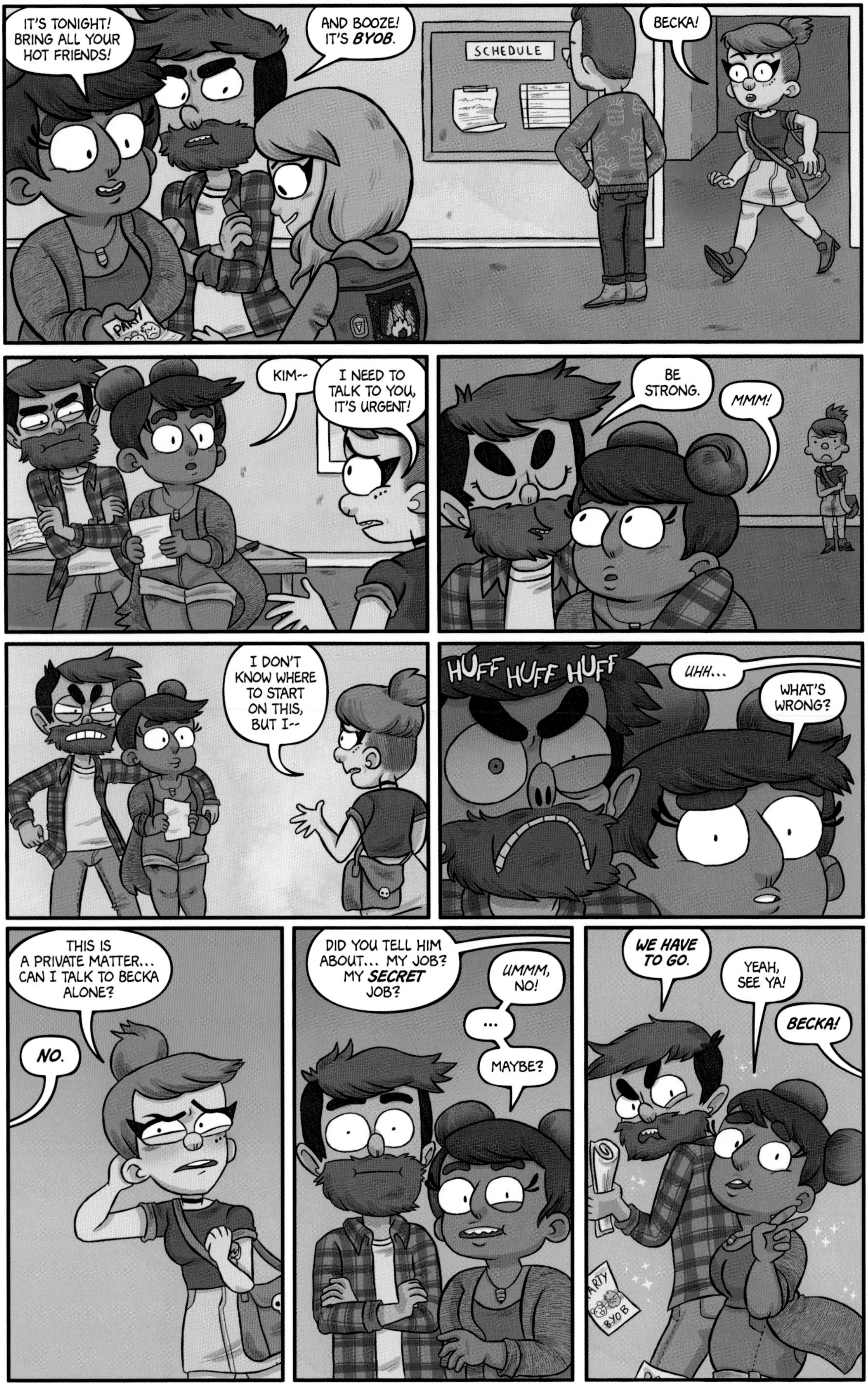
IT'S TONIGHT! BRING ALL YOUR HOT FRIENDS!
AND BOOZE! IT'S *BYOB*.
SCHEDULE
BECKA!
PARTY
KIM--
I NEED TO TALK TO YOU, IT'S URGENT!
BE STRONG.
MMM!
I DON'T KNOW WHERE TO START ON THIS, BUT I--
HUFF HUFF HUFF
UHH...
WHAT'S WRONG?
THIS IS A PRIVATE MATTER... CAN I TALK TO BECKA ALONE?
NO.
DID YOU TELL HIM ABOUT... MY JOB? MY *SECRET* JOB?
UMMM, NO!
...
MAYBE?
WE HAVE TO GO.
YEAH, SEE YA!
BECKA!
PARTY
BYOB

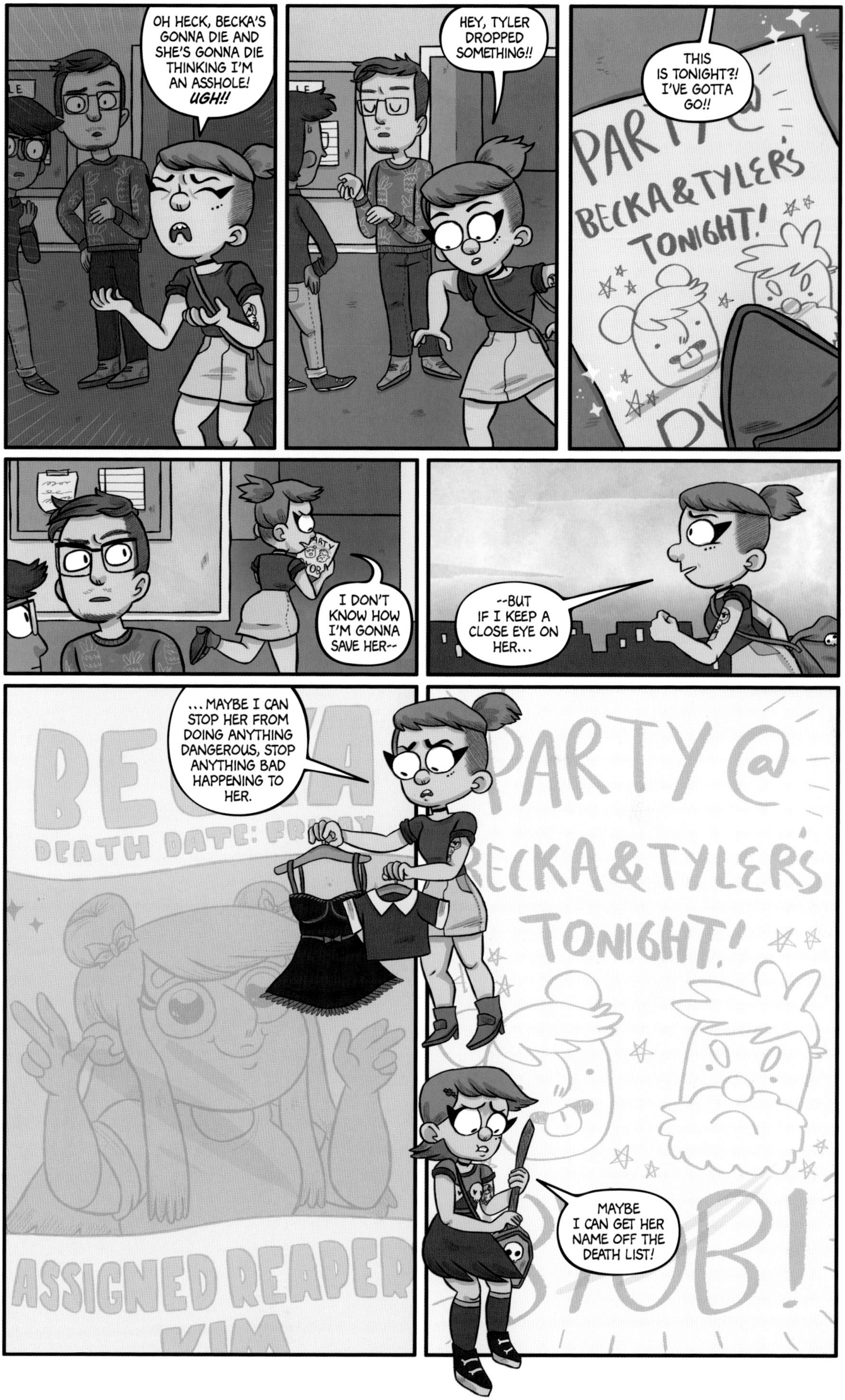
OH HECK, BECKA'S GONNA DIE AND SHE'S GONNA DIE THINKING I'M AN ASSHOLE! UGH!!
HEY, TYLER DROPPED SOMETHING!!
THIS IS TONIGHT?! I'VE GOTTA GO!!
PARTY @ BECKA&TYLER'S TONIGHT!
I DON'T KNOW HOW I'M GONNA SAVE HER--
--BUT IF I KEEP A CLOSE EYE ON HER...
...MAYBE I CAN STOP HER FROM DOING ANYTHING DANGEROUS, STOP ANYTHING BAD HAPPENING TO HER.
DEATH DATE: FRI
ASSIGNED REAPER
PARTY @ BECKA&TYLER'S TONIGHT!
MAYBE I CAN GET HER NAME OFF THE DEATH LIST!

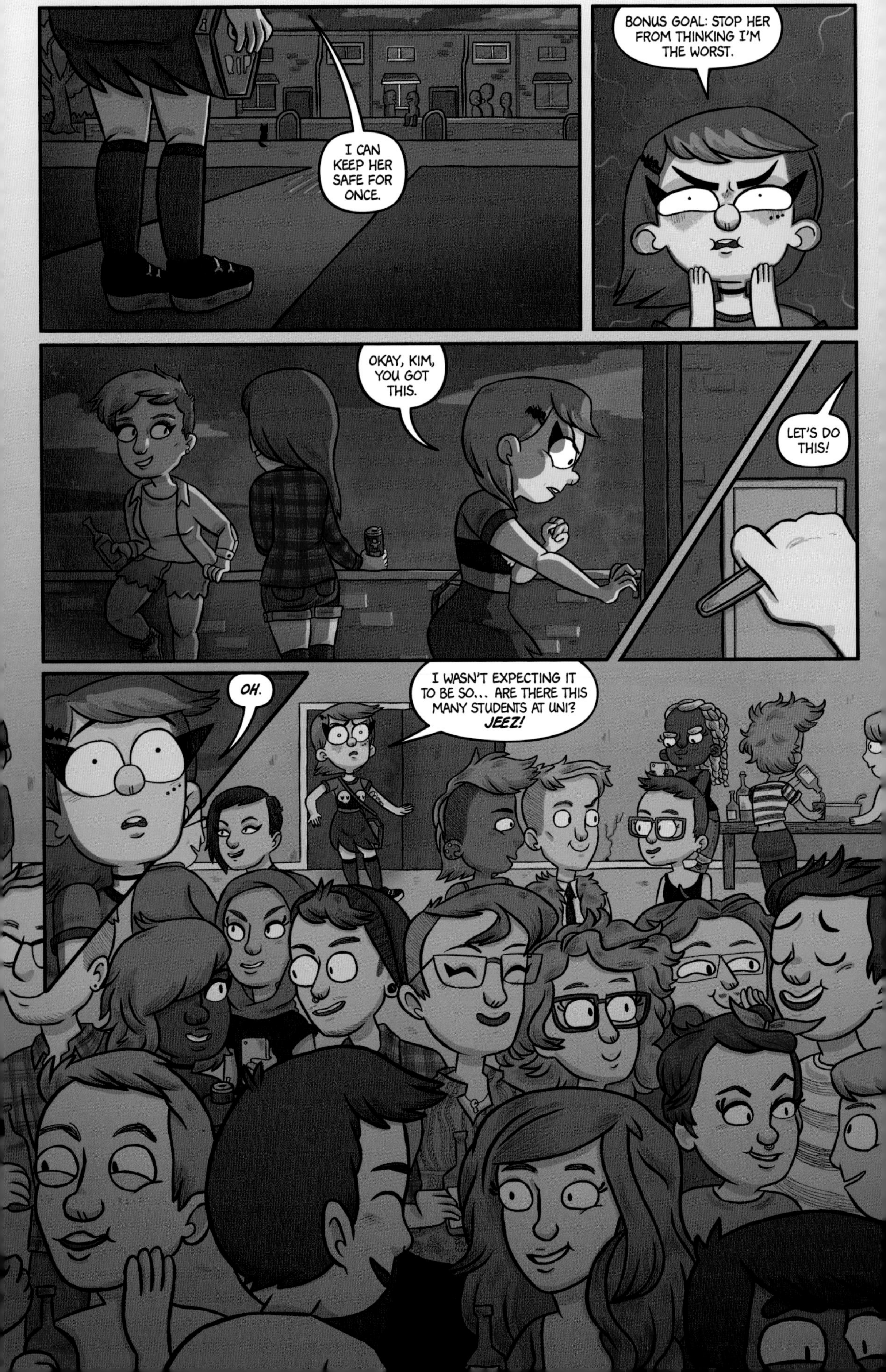
I CAN KEEP HER SAFE FOR ONCE.
BONUS GOAL: STOP HER FROM THINKING I'M THE WORST.
OKAY, KIM, YOU GOT THIS.
LET'S DO THIS!
OH.
I WASN'T EXPECTING IT TO BE SO... ARE THERE THIS MANY STUDENTS AT UNI? JEEZ!

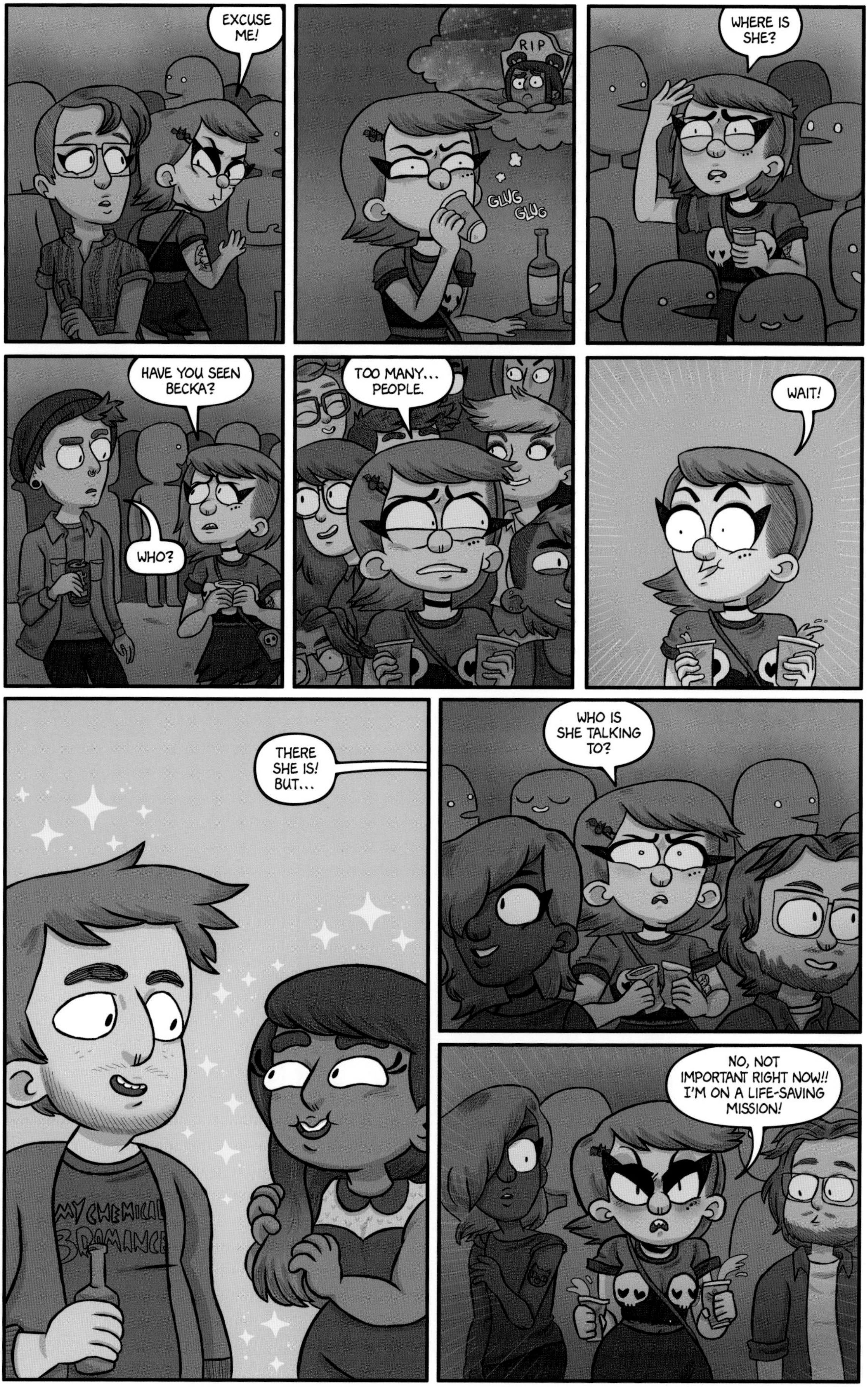
EXCUSE ME!
RIP
GLUG GLUG
WHERE IS SHE?
HAVE YOU SEEN BECKA?
WHO?
TOO MANY... PEOPLE.
WAIT!
THERE SHE IS! BUT...
MY CHEMICAL ROMANCE
WHO IS SHE TALKING TO?
NO, NOT IMPORTANT RIGHT NOW!! I'M ON A LIFE-SAVING MISSION!

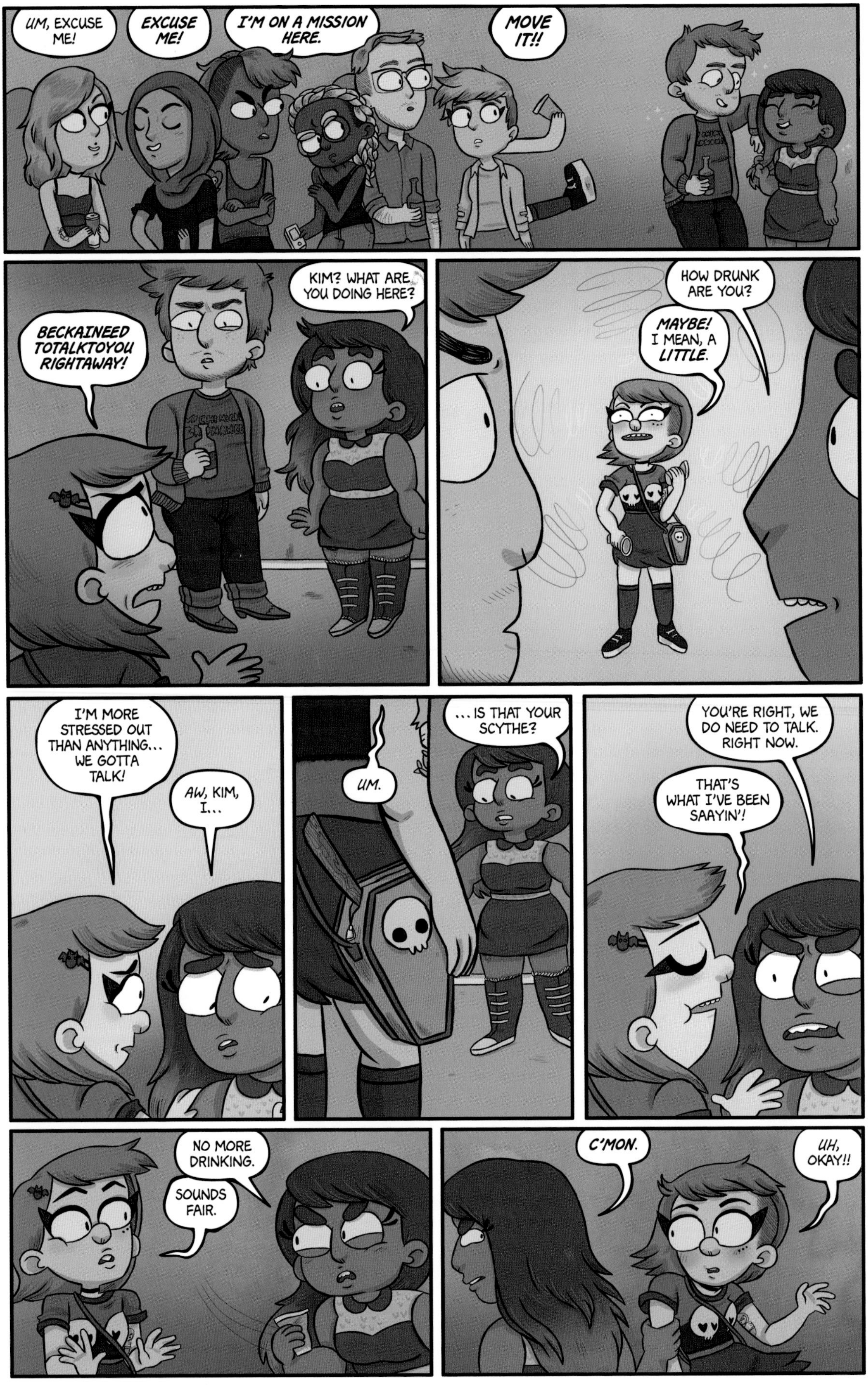
UM, EXCUSE ME!
EXCUSE ME!
I'M ON A MISSION HERE.
MOVE IT!!
KIM? WHAT ARE YOU DOING HERE?
BECKAINEED TOTALKTOYOU RIGHTAWAY!
HOW DRUNK ARE YOU?
MAYBE! I MEAN, A LITTLE.
I'M MORE STRESSED OUT THAN ANYTHING... WE GOTTA TALK!
AW, KIM, I...
...IS THAT YOUR SCYTHE?
UM.
YOU'RE RIGHT, WE DO NEED TO TALK. RIGHT NOW.
THAT'S WHAT I'VE BEEN SAAYIN'!
NO MORE DRINKING.
SOUNDS FAIR.
C'MON.
UH, OKAY!!

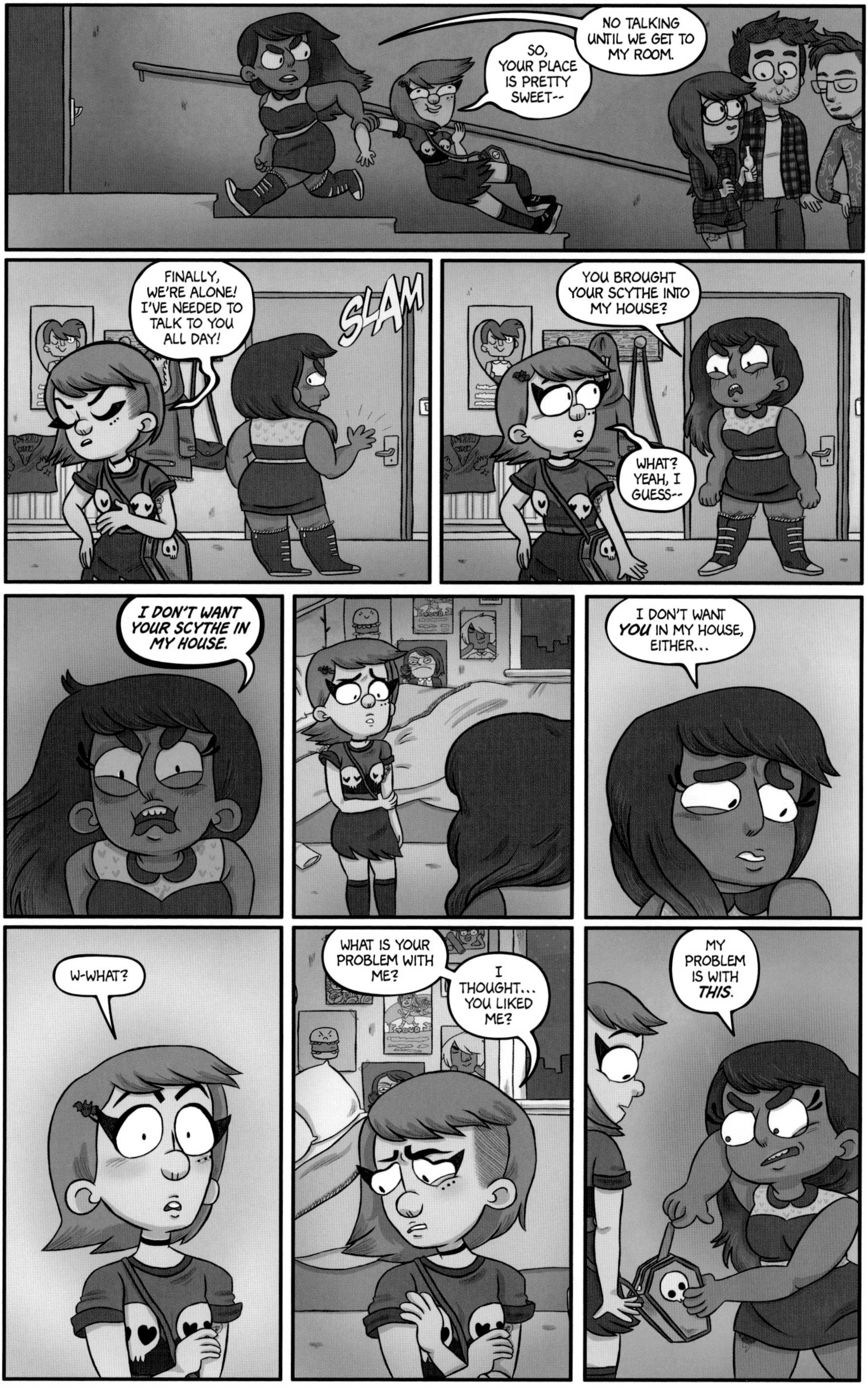

SO, YOUR PLACE IS PRETTY SWEET--
NO TALKING UNTIL WE GET TO MY ROOM.
FINALLY, WE'RE ALONE! I'VE NEEDED TO TALK TO YOU ALL DAY!
SLAM
YOU BROUGHT YOUR SCYTHE INTO MY HOUSE?
WHAT? YEAH, I GUESS--
I DON'T WANT YOUR SCYTHE IN MY HOUSE.
I DON'T WANT YOU IN MY HOUSE, EITHER...
W-WHAT?
WHAT IS YOUR PROBLEM WITH ME?
I THOUGHT... YOU LIKED ME?
MY PROBLEM IS WITH THIS.

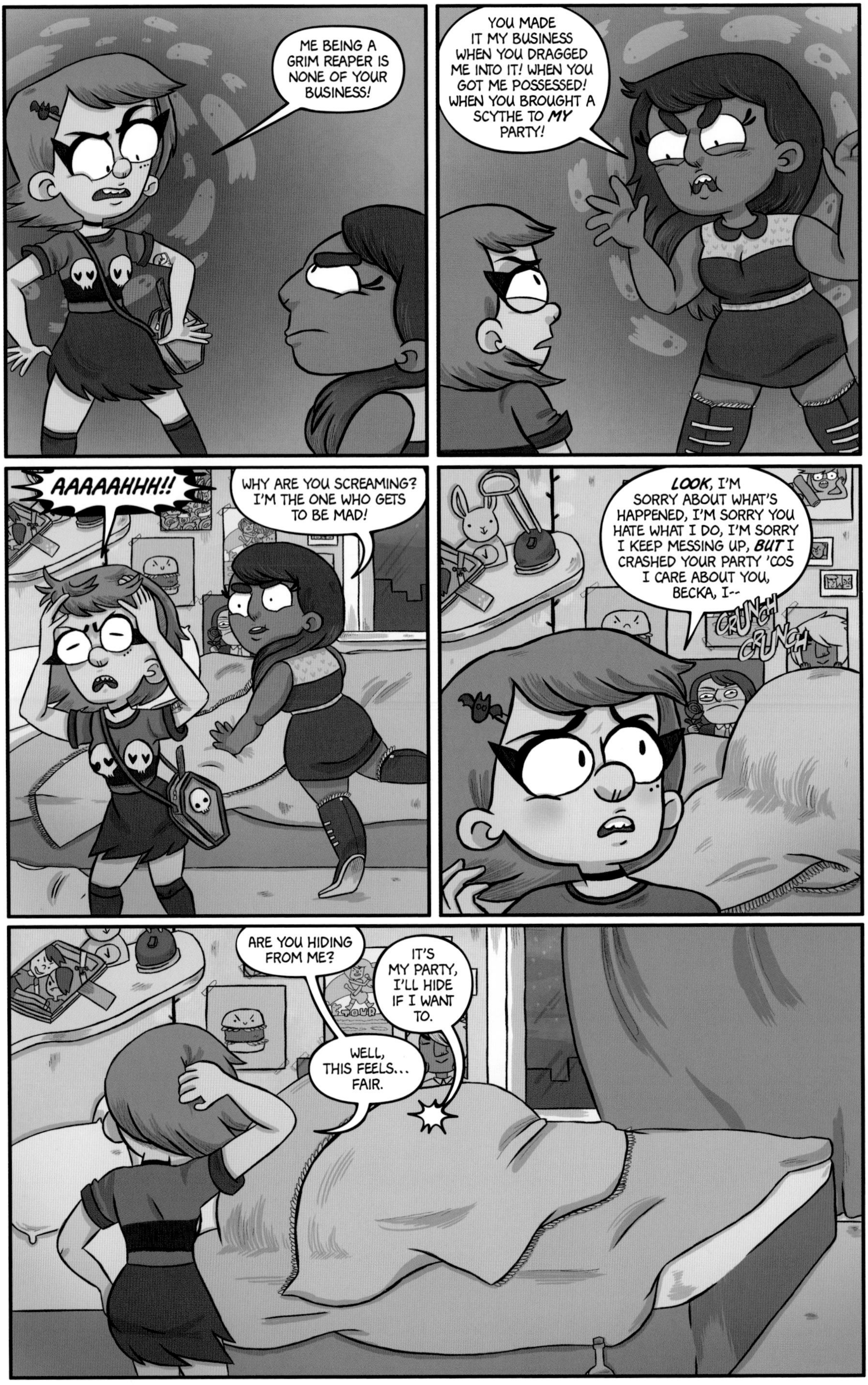
ME BEING A GRIM REAPER IS NONE OF YOUR BUSINESS!
YOU MADE IT MY BUSINESS WHEN YOU DRAGGED ME INTO IT! WHEN YOU GOT ME POSSESSED! WHEN YOU BROUGHT A SCYTHE TO *MY* PARTY!
AAAAAHHH!!
WHY ARE YOU SCREAMING? I'M THE ONE WHO GETS TO BE MAD!
LOOK, I'M SORRY ABOUT WHAT'S HAPPENED, I'M SORRY YOU HATE WHAT I DO, I'M SORRY I KEEP MESSING UP, *BUT* I CRASHED YOUR PARTY 'COS I CARE ABOUT YOU, BECKA, I--
CRUNCH
CRUNCH
ARE YOU HIDING FROM ME?
IT'S MY PARTY, I'LL HIDE IF I WANT TO.
WELL, THIS FEELS... FAIR.

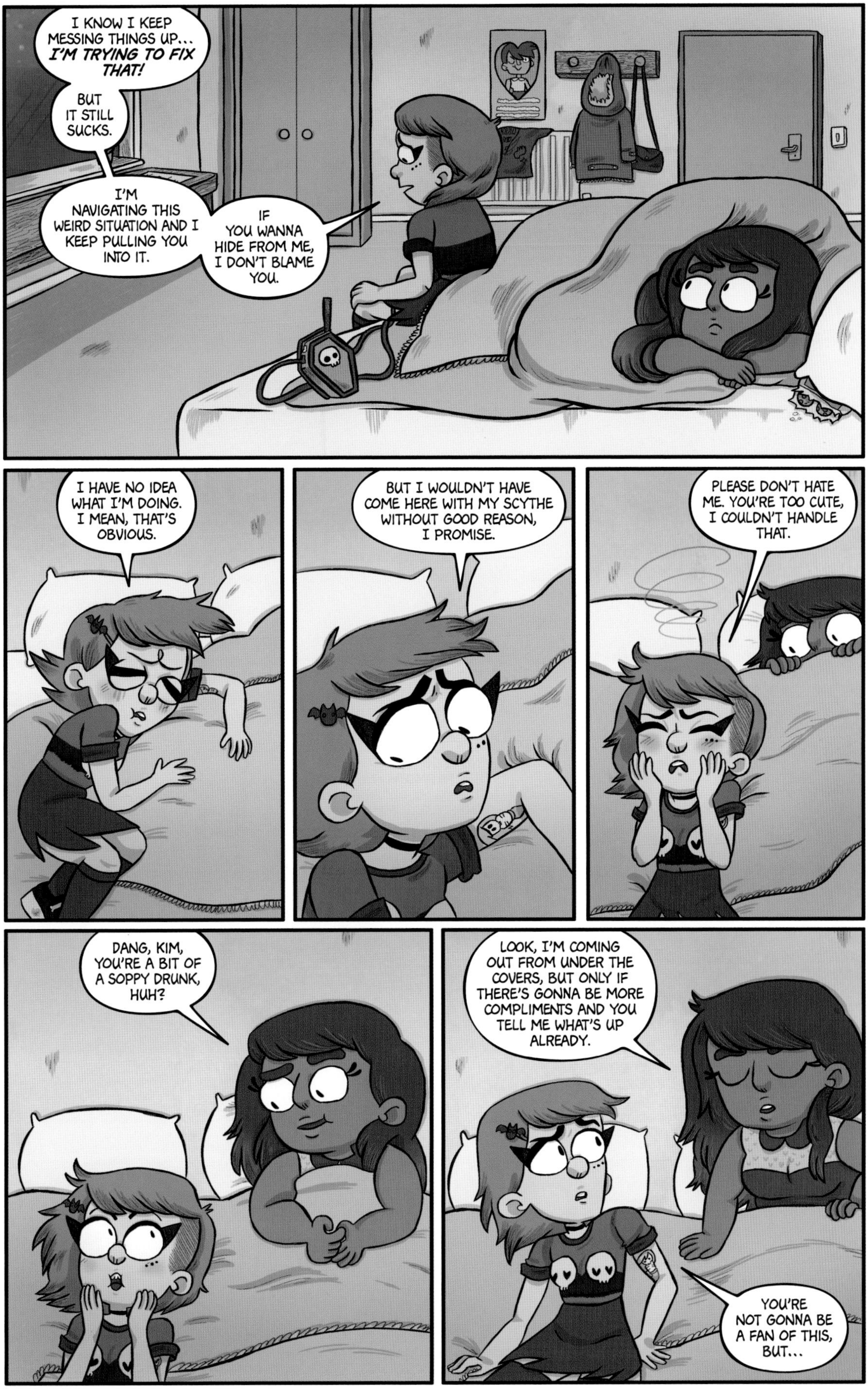
I KNOW I KEEP MESSING THINGS UP... *I'M TRYING TO FIX THAT!*
BUT IT STILL SUCKS.
I'M NAVIGATING THIS WEIRD SITUATION AND I KEEP PULLING YOU INTO IT.
IF YOU WANNA HIDE FROM ME, I DON'T BLAME YOU.
I HAVE NO IDEA WHAT I'M DOING. I MEAN, THAT'S OBVIOUS.
BUT I WOULDN'T HAVE COME HERE WITH MY SCYTHE WITHOUT GOOD REASON, I PROMISE.
PLEASE DON'T HATE ME. YOU'RE TOO CUTE, I COULDN'T HANDLE THAT.
DANG, KIM, YOU'RE A BIT OF A SOPPY DRUNK, HUH?
LOOK, I'M COMING OUT FROM UNDER THE COVERS, BUT ONLY IF THERE'S GONNA BE MORE COMPLIMENTS AND YOU TELL ME WHAT'S UP ALREADY.
YOU'RE NOT GONNA BE A FAN OF THIS, BUT...

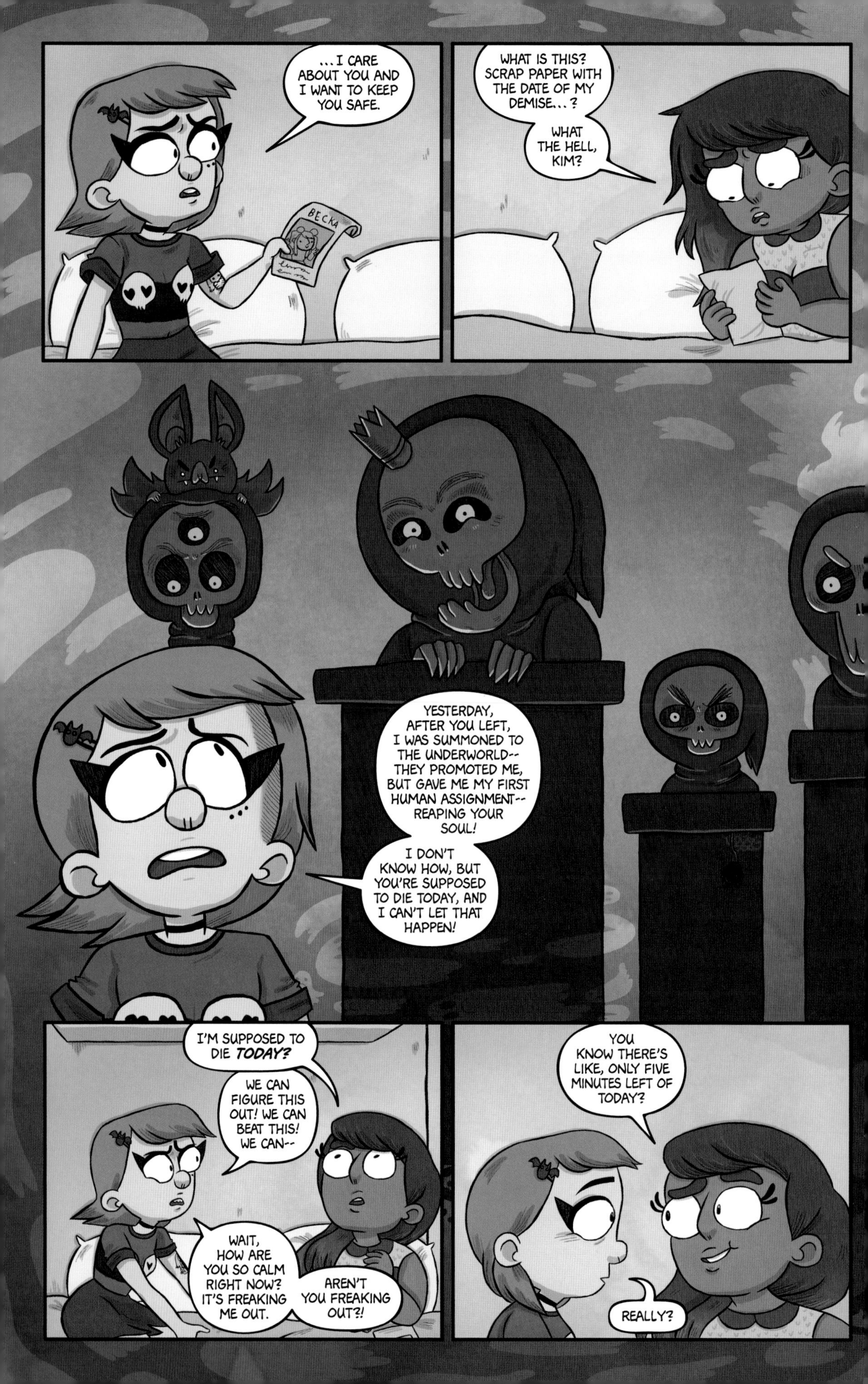

...I CARE ABOUT YOU AND I WANT TO KEEP YOU SAFE.
BECKA
WHAT IS THIS? SCRAP PAPER WITH THE DATE OF MY DEMISE...?
WHAT THE HELL, KIM?
YESTERDAY, AFTER YOU LEFT, I WAS SUMMONED TO THE UNDERWORLD-- THEY PROMOTED ME, BUT GAVE ME MY FIRST HUMAN ASSIGNMENT-- REAPING YOUR SOUL!
I DON'T KNOW HOW, BUT YOU'RE SUPPOSED TO DIE TODAY, AND I CAN'T LET THAT HAPPEN!
I'M SUPPOSED TO DIE ***TODAY?***
WE CAN FIGURE THIS OUT! WE CAN BEAT THIS! WE CAN--
WAIT, HOW ARE YOU SO CALM RIGHT NOW? IT'S FREAKING ME OUT.
AREN'T YOU FREAKING OUT?!
YOU KNOW THERE'S LIKE, ONLY FIVE MINUTES LEFT OF TODAY?
REALLY?

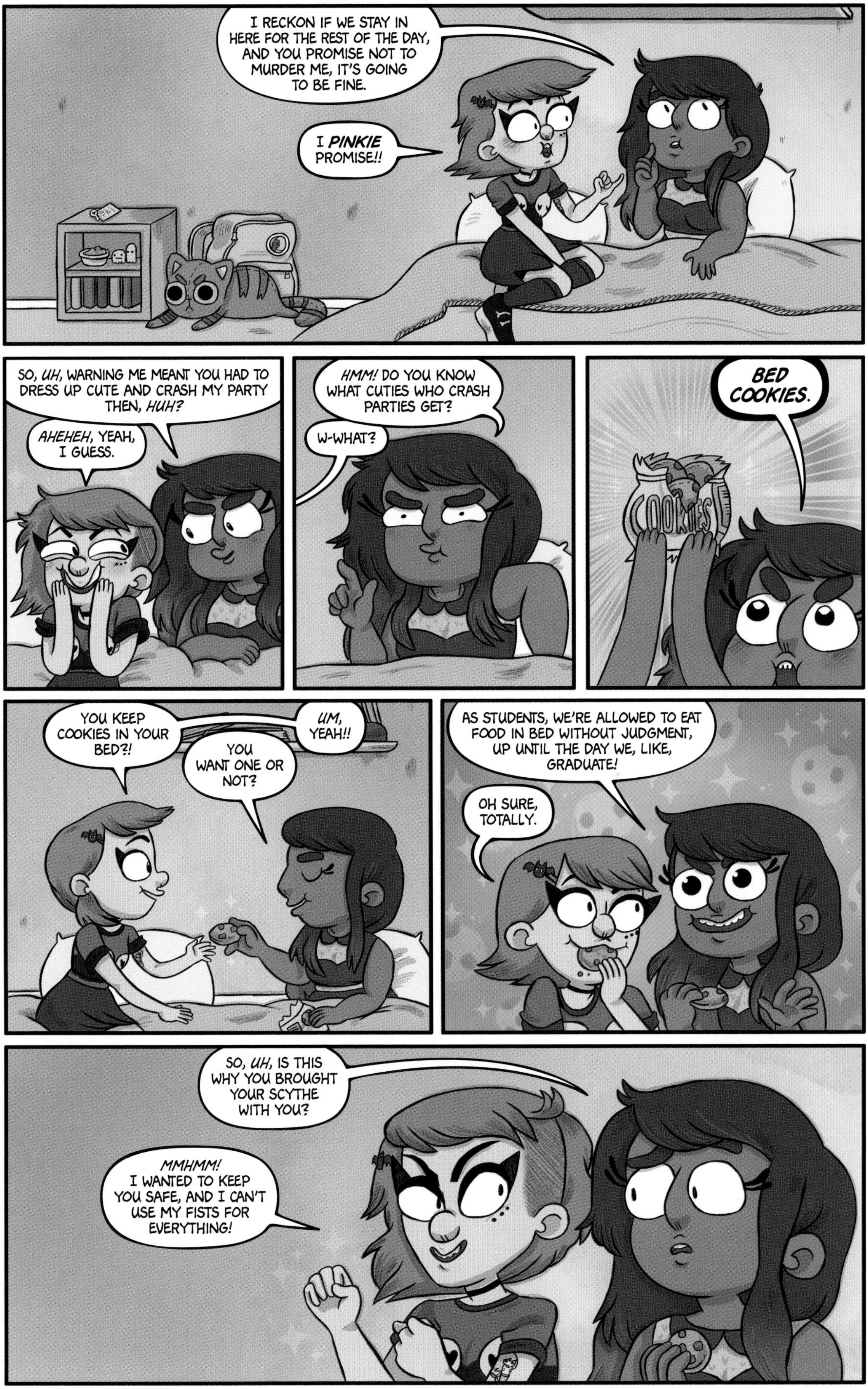
I RECKON IF WE STAY IN HERE FOR THE REST OF THE DAY, AND YOU PROMISE NOT TO MURDER ME, IT'S GOING TO BE FINE.
I *PINKIE* PROMISE!!
SO, *UH*, WARNING ME MEANT YOU HAD TO DRESS UP CUTE AND CRASH MY PARTY THEN, *HUH?*
AHEHEH, YEAH, I GUESS.
HMM! DO YOU KNOW WHAT CUTIES WHO CRASH PARTIES GET?
W-WHAT?
BED COOKIES.
COOKIES
YOU KEEP COOKIES IN YOUR BED?!
UM, YEAH!!
YOU WANT ONE OR NOT?
AS STUDENTS, WE'RE ALLOWED TO EAT FOOD IN BED WITHOUT JUDGMENT, UP UNTIL THE DAY WE, LIKE, GRADUATE!
OH SURE, TOTALLY.
SO, *UH*, IS THIS WHY YOU BROUGHT YOUR SCYTHE WITH YOU?
MMHMM! I WANTED TO KEEP YOU SAFE, AND I CAN'T USE MY FISTS FOR EVERYTHING!

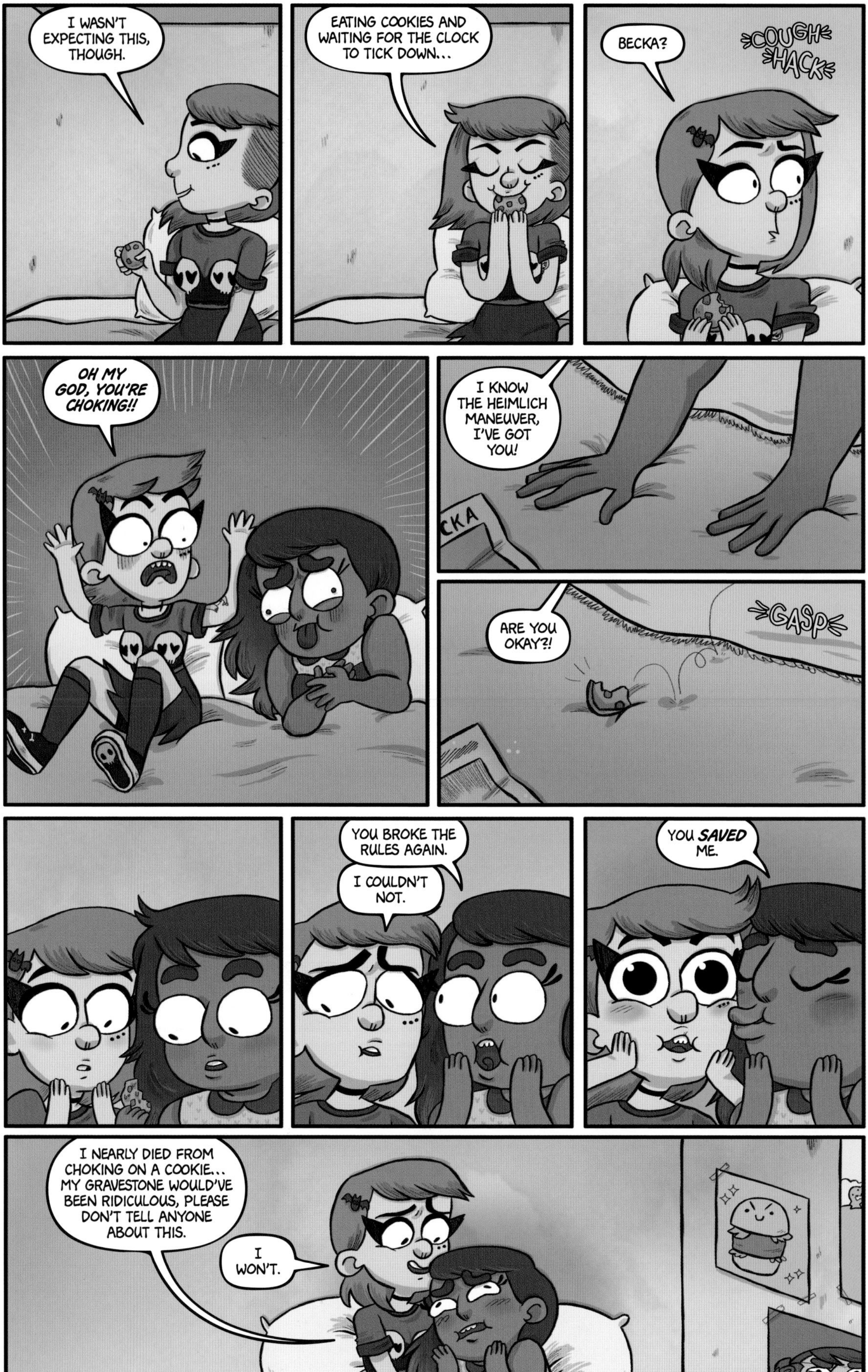
I WASN'T EXPECTING THIS, THOUGH.
EATING COOKIES AND WAITING FOR THE CLOCK TO TICK DOWN...
BECKA?
COUGH
HACK
OH MY GOD, YOU'RE CHOKING!!
I KNOW THE HEIMLICH MANEUVER, I'VE GOT YOU!
CKA
ARE YOU OKAY?!
GASP
YOU BROKE THE RULES AGAIN.
I COULDN'T NOT.
YOU **SAVED** ME.
I NEARLY DIED FROM CHOKING ON A COOKIE... MY GRAVESTONE WOULD'VE BEEN RIDICULOUS, PLEASE DON'T TELL ANYONE ABOUT THIS.
I WON'T.

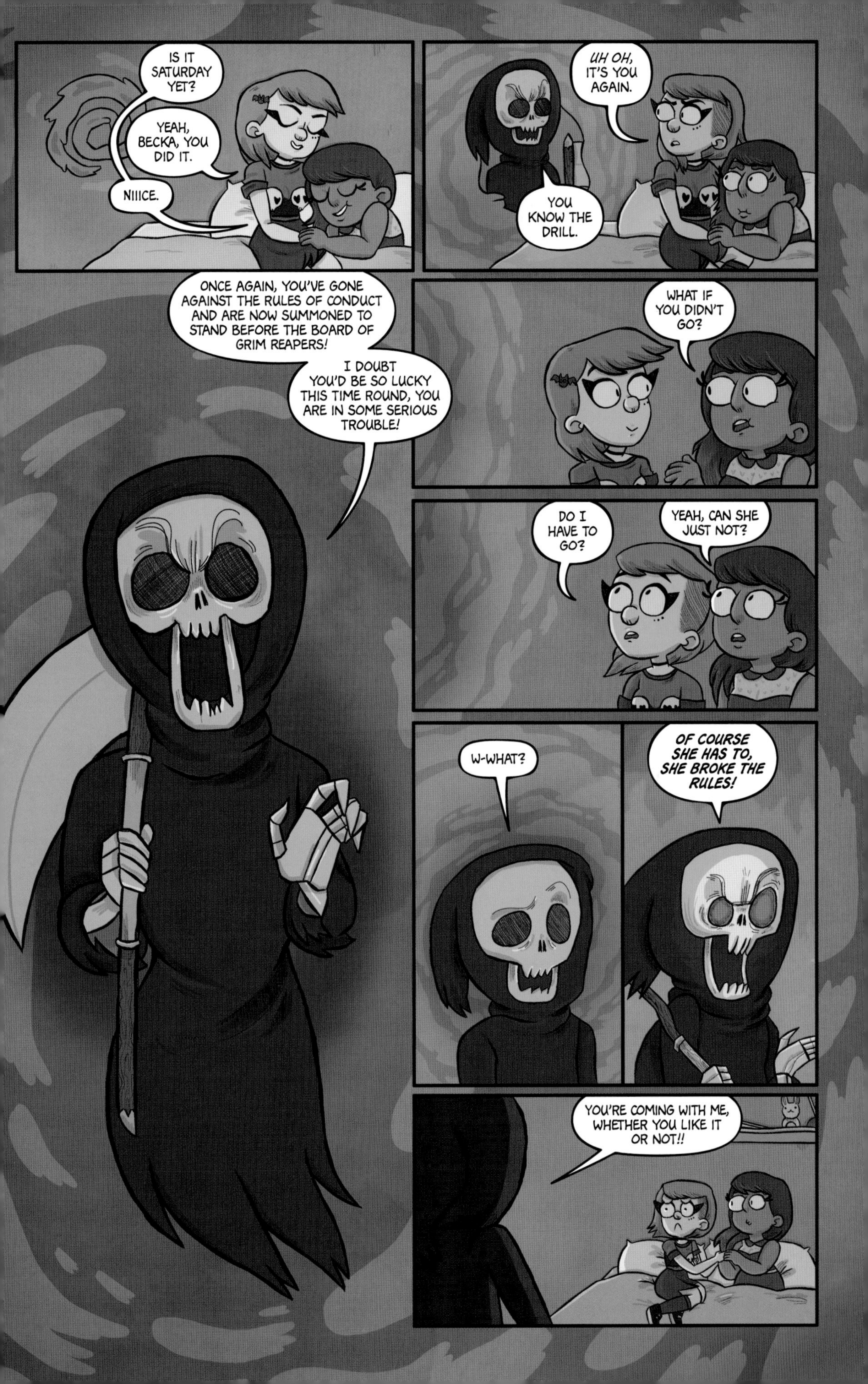
IS IT SATURDAY YET?
YEAH, BECKA, YOU DID IT.
NIIICE.
UH OH, IT'S YOU AGAIN.
YOU KNOW THE DRILL.
ONCE AGAIN, YOU'VE GONE AGAINST THE RULES OF CONDUCT AND ARE NOW SUMMONED TO STAND BEFORE THE BOARD OF GRIM REAPERS!
I DOUBT YOU'D BE SO LUCKY THIS TIME ROUND, YOU ARE IN SOME SERIOUS TROUBLE!
WHAT IF YOU DIDN'T GO?
DO I HAVE TO GO?
YEAH, CAN SHE JUST NOT?
W-WHAT?
OF COURSE SHE HAS TO, SHE BROKE THE RULES!
YOU'RE COMING WITH ME, WHETHER YOU LIKE IT OR NOT!!

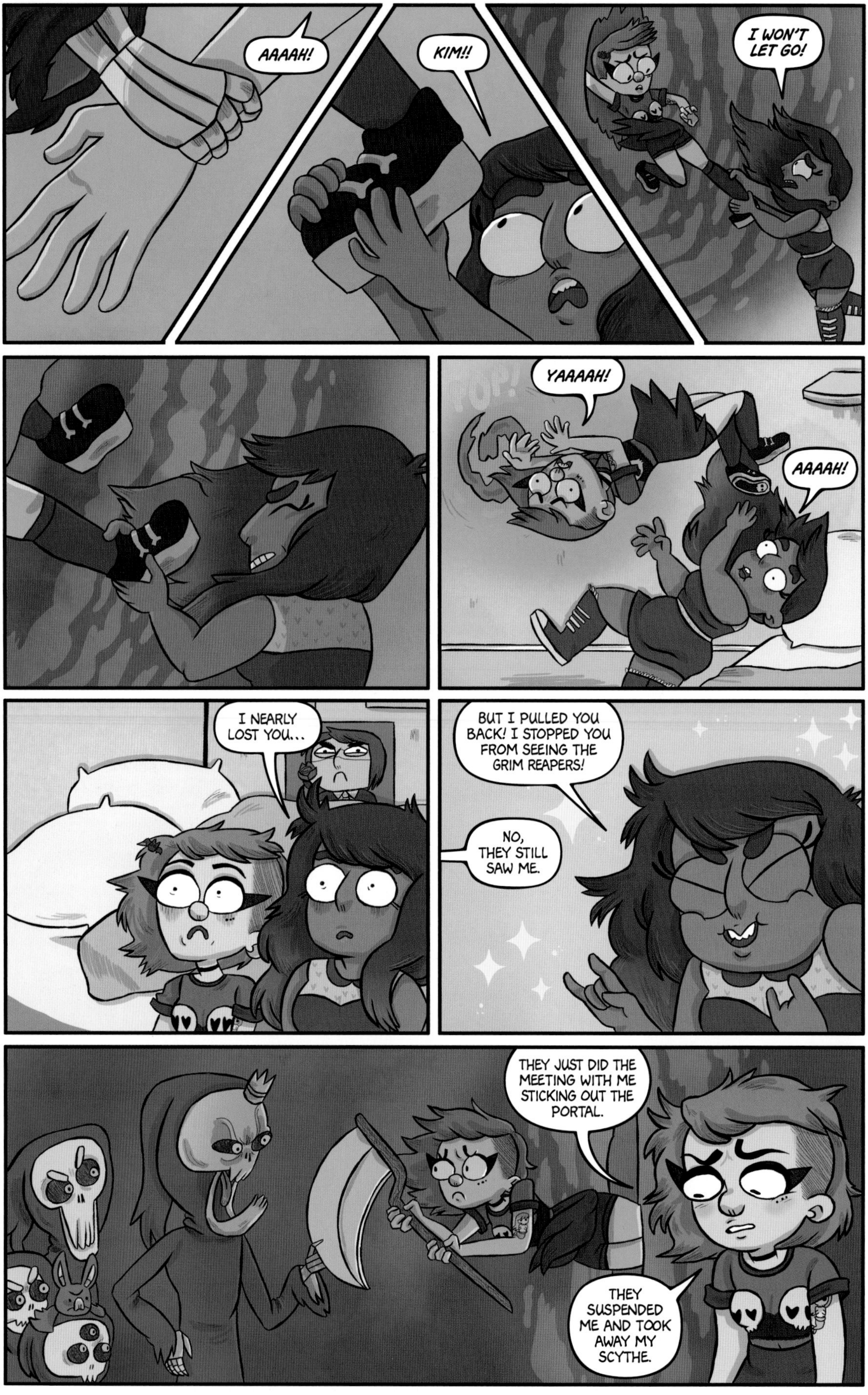
AAAAH!
KIM!!
I WON'T LET GO!
POP!
YAAAAH!
AAAAH!
I NEARLY LOST YOU...
BUT I PULLED YOU BACK! I STOPPED YOU FROM SEEING THE GRIM REAPERS!
NO, THEY STILL SAW ME.
THEY JUST DID THE MEETING WITH ME STICKING OUT THE PORTAL.
THEY SUSPENDED ME AND TOOK AWAY MY SCYTHE.

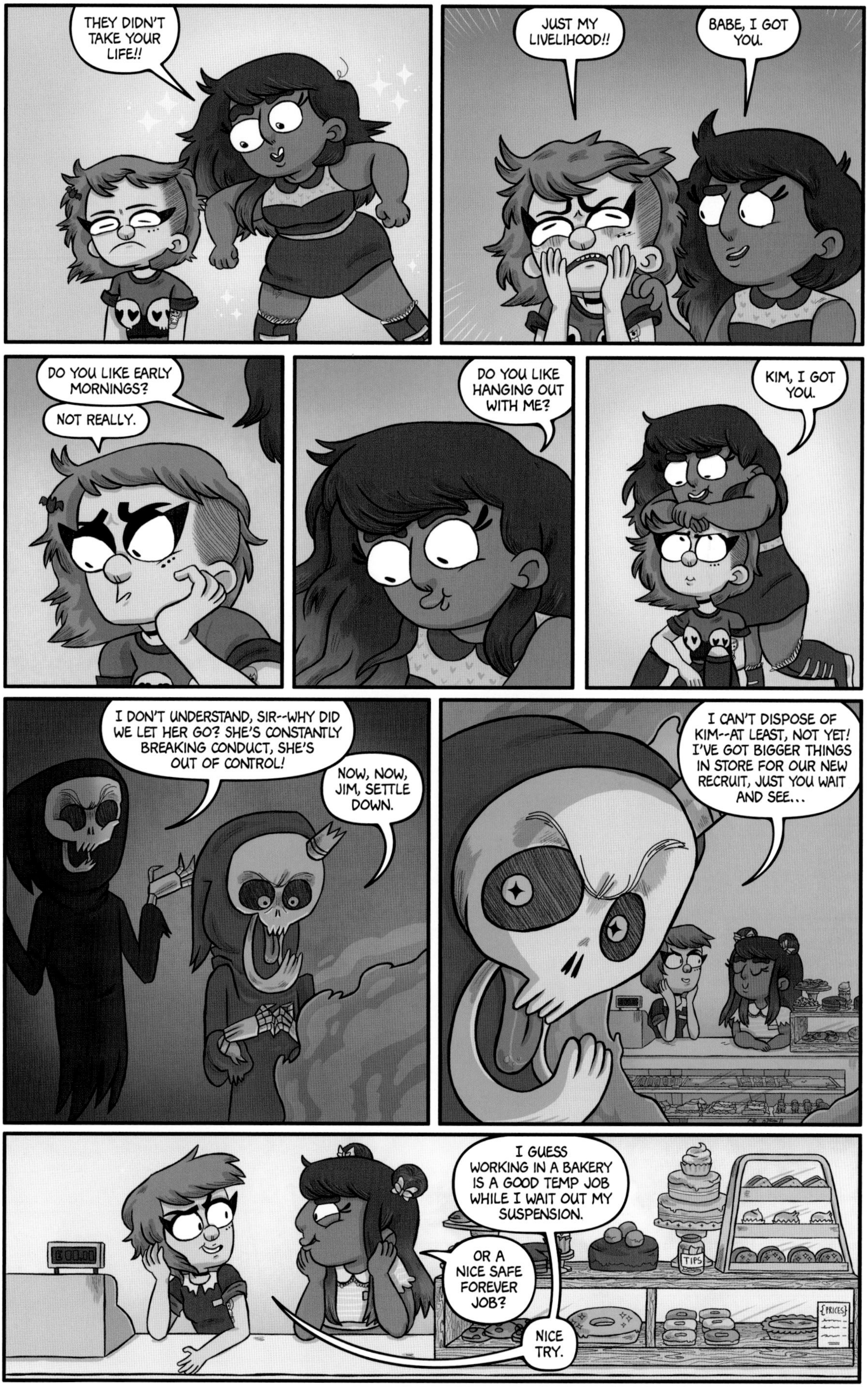
THEY DIDN'T TAKE YOUR LIFE!!
JUST MY LIVELIHOOD!!
BABE, I GOT YOU.
DO YOU LIKE EARLY MORNINGS?
NOT REALLY.
DO YOU LIKE HANGING OUT WITH ME?
KIM, I GOT YOU.
I DON'T UNDERSTAND, SIR--WHY DID WE LET HER GO? SHE'S CONSTANTLY BREAKING CONDUCT, SHE'S OUT OF CONTROL!
NOW, NOW, JIM, SETTLE DOWN.
I CAN'T DISPOSE OF KIM--AT LEAST, NOT YET! I'VE GOT BIGGER THINGS IN STORE FOR OUR NEW RECRUIT, JUST YOU WAIT AND SEE...
I GUESS WORKING IN A BAKERY IS A GOOD TEMP JOB WHILE I WAIT OUT MY SUSPENSION.
OR A NICE SAFE FOREVER JOB?
NICE TRY.
TIPS
PRICES

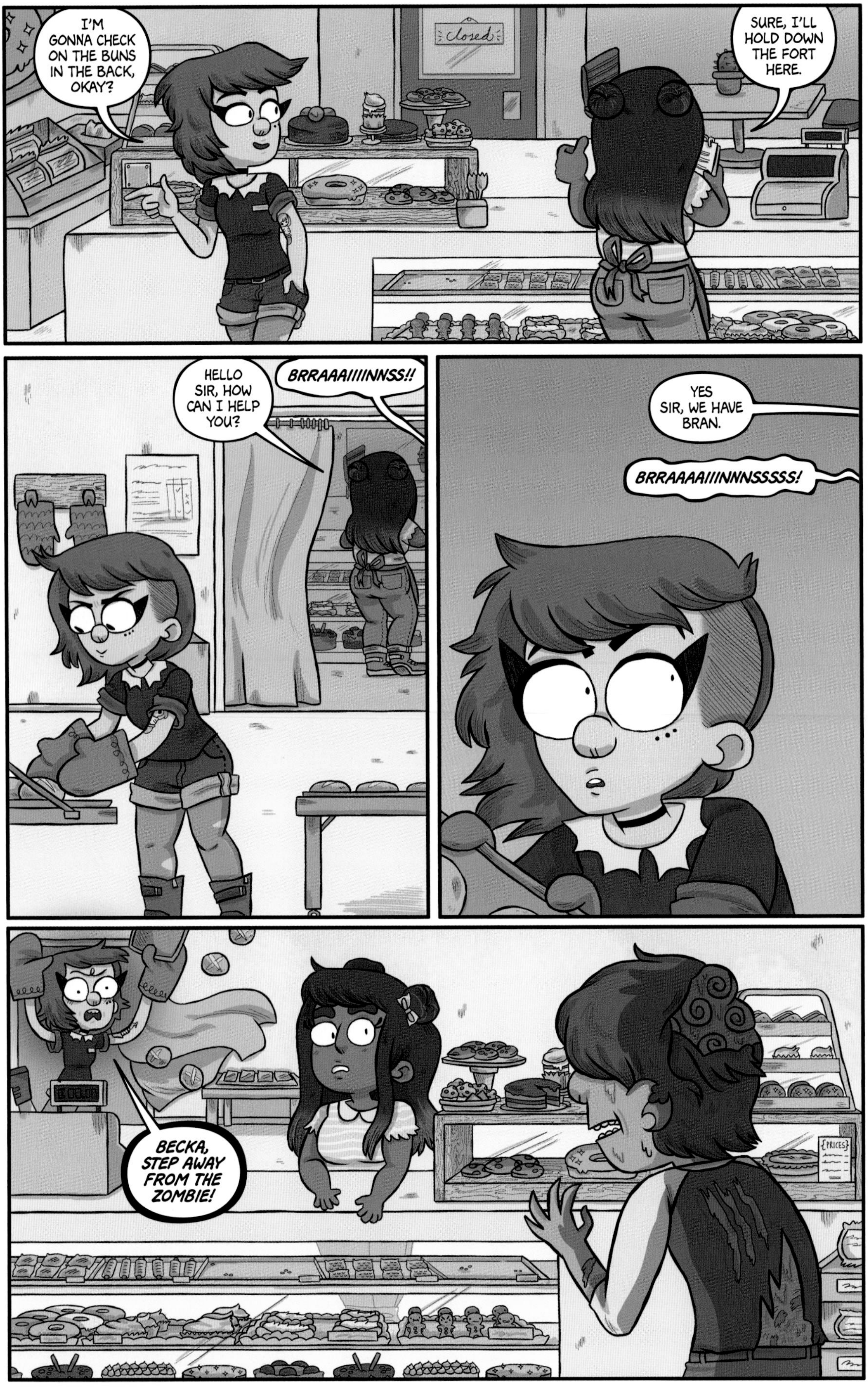

I'M GONNA CHECK ON THE BUNS IN THE BACK, OKAY?
closed
SURE, I'LL HOLD DOWN THE FORT HERE.
HELLO SIR, HOW CAN I HELP YOU?
BRRAAAIIIINNSS!!
YES SIR, WE HAVE BRAN.
BRRAAAAIIIINNNSSSSS!
BECKA, STEP AWAY FROM THE ZOMBIE!

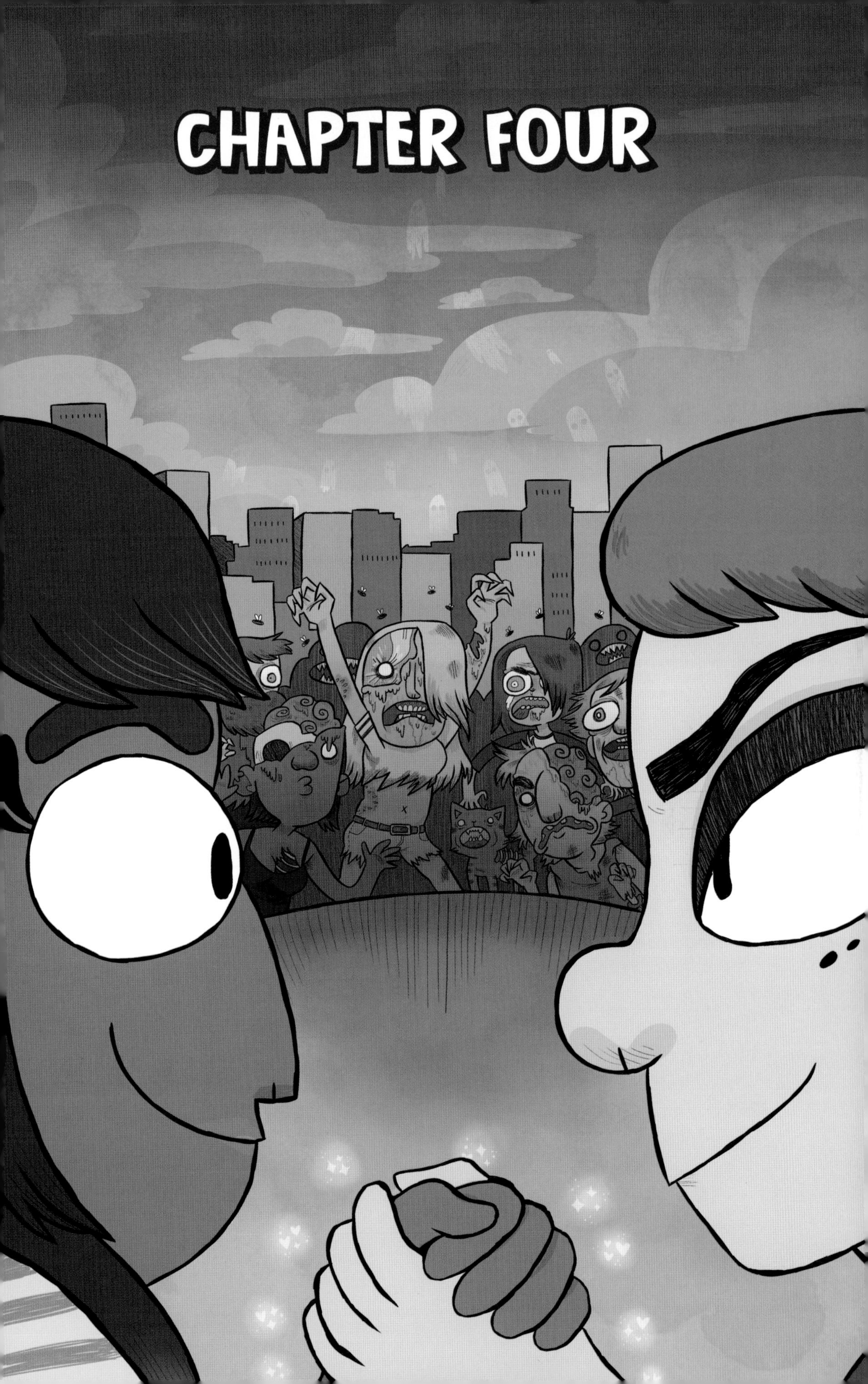
CHAPTER FOUR

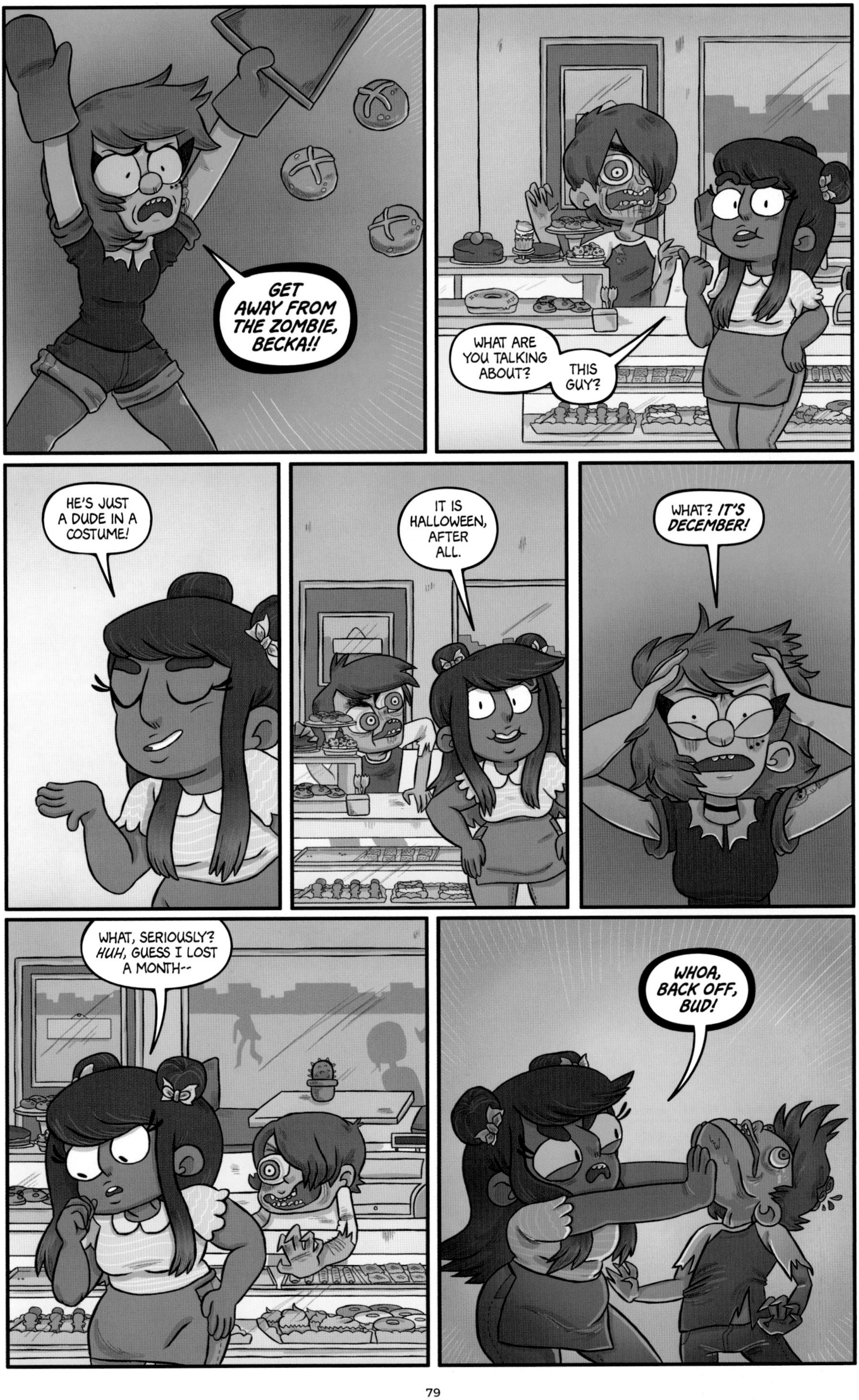
GET AWAY FROM THE ZOMBIE, BECKA!!
WHAT ARE YOU TALKING ABOUT?
THIS GUY?
HE'S JUST A DUDE IN A COSTUME!
IT IS HALLOWEEN, AFTER ALL.
WHAT? *IT'S DECEMBER!*
WHAT, SERIOUSLY? *HUH*, GUESS I LOST A MONTH--
WHOA, BACK OFF, BUD!

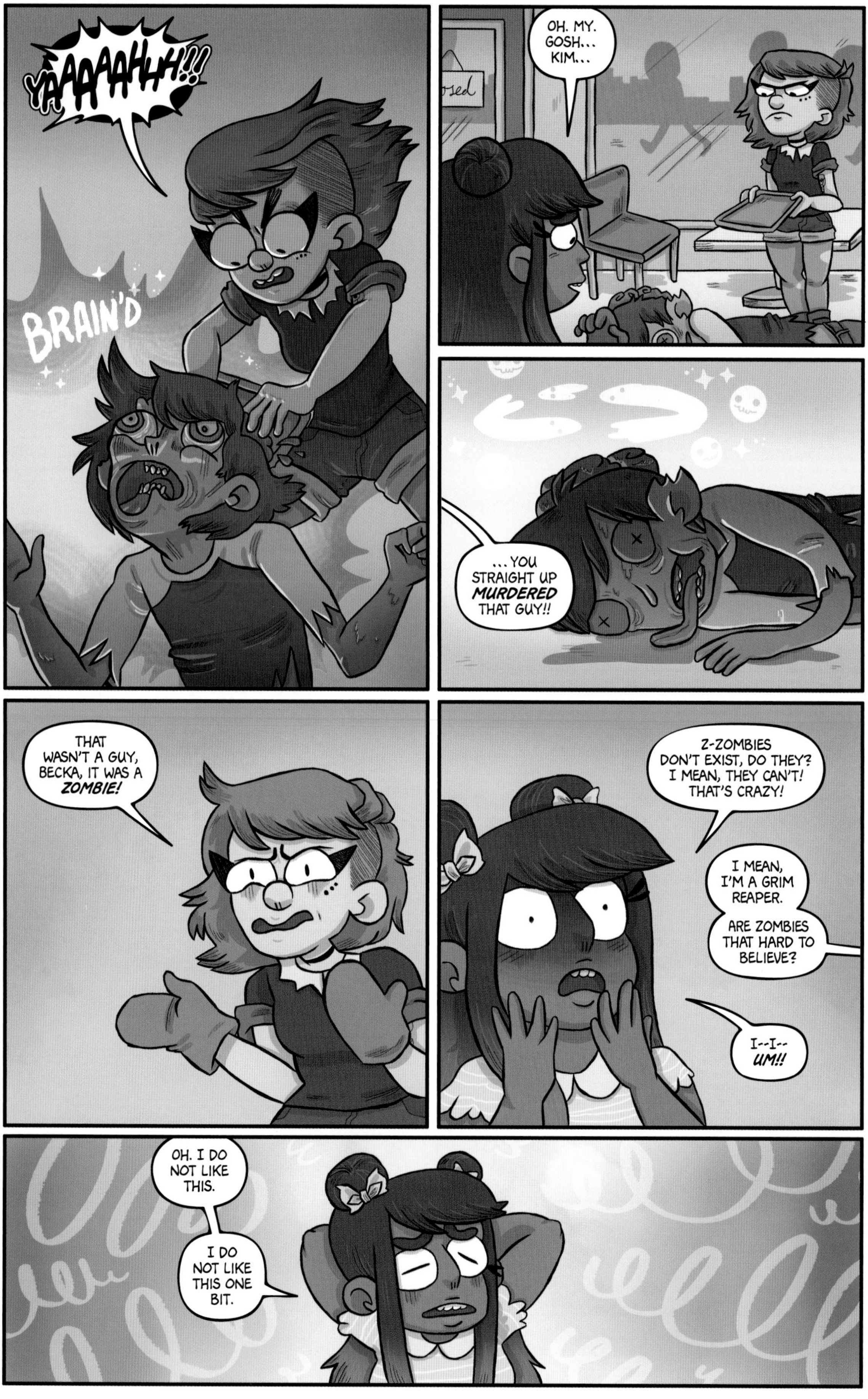
YAAAAAHHH!!!
BRAIN'D
OH. MY. GOSH... KIM...
...YOU STRAIGHT UP *MURDERED* THAT GUY!!
THAT WASN'T A GUY, BECKA, IT WAS A *ZOMBIE!*
Z-ZOMBIES DON'T EXIST, DO THEY? I MEAN, THEY CAN'T! THAT'S CRAZY!
I MEAN, I'M A GRIM REAPER.
ARE ZOMBIES THAT HARD TO BELIEVE?
I--I-- *UM!!*
OH. I DO NOT LIKE THIS.
I DO NOT LIKE THIS ONE BIT.

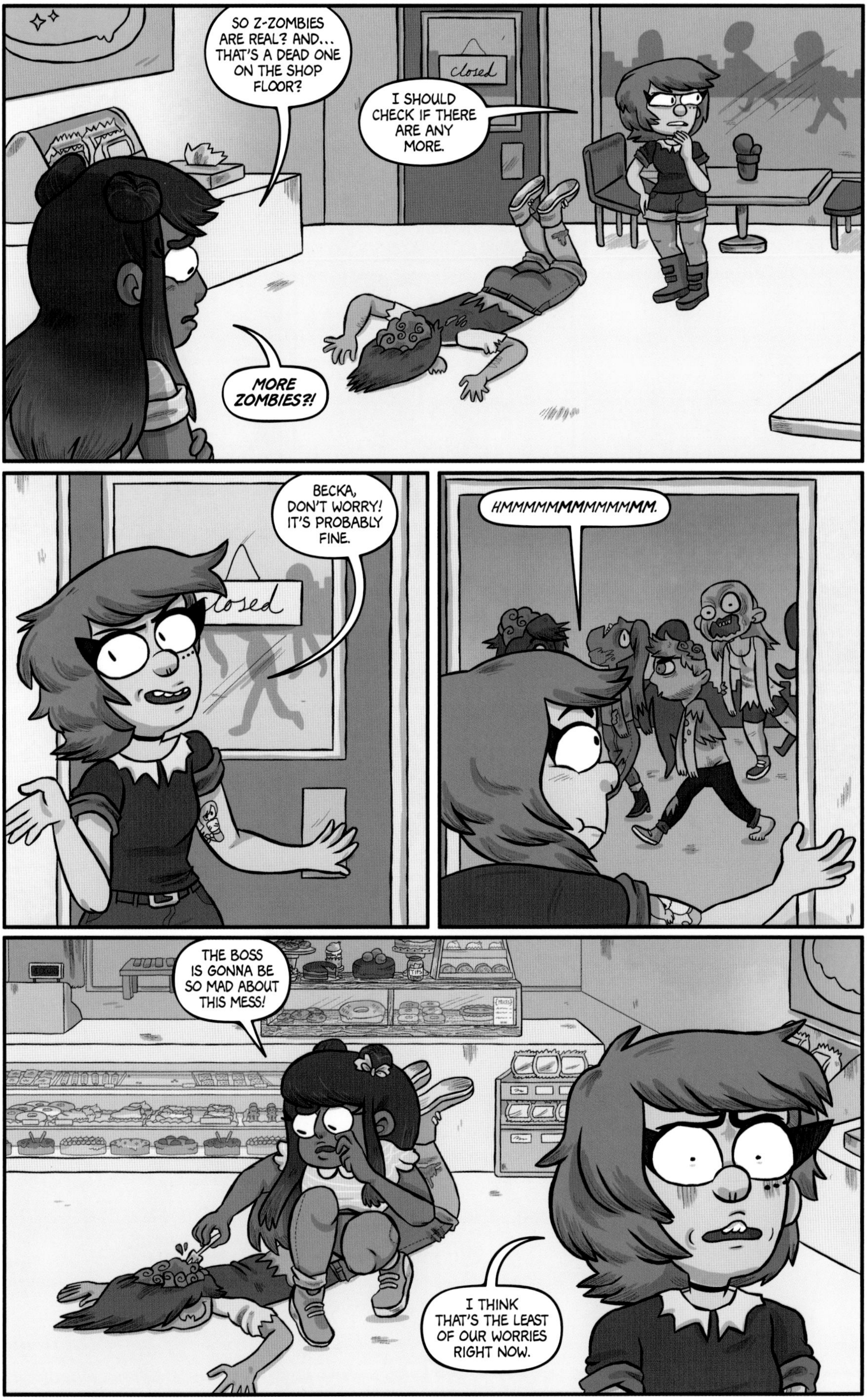
SO Z-ZOMBIES ARE REAL? AND... THAT'S A DEAD ONE ON THE SHOP FLOOR?
closed
I SHOULD CHECK IF THERE ARE ANY MORE.
MORE ZOMBIES?!
BECKA, DON'T WORRY! IT'S PROBABLY FINE.
closed
HMMMMMMMMMMMMMM.
THE BOSS IS GONNA BE SO MAD ABOUT THIS MESS!
TIPS
I THINK THAT'S THE LEAST OF OUR WORRIES RIGHT NOW.

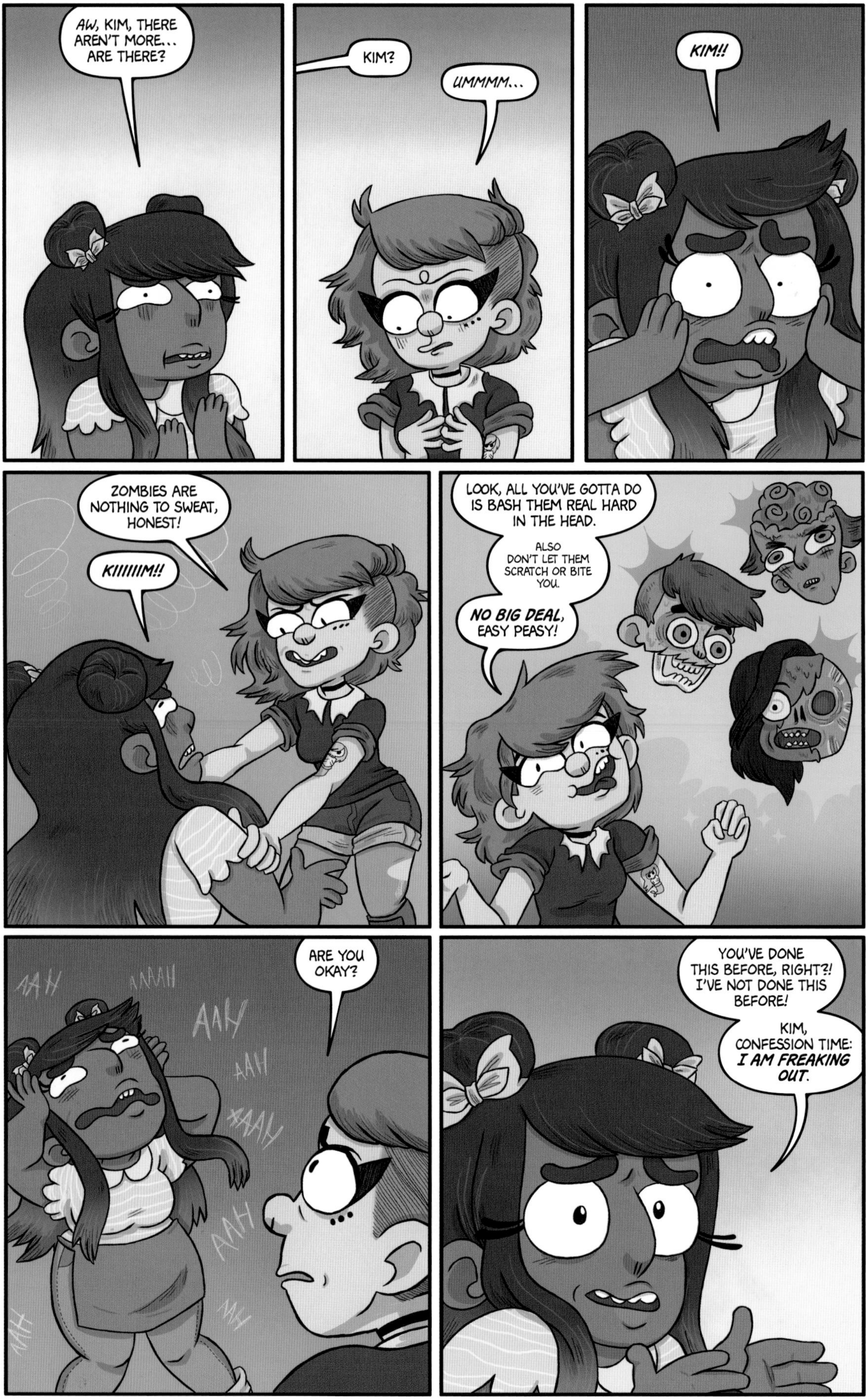
AW, KIM, THERE AREN'T MORE... ARE THERE?
KIM?
UMMMM...
KIM!!
ZOMBIES ARE NOTHING TO SWEAT, HONEST!
KIIIIIIM!!
LOOK, ALL YOU'VE GOTTA DO IS BASH THEM REAL HARD IN THE HEAD.
ALSO DON'T LET THEM SCRATCH OR BITE YOU.
NO BIG DEAL, EASY PEASY!
ARE YOU OKAY?
YOU'VE DONE THIS BEFORE, RIGHT?! I'VE NOT DONE THIS BEFORE!
KIM, CONFESSION TIME: I AM FREAKING OUT.

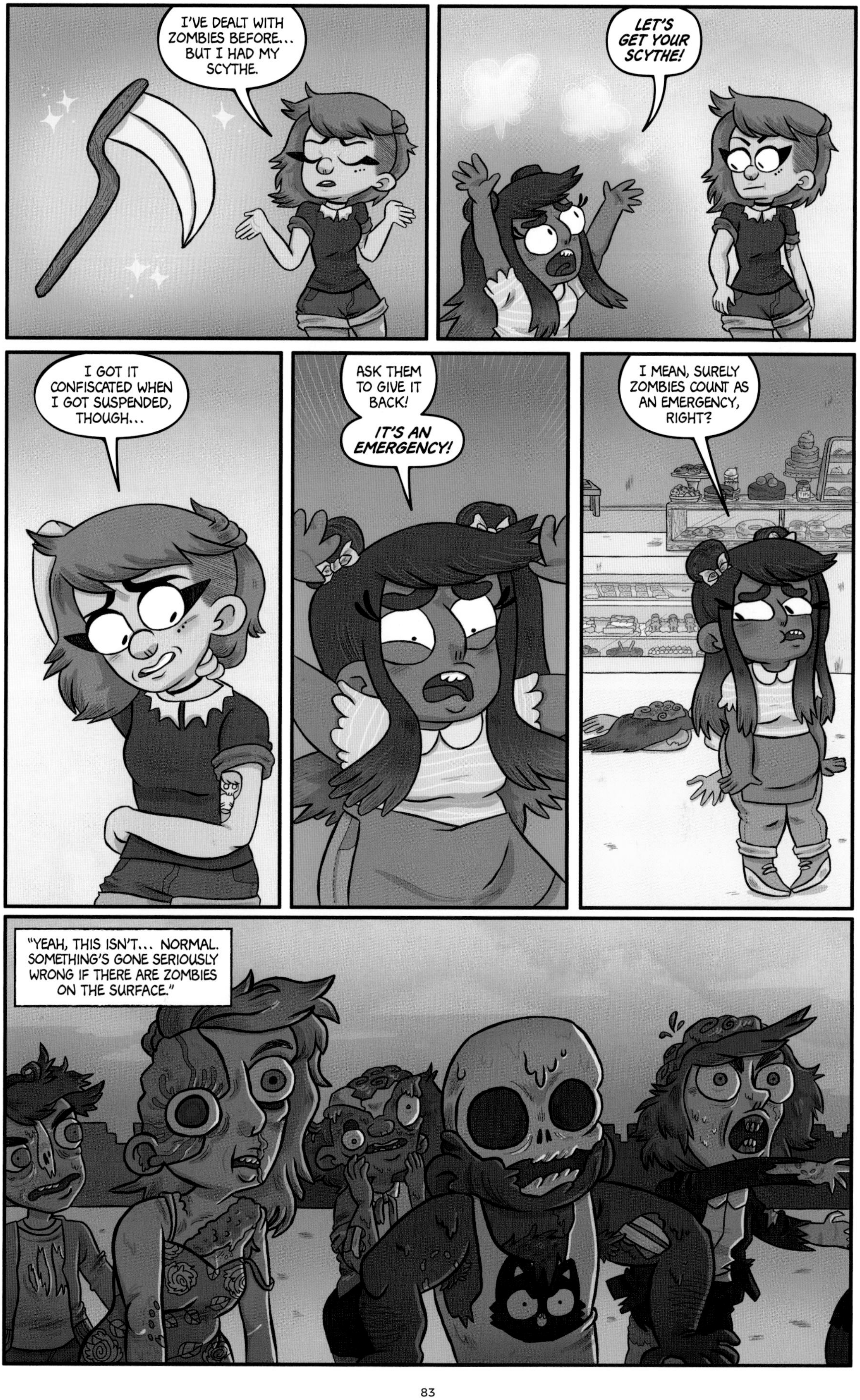
I'VE DEALT WITH ZOMBIES BEFORE... BUT I HAD MY SCYTHE.
LET'S GET YOUR SCYTHE!
I GOT IT CONFISCATED WHEN I GOT SUSPENDED, THOUGH...
ASK THEM TO GIVE IT BACK!
IT'S AN EMERGENCY!
I MEAN, SURELY ZOMBIES COUNT AS AN EMERGENCY, RIGHT?
"YEAH, THIS ISN'T... NORMAL. SOMETHING'S GONE SERIOUSLY WRONG IF THERE ARE ZOMBIES ON THE SURFACE."

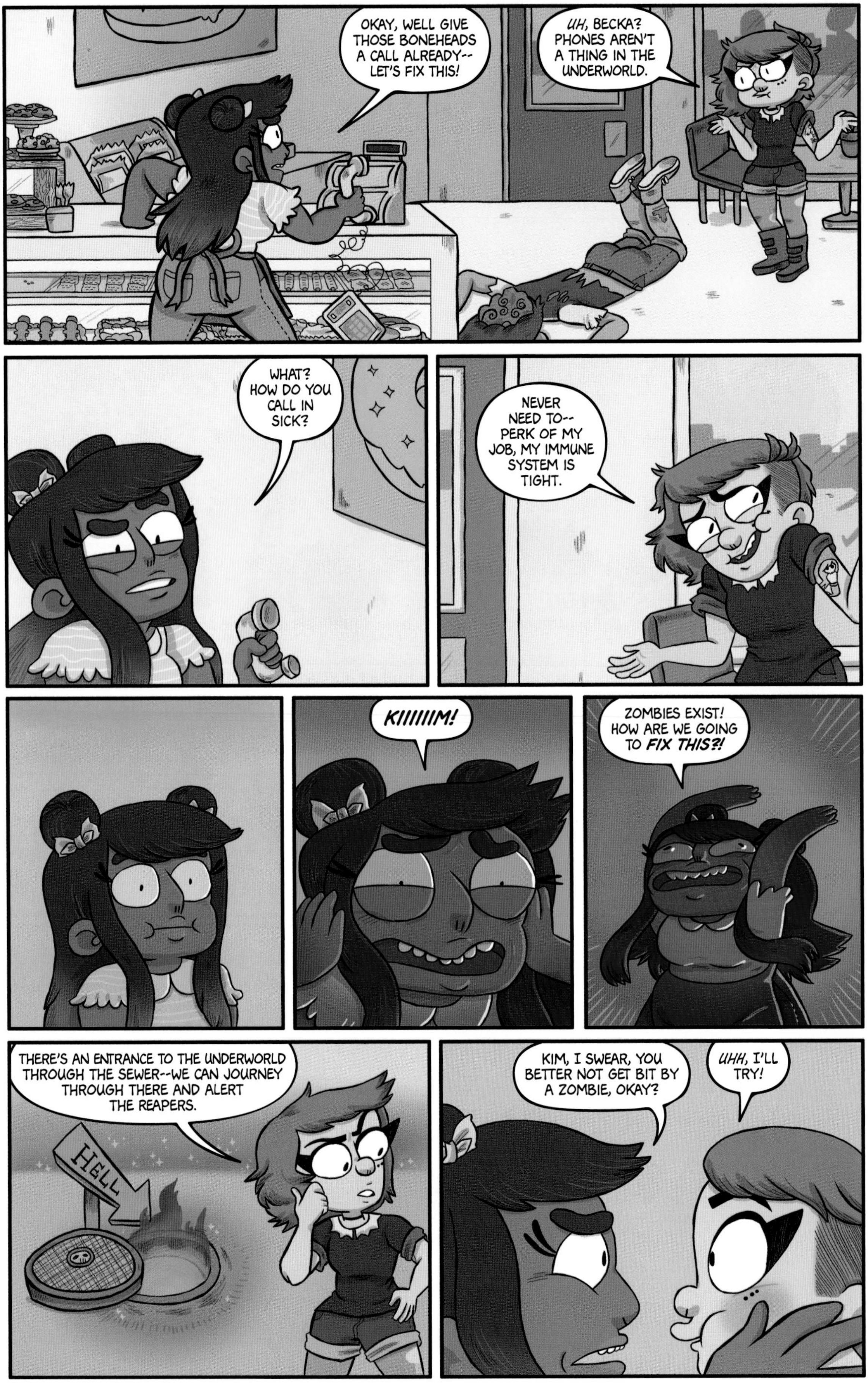
OKAY, WELL GIVE THOSE BONEHEADS A CALL ALREADY-- LET'S FIX THIS!
UH, BECKA? PHONES AREN'T A THING IN THE UNDERWORLD.
WHAT? HOW DO YOU CALL IN SICK?
NEVER NEED TO-- PERK OF MY JOB, MY IMMUNE SYSTEM IS TIGHT.
KIIIIIIM!
ZOMBIES EXIST! HOW ARE WE GOING TO FIX THIS?!
THERE'S AN ENTRANCE TO THE UNDERWORLD THROUGH THE SEWER--WE CAN JOURNEY THROUGH THERE AND ALERT THE REAPERS.
HELL
KIM, I SWEAR, YOU BETTER NOT GET BIT BY A ZOMBIE, OKAY?
UHH, I'LL TRY!

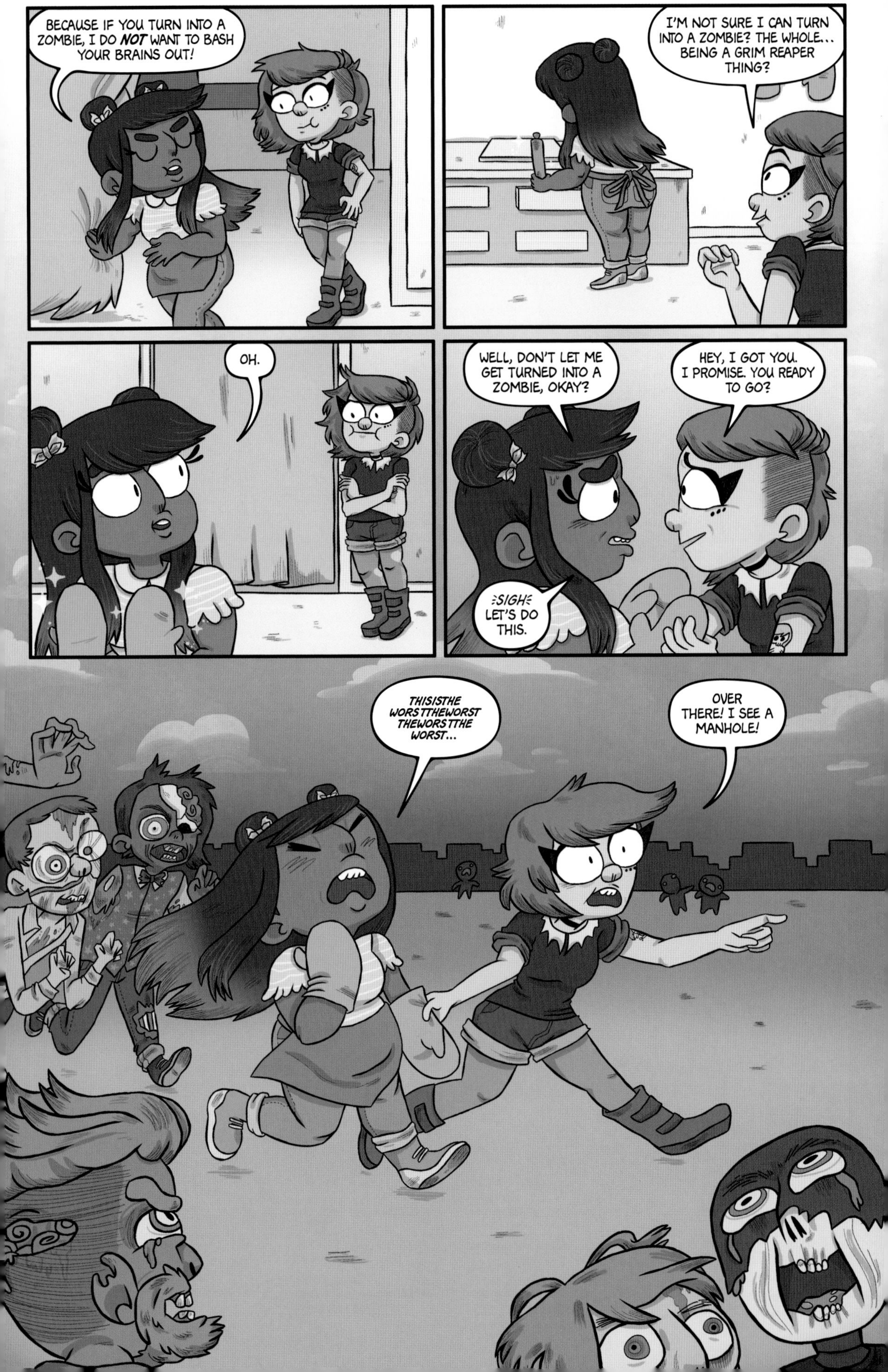
BECAUSE IF YOU TURN INTO A ZOMBIE, I DO **NOT** WANT TO BASH YOUR BRAINS OUT!
I'M NOT SURE I CAN TURN INTO A ZOMBIE? THE WHOLE... BEING A GRIM REAPER THING?
OH.
WELL, DON'T LET ME GET TURNED INTO A ZOMBIE, OKAY?
HEY, I GOT YOU. I PROMISE. YOU READY TO GO?
SIGH LET'S DO THIS.
THISISTHE WORSTTHEWORST THEWORSTTHE WORST...
OVER THERE! I SEE A MANHOLE!

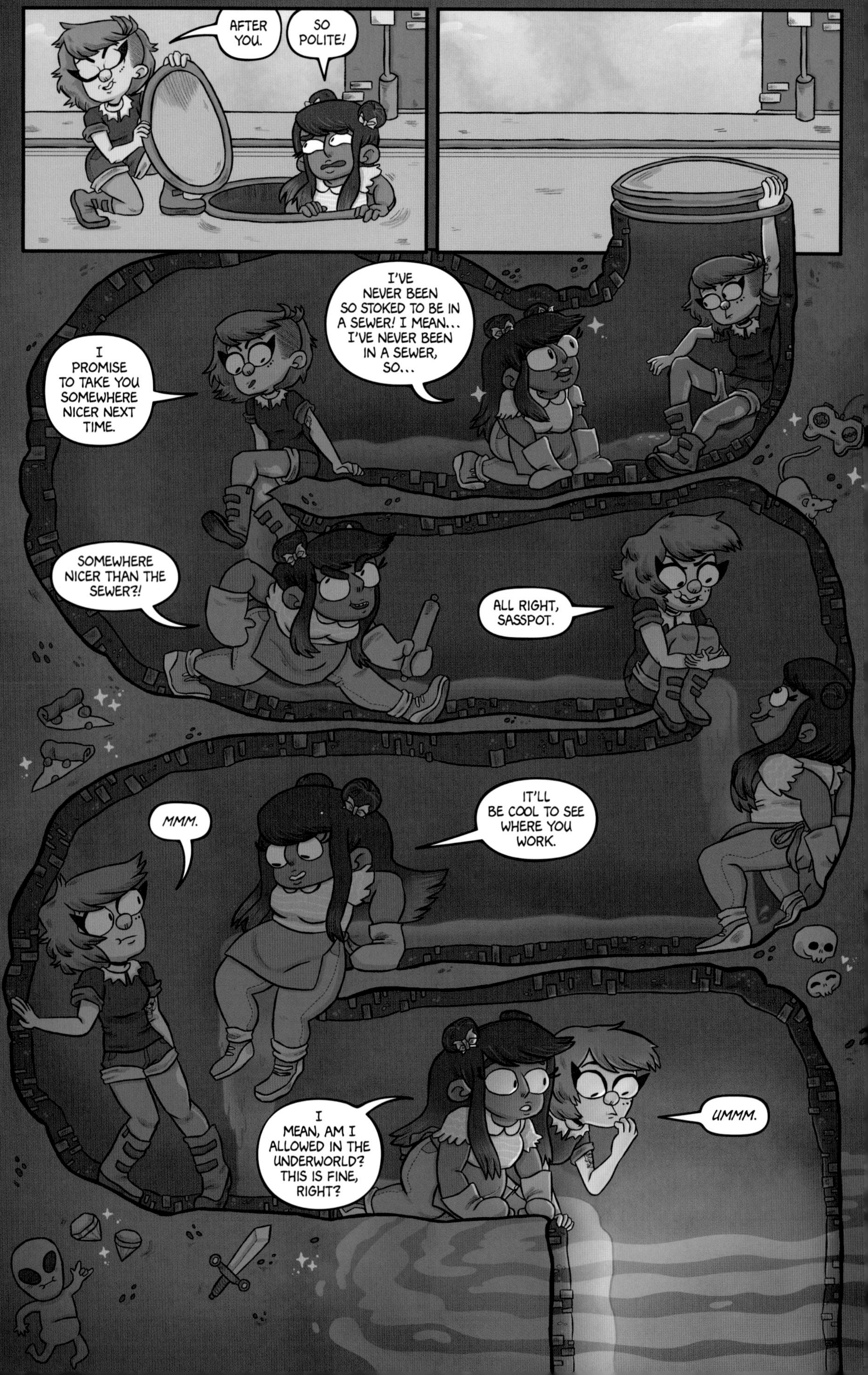
AFTER YOU.
SO POLITE!
I'VE NEVER BEEN SO STOKED TO BE IN A SEWER! I MEAN... I'VE NEVER BEEN IN A SEWER, SO...
I PROMISE TO TAKE YOU SOMEWHERE NICER NEXT TIME.
SOMEWHERE NICER THAN THE SEWER?!
ALL RIGHT, SASSPOT.
IT'LL BE COOL TO SEE WHERE YOU WORK.
MMM.
I MEAN, AM I ALLOWED IN THE UNDERWORLD? THIS IS FINE, RIGHT?
UMMM.

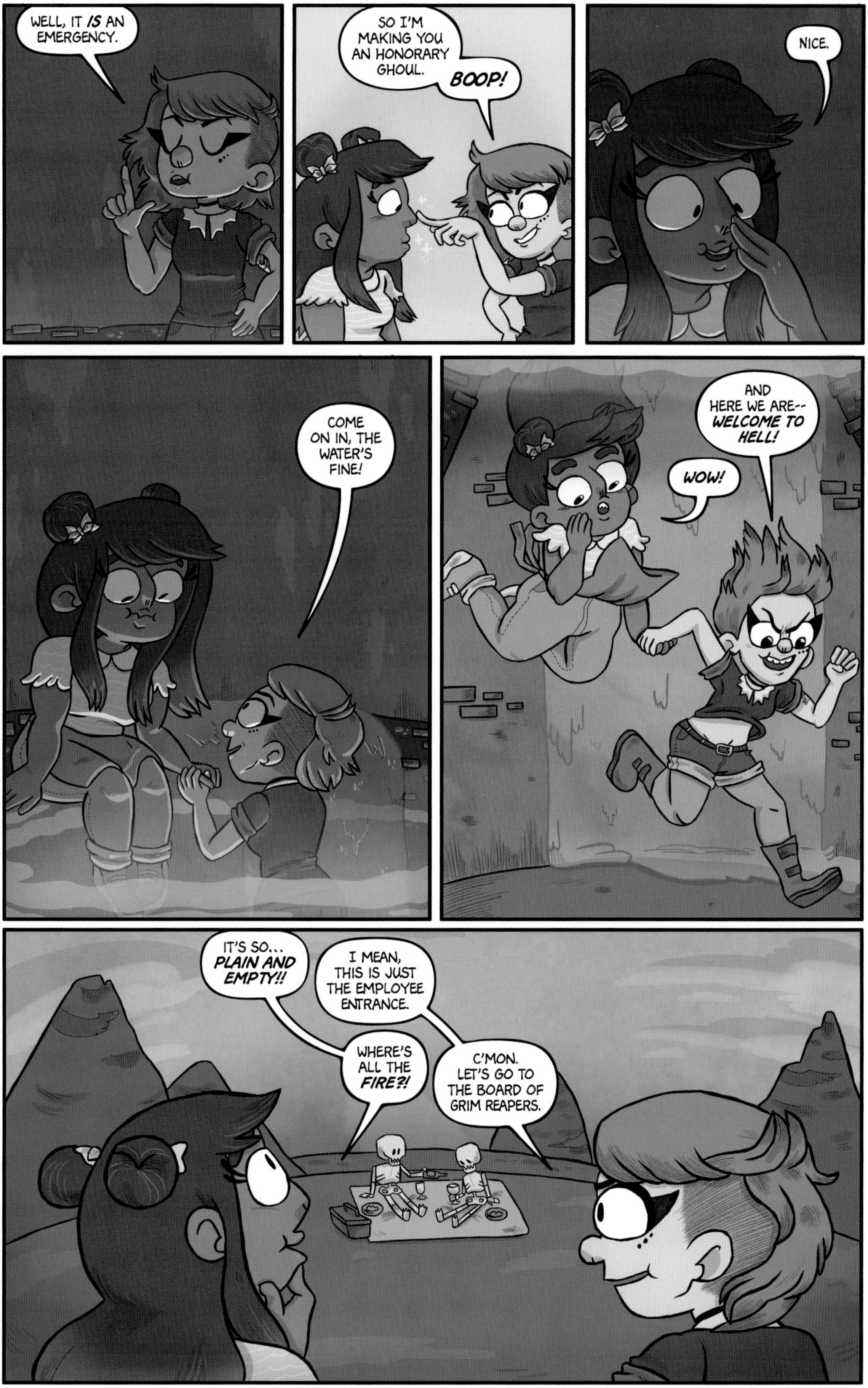
WELL, IT *IS* AN EMERGENCY.
SO I'M MAKING YOU AN HONORARY GHOUL.
BOOP!
NICE.
COME ON IN, THE WATER'S FINE!
AND HERE WE ARE-- *WELCOME TO HELL!*
WOW!
IT'S SO... *PLAIN AND EMPTY!!*
I MEAN, THIS IS JUST THE EMPLOYEE ENTRANCE.
WHERE'S ALL THE *FIRE?!*
C'MON. LET'S GO TO THE BOARD OF GRIM REAPERS.

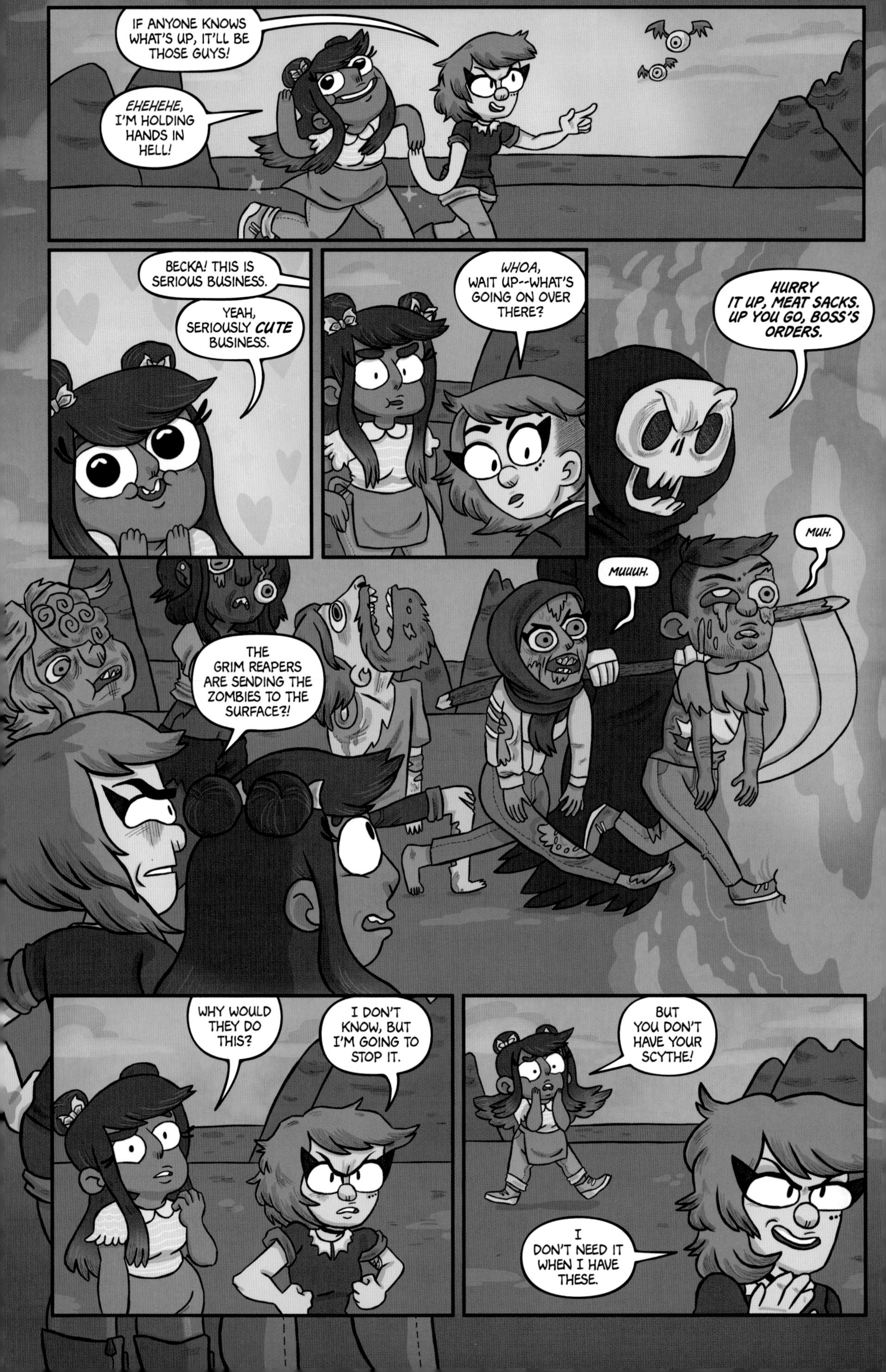
IF ANYONE KNOWS WHAT'S UP, IT'LL BE THOSE GUYS!
EHEHEHE, I'M HOLDING HANDS IN HELL!
BECKA! THIS IS SERIOUS BUSINESS.
YEAH, SERIOUSLY CUTE BUSINESS.
WHOA, WAIT UP--WHAT'S GOING ON OVER THERE?
HURRY IT UP, MEAT SACKS. UP YOU GO, BOSS'S ORDERS.
MUH.
MUUUH.
THE GRIM REAPERS ARE SENDING THE ZOMBIES TO THE SURFACE?!
WHY WOULD THEY DO THIS?
I DON'T KNOW, BUT I'M GOING TO STOP IT.
BUT YOU DON'T HAVE YOUR SCYTHE!
I DON'T NEED IT WHEN I HAVE THESE.

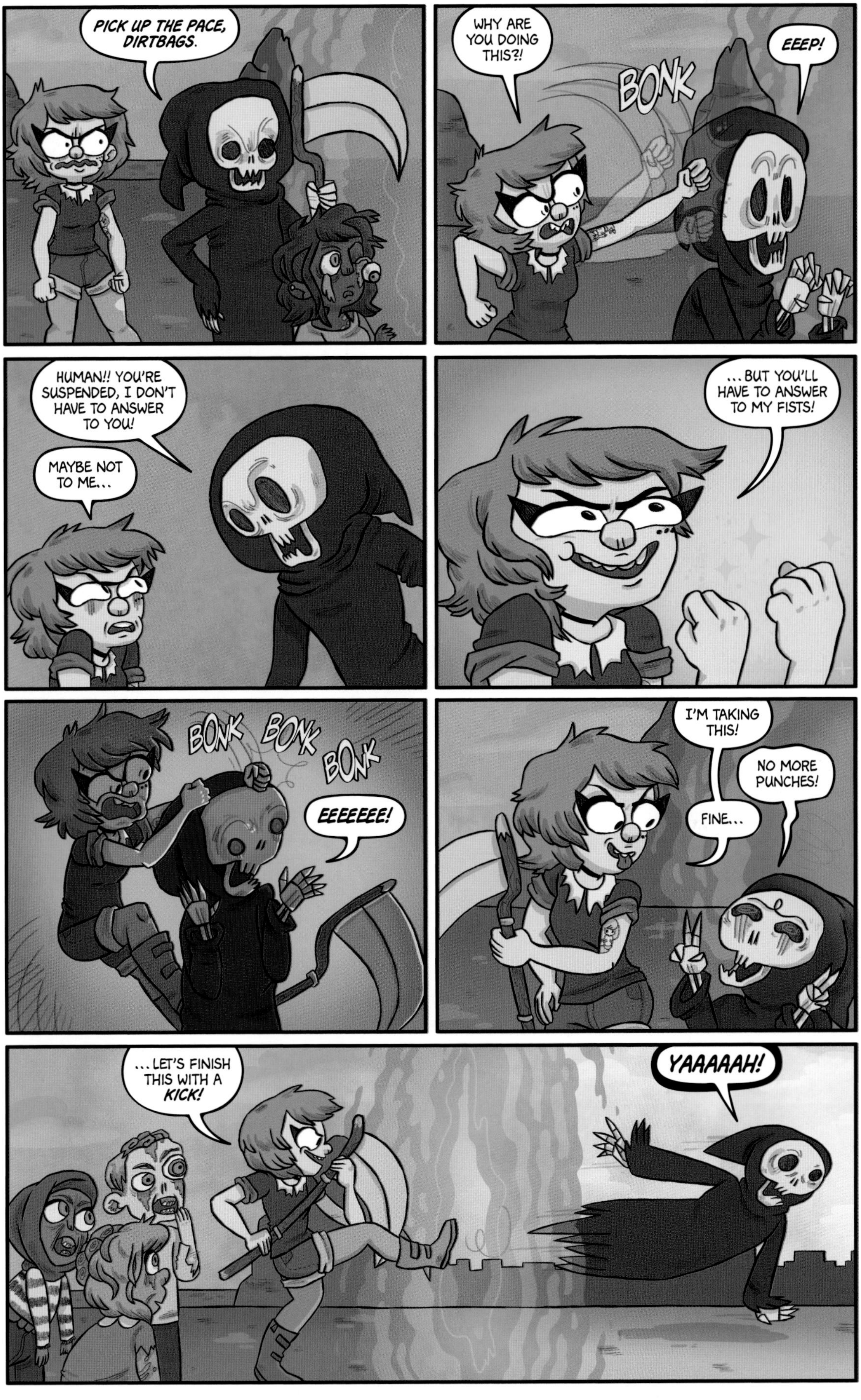
PICK UP THE PACE, DIRTBAGS.
WHY ARE YOU DOING THIS?!
BONK
EEEP!
HUMAN!! YOU'RE SUSPENDED, I DON'T HAVE TO ANSWER TO YOU!
MAYBE NOT TO ME...
...BUT YOU'LL HAVE TO ANSWER TO MY FISTS!
BONK BONK BONK
EEEEEEE!
I'M TAKING THIS!
NO MORE PUNCHES!
FINE...
...LET'S FINISH THIS WITH A KICK!
YAAAAAH!

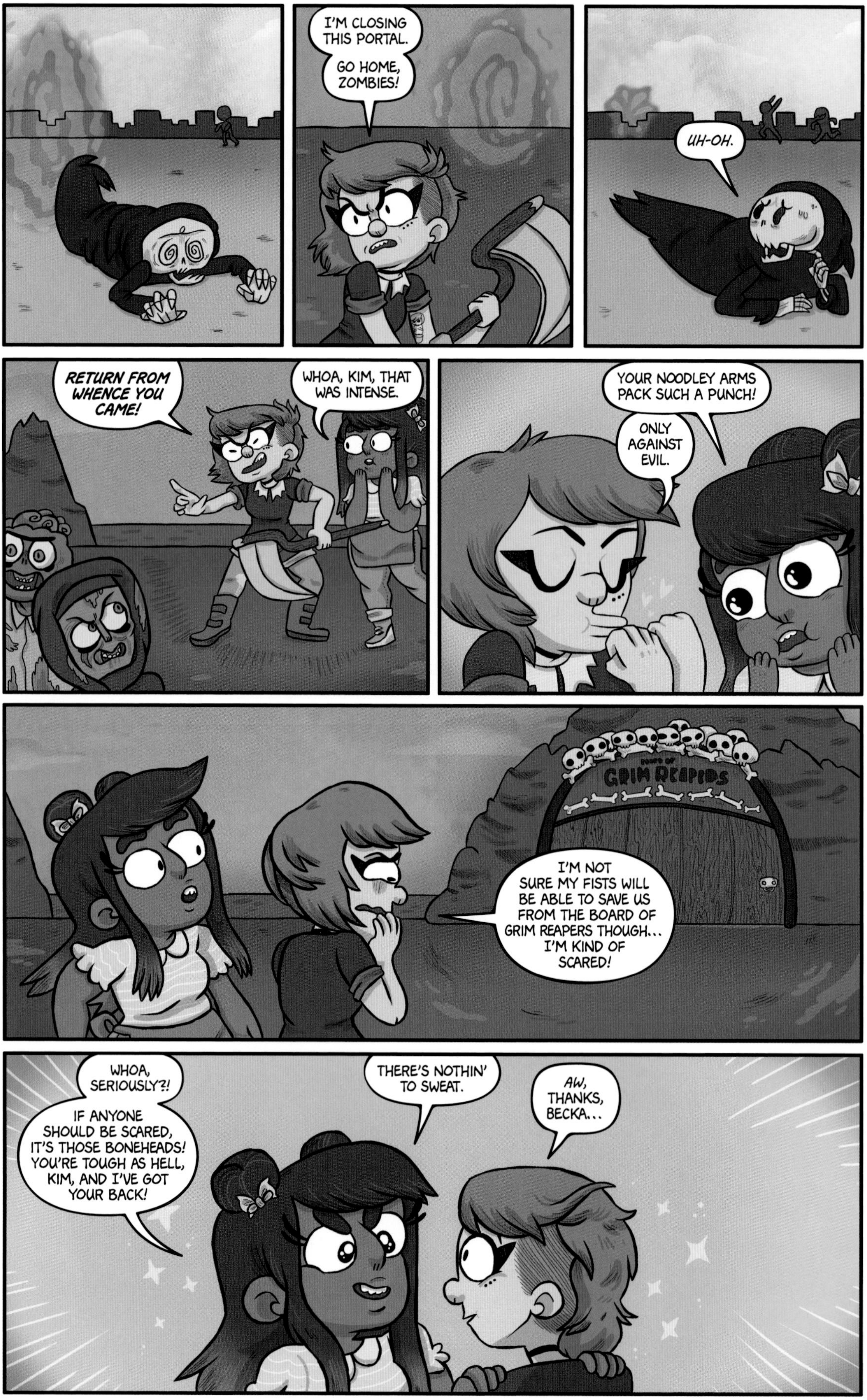
I'M CLOSING THIS PORTAL.
GO HOME, ZOMBIES!
UH-OH.
RETURN FROM WHENCE YOU CAME!
WHOA, KIM, THAT WAS INTENSE.
YOUR NOODLEY ARMS PACK SUCH A PUNCH!
ONLY AGAINST EVIL.
GRIM REAPERS
I'M NOT SURE MY FISTS WILL BE ABLE TO SAVE US FROM THE BOARD OF GRIM REAPERS THOUGH… I'M KIND OF SCARED!
WHOA, SERIOUSLY?!
IF ANYONE SHOULD BE SCARED, IT'S THOSE BONEHEADS! YOU'RE TOUGH AS HELL, KIM, AND I'VE GOT YOUR BACK!
THERE'S NOTHIN' TO SWEAT.
AW, THANKS, BECKA…

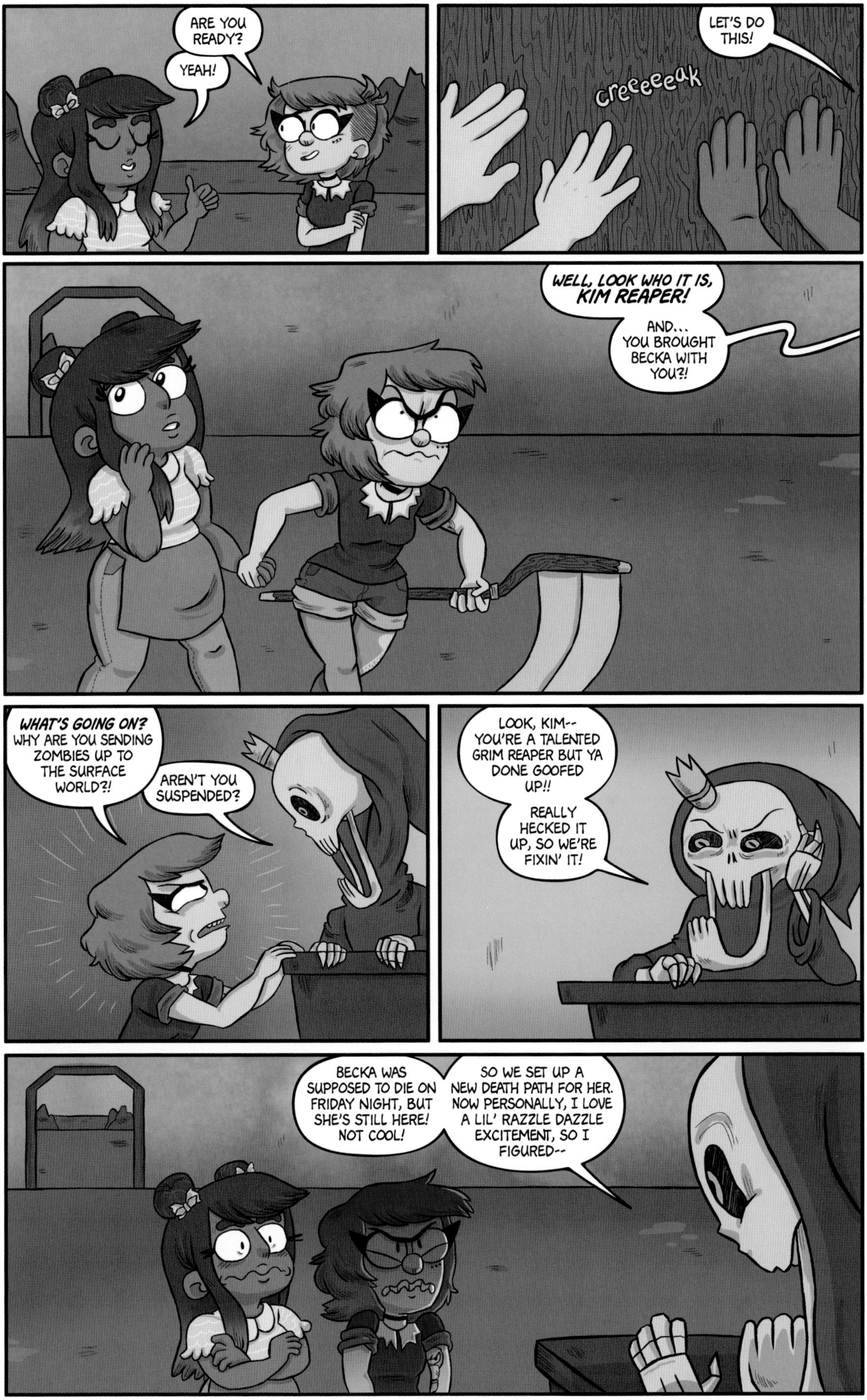

ARE YOU READY?
YEAH!
LET'S DO THIS!
creeeeeak
WELL, LOOK WHO IT IS, KIM REAPER!
AND... YOU BROUGHT BECKA WITH YOU?!
WHAT'S GOING ON? WHY ARE YOU SENDING ZOMBIES UP TO THE SURFACE WORLD?!
AREN'T YOU SUSPENDED?
LOOK, KIM-- YOU'RE A TALENTED GRIM REAPER BUT YA DONE GOOFED UP!!
REALLY HECKED IT UP, SO WE'RE FIXIN' IT!
BECKA WAS SUPPOSED TO DIE ON FRIDAY NIGHT, BUT SHE'S STILL HERE! NOT COOL!
SO WE SET UP A NEW DEATH PATH FOR HER. NOW PERSONALLY, I LOVE A LIL' RAZZLE DAZZLE EXCITEMENT, SO I FIGURED--

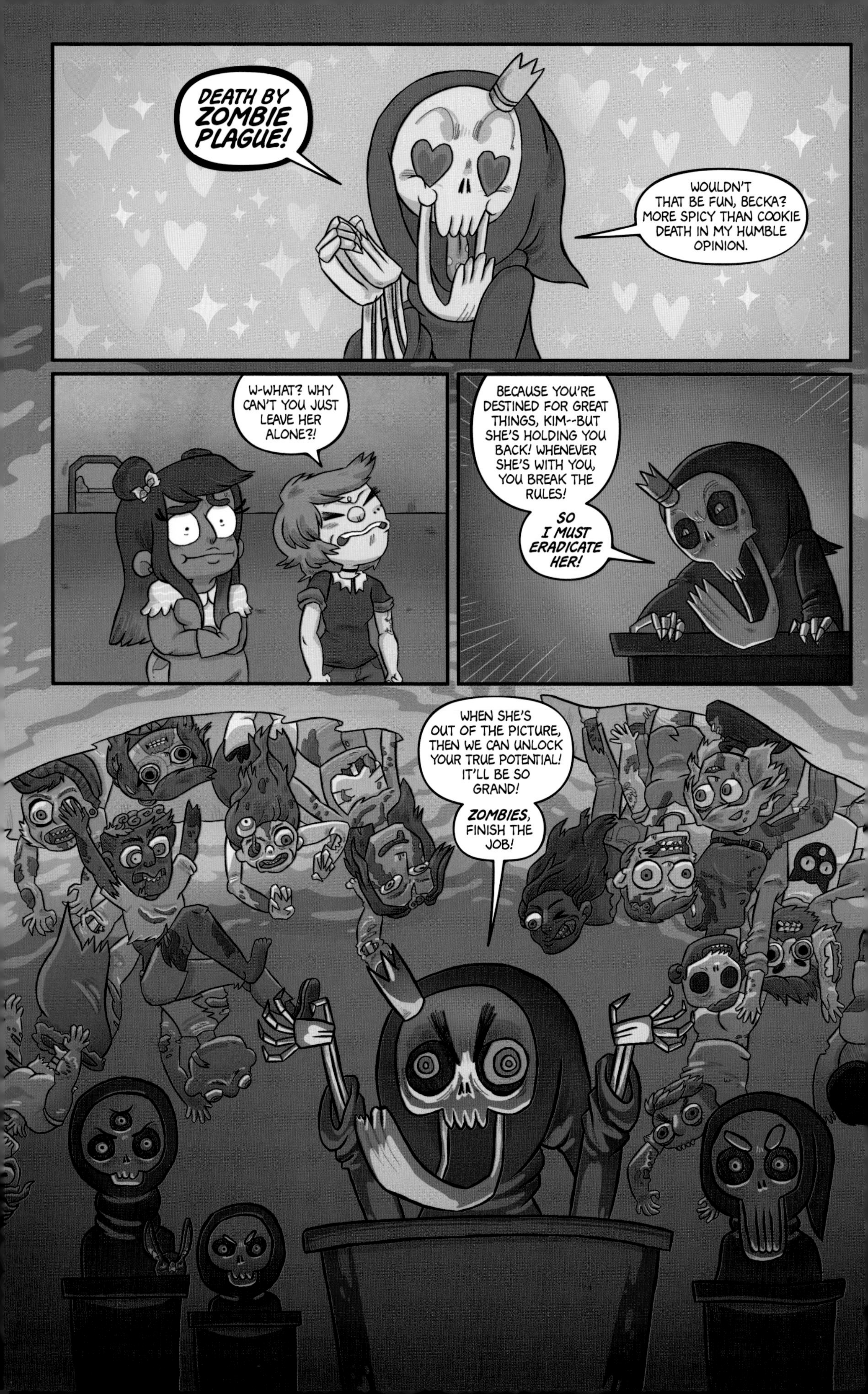
DEATH BY ZOMBIE PLAGUE!
WOULDN'T THAT BE FUN, BECKA? MORE SPICY THAN COOKIE DEATH IN MY HUMBLE OPINION.
W-WHAT? WHY CAN'T YOU JUST LEAVE HER ALONE?!
BECAUSE YOU'RE DESTINED FOR GREAT THINGS, KIM--BUT SHE'S HOLDING YOU BACK! WHENEVER SHE'S WITH YOU, YOU BREAK THE RULES!
SO I MUST ERADICATE HER!
WHEN SHE'S OUT OF THE PICTURE, THEN WE CAN UNLOCK YOUR TRUE POTENTIAL! IT'LL BE SO GRAND!
ZOMBIES, FINISH THE JOB!

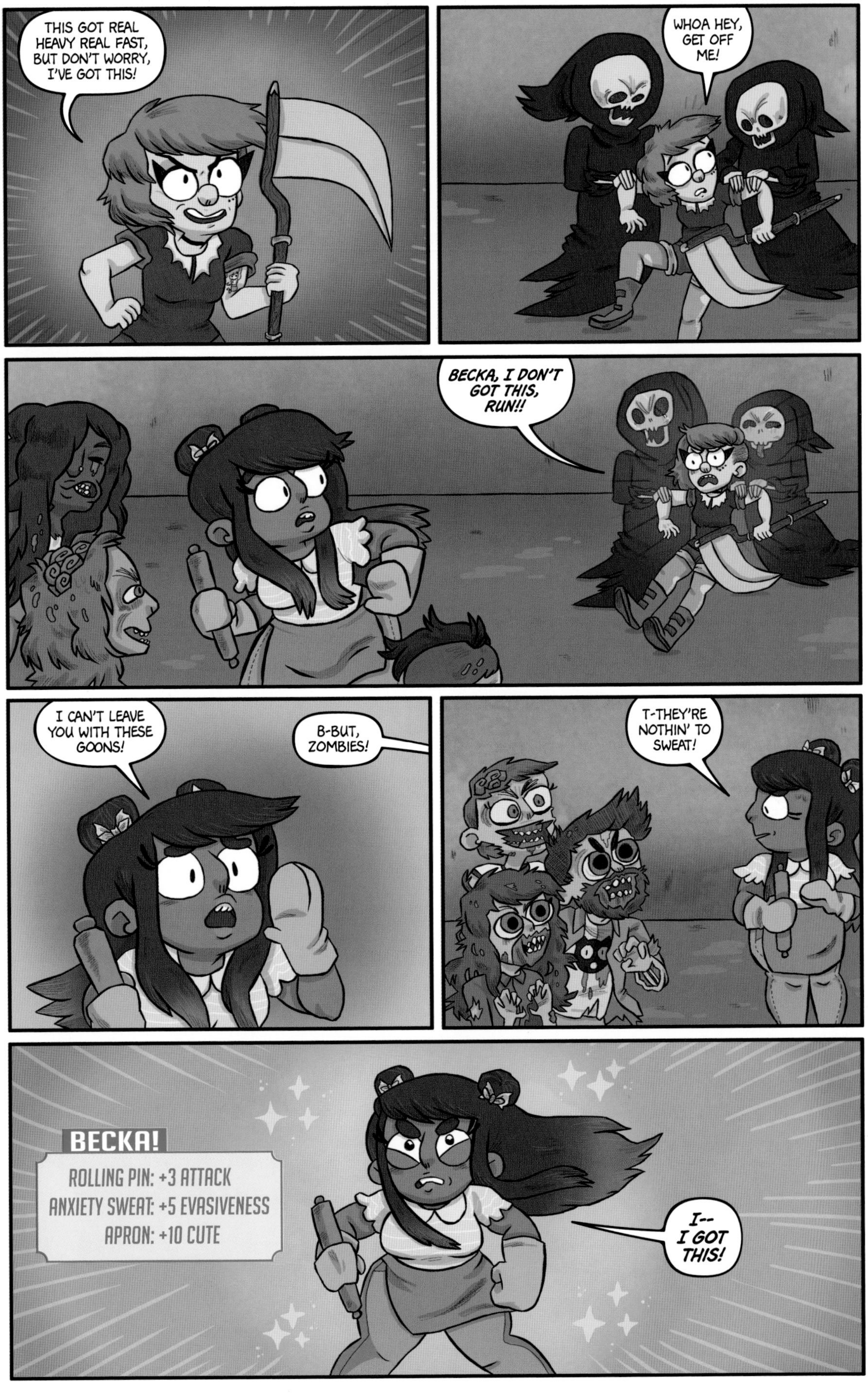
THIS GOT REAL HEAVY REAL FAST, BUT DON'T WORRY, I'VE GOT THIS!
WHOA HEY, GET OFF ME!
BECKA, I DON'T GOT THIS, RUN!!
I CAN'T LEAVE YOU WITH THESE GOONS!
B-BUT, ZOMBIES!
T-THEY'RE NOTHIN' TO SWEAT!
BECKA!
ROLLING PIN: +3 ATTACK
ANXIETY SWEAT: +5 EVASIVENESS
APRON: +10 CUTE
I-- I GOT THIS!

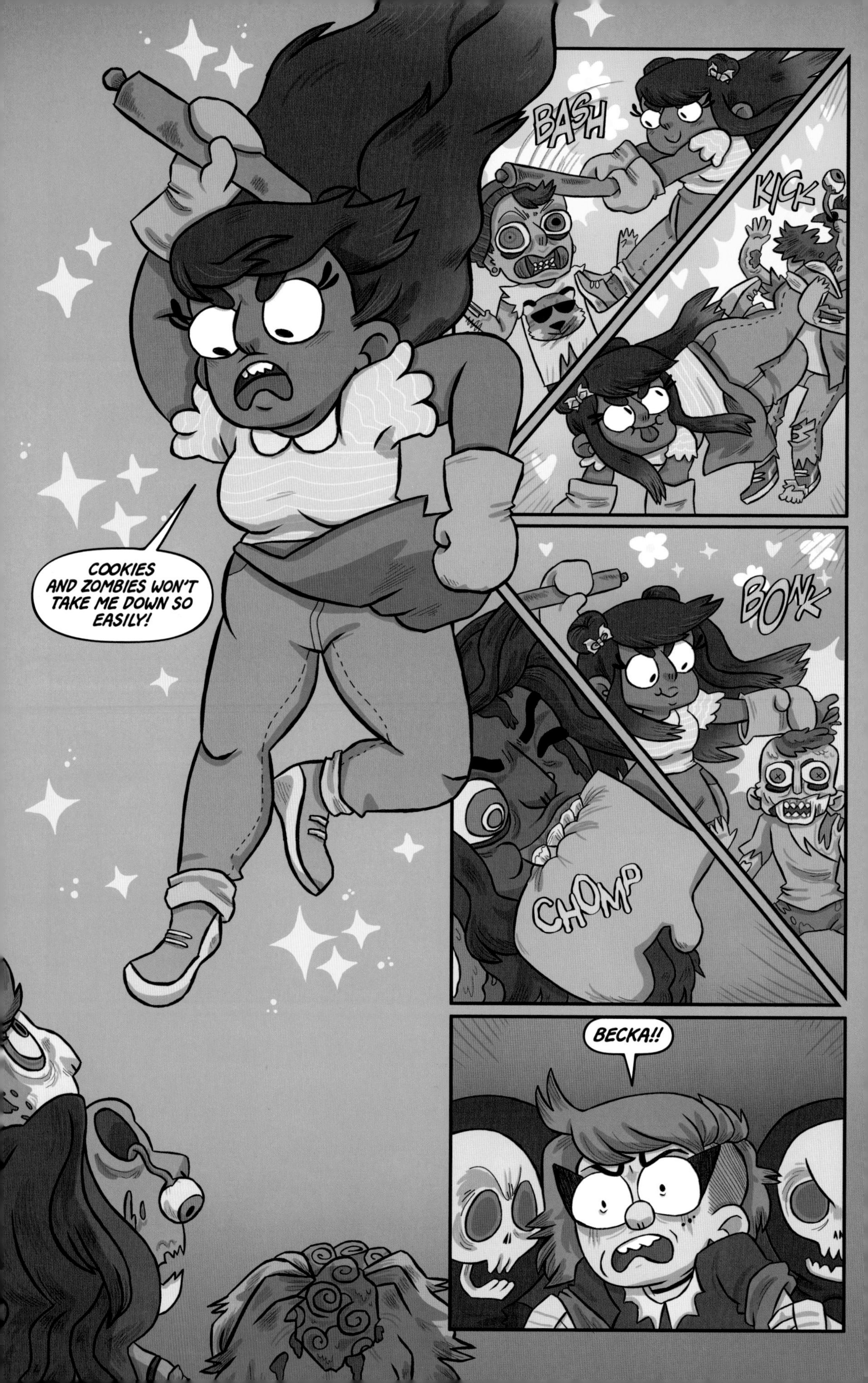
COOKIES AND ZOMBIES WON'T TAKE ME DOWN SO EASILY!
BASH
KICK
BONK
CHOMP
BECKA!!

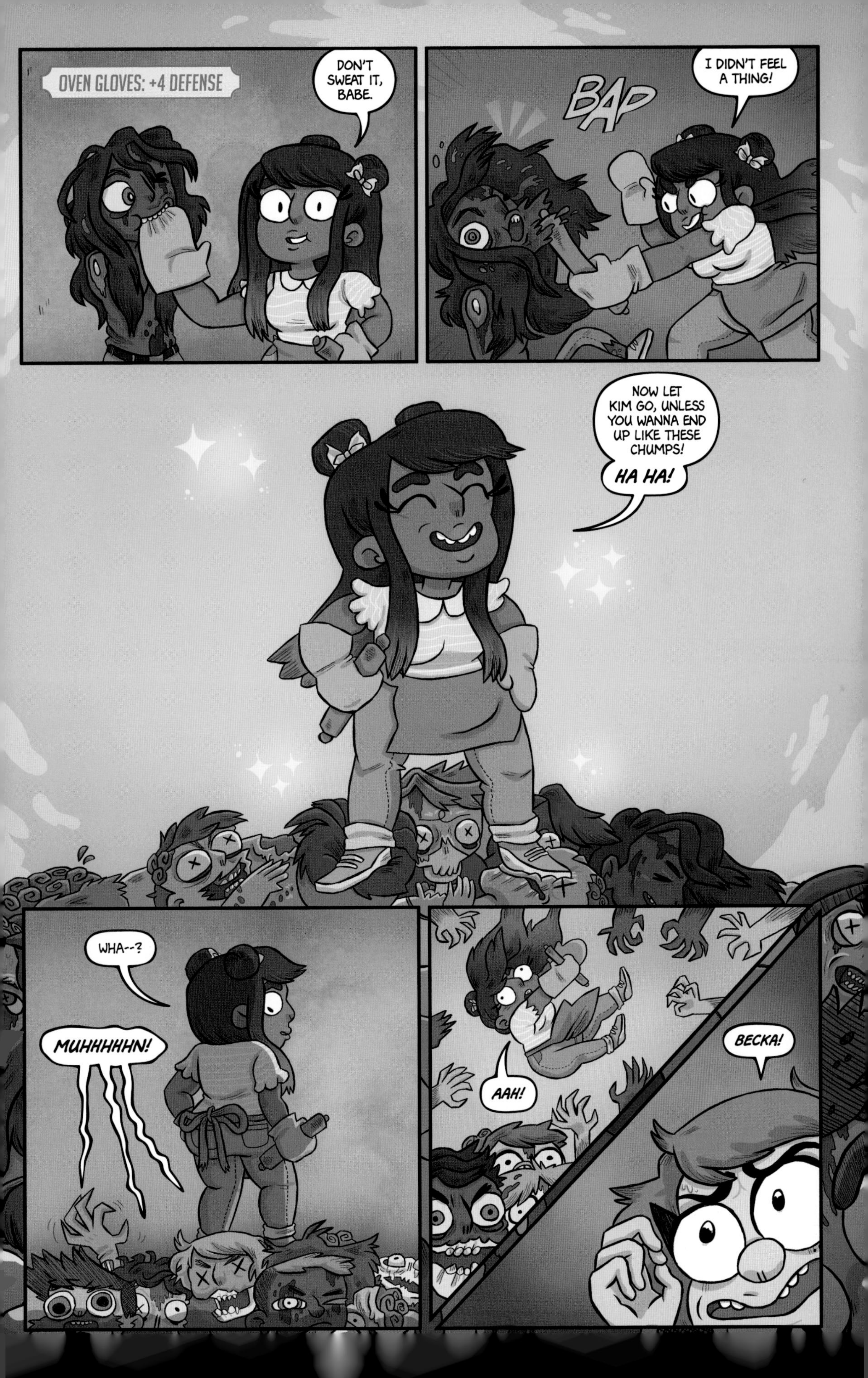
OVEN GLOVES: +4 DEFENSE
DON'T SWEAT IT, BABE.
BAP
I DIDN'T FEEL A THING!
NOW LET KIM GO, UNLESS YOU WANNA END UP LIKE THESE CHUMPS!
HA HA!
WHA--?
MUHHHHHN!
AAH!
BECKA!

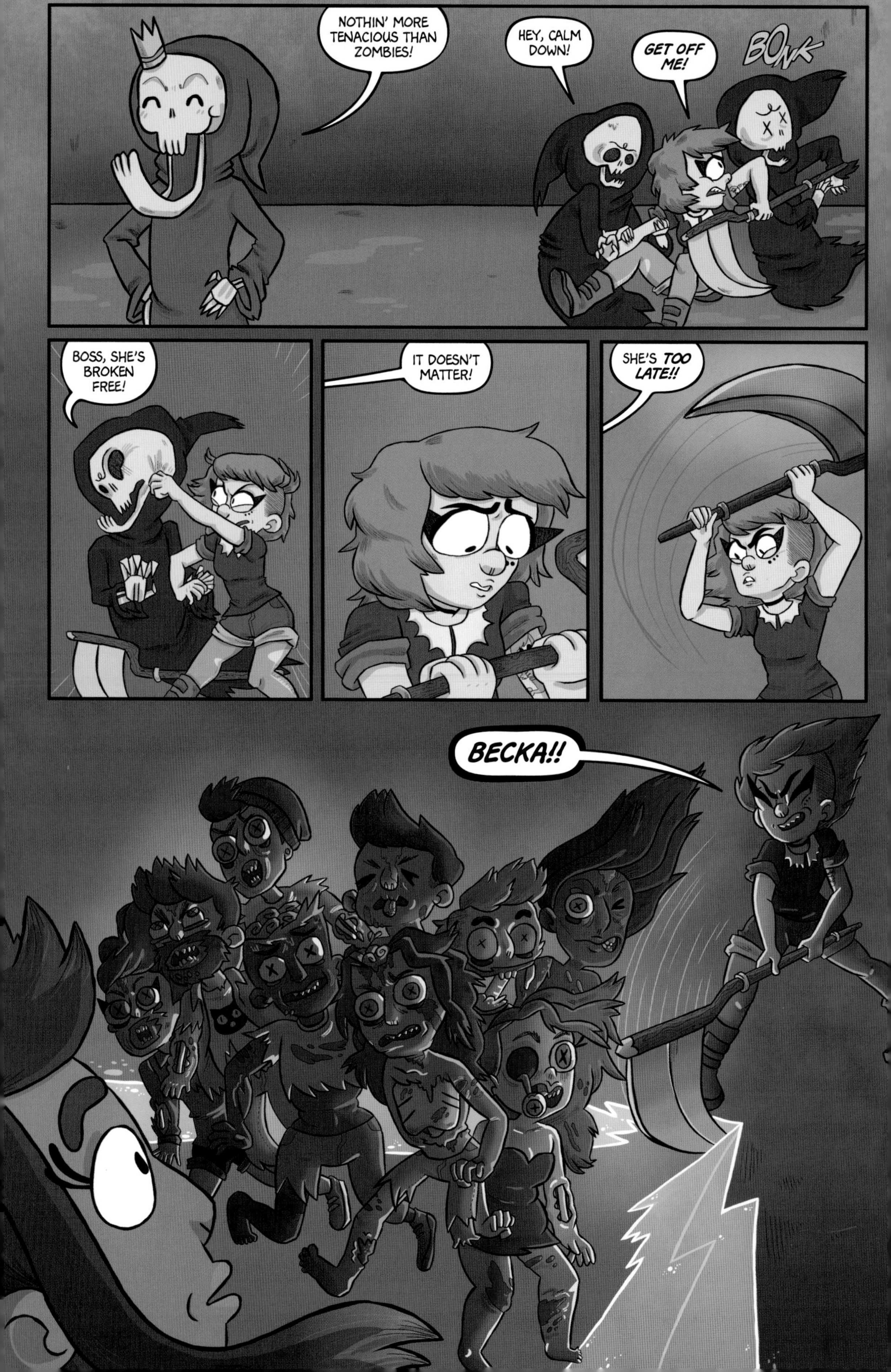
NOTHIN' MORE TENACIOUS THAN ZOMBIES!
HEY, CALM DOWN!
GET OFF ME!
BONK
BOSS, SHE'S BROKEN FREE!
IT DOESN'T MATTER!
SHE'S TOO LATE!!
BECKA!!

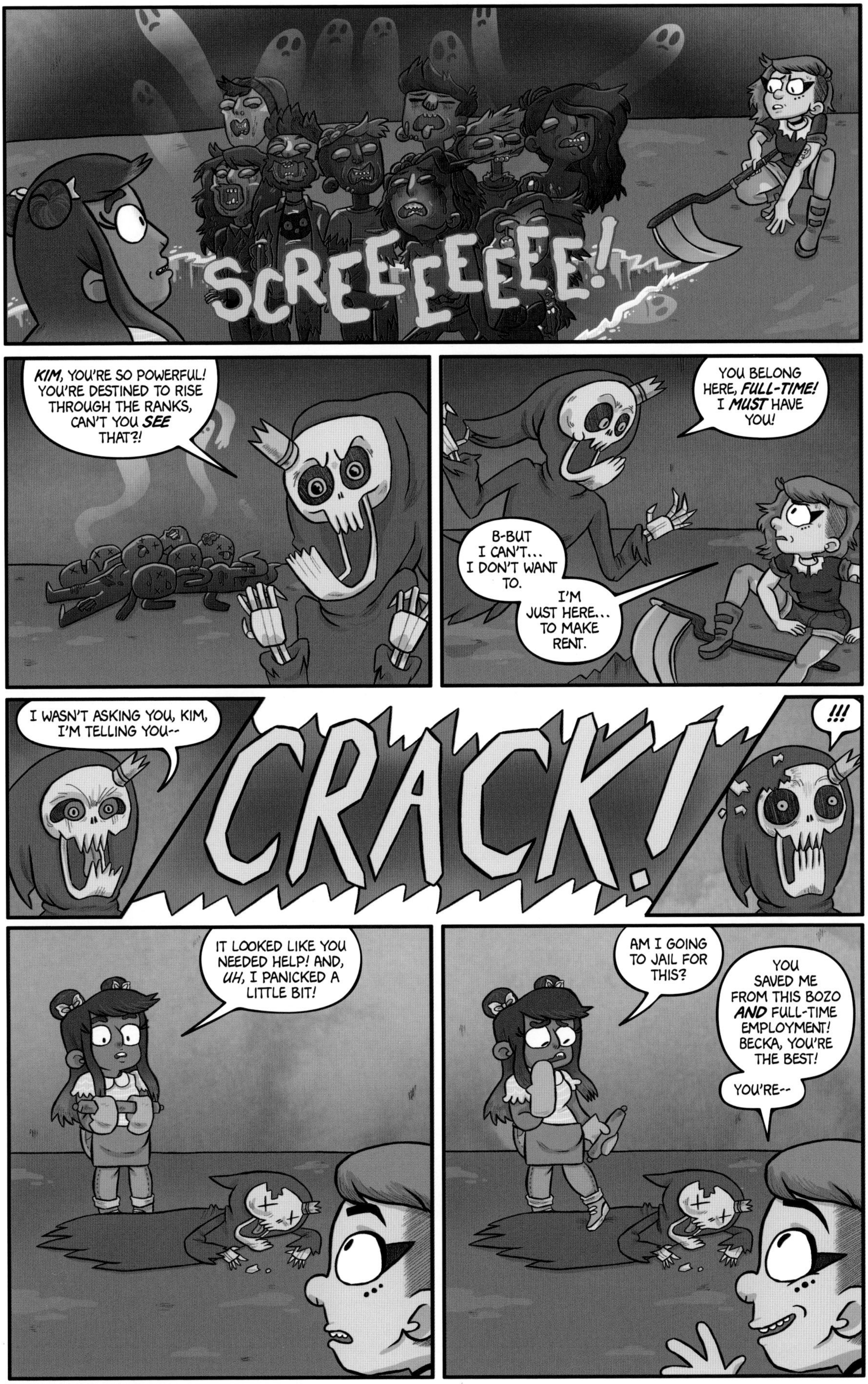
SCREEEEEEE!
KIM, YOU'RE SO POWERFUL! YOU'RE DESTINED TO RISE THROUGH THE RANKS, CAN'T YOU SEE THAT?!
YOU BELONG HERE, FULL-TIME! I MUST HAVE YOU!
B-BUT I CAN'T... I DON'T WANT TO.
I'M JUST HERE... TO MAKE RENT.
I WASN'T ASKING YOU, KIM, I'M TELLING YOU--
CRACK!
!!!
IT LOOKED LIKE YOU NEEDED HELP! AND, UH, I PANICKED A LITTLE BIT!
AM I GOING TO JAIL FOR THIS?
YOU SAVED ME FROM THIS BOZO AND FULL-TIME EMPLOYMENT! BECKA, YOU'RE THE BEST!
YOU'RE--

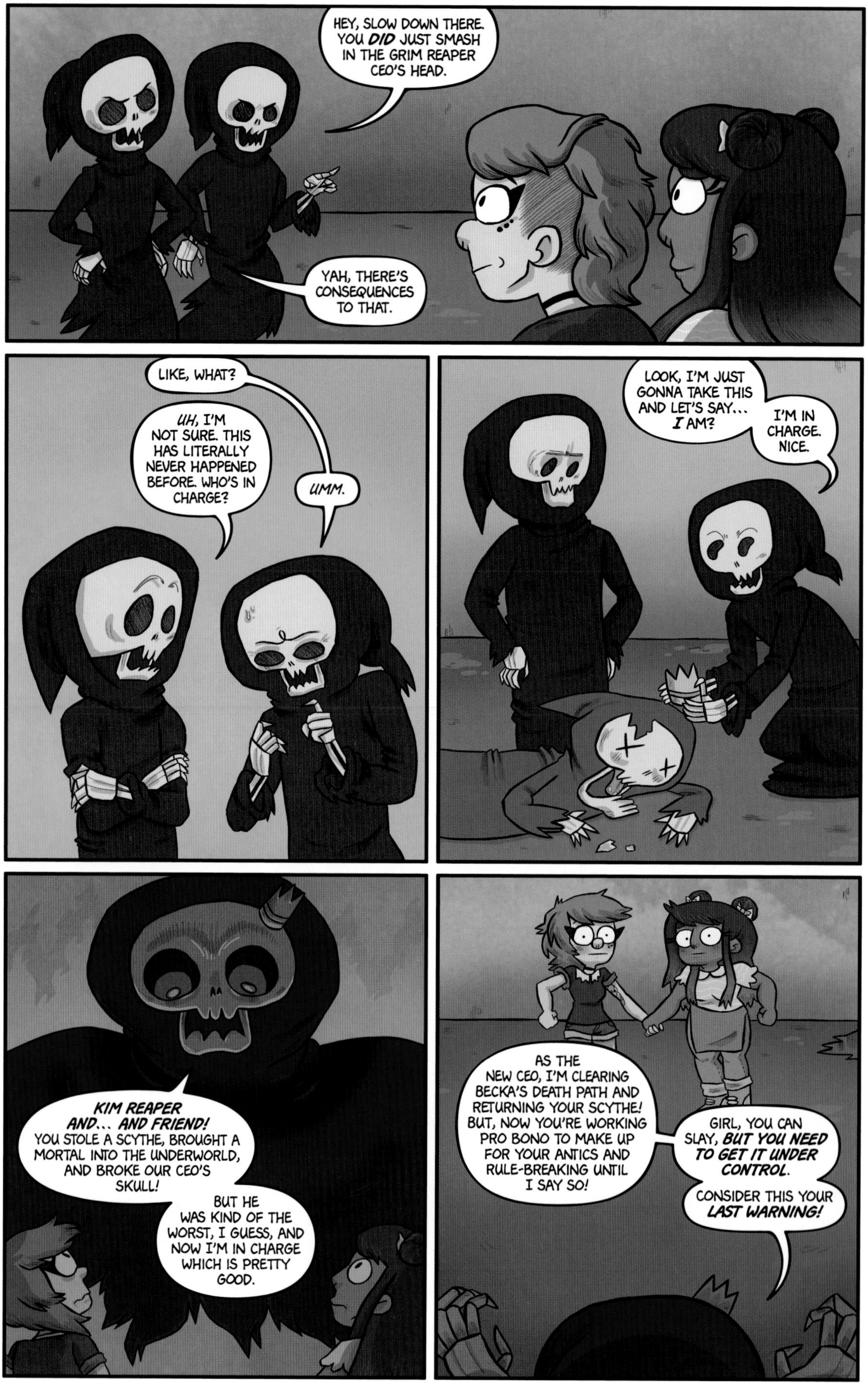
HEY, SLOW DOWN THERE. YOU DID JUST SMASH IN THE GRIM REAPER CEO'S HEAD.
YAH, THERE'S CONSEQUENCES TO THAT.
LIKE, WHAT?
UH, I'M NOT SURE. THIS HAS LITERALLY NEVER HAPPENED BEFORE. WHO'S IN CHARGE?
UMM.
LOOK, I'M JUST GONNA TAKE THIS AND LET'S SAY... I AM?
I'M IN CHARGE. NICE.
KIM REAPER AND... AND FRIEND! YOU STOLE A SCYTHE, BROUGHT A MORTAL INTO THE UNDERWORLD, AND BROKE OUR CEO'S SKULL!
BUT HE WAS KIND OF THE WORST, I GUESS, AND NOW I'M IN CHARGE WHICH IS PRETTY GOOD.
AS THE NEW CEO, I'M CLEARING BECKA'S DEATH PATH AND RETURNING YOUR SCYTHE! BUT, NOW YOU'RE WORKING PRO BONO TO MAKE UP FOR YOUR ANTICS AND RULE-BREAKING UNTIL I SAY SO!
GIRL, YOU CAN SLAY, BUT YOU NEED TO GET IT UNDER CONTROL.
CONSIDER THIS YOUR LAST WARNING!

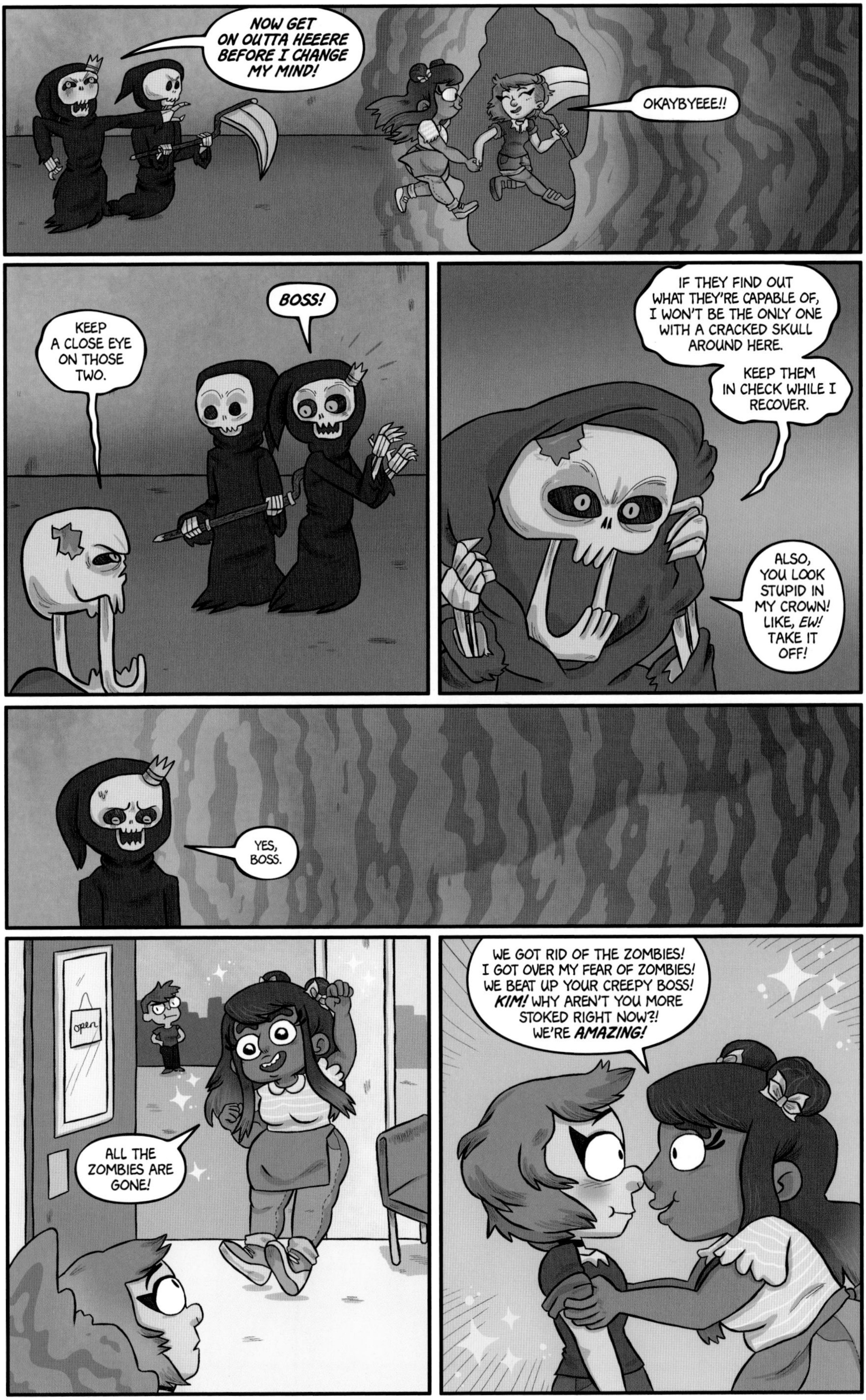
NOW GET ON OUTTA HEEERE BEFORE I CHANGE MY MIND!
OKAYBYEEE!!
KEEP A CLOSE EYE ON THOSE TWO.
BOSS!
IF THEY FIND OUT WHAT THEY'RE CAPABLE OF, I WON'T BE THE ONLY ONE WITH A CRACKED SKULL AROUND HERE.
KEEP THEM IN CHECK WHILE I RECOVER.
ALSO, YOU LOOK STUPID IN MY CROWN! LIKE, EW! TAKE IT OFF!
YES, BOSS.
open
ALL THE ZOMBIES ARE GONE!
WE GOT RID OF THE ZOMBIES! I GOT OVER MY FEAR OF ZOMBIES! WE BEAT UP YOUR CREEPY BOSS! KIM! WHY AREN'T YOU MORE STOKED RIGHT NOW?! WE'RE AMAZING!

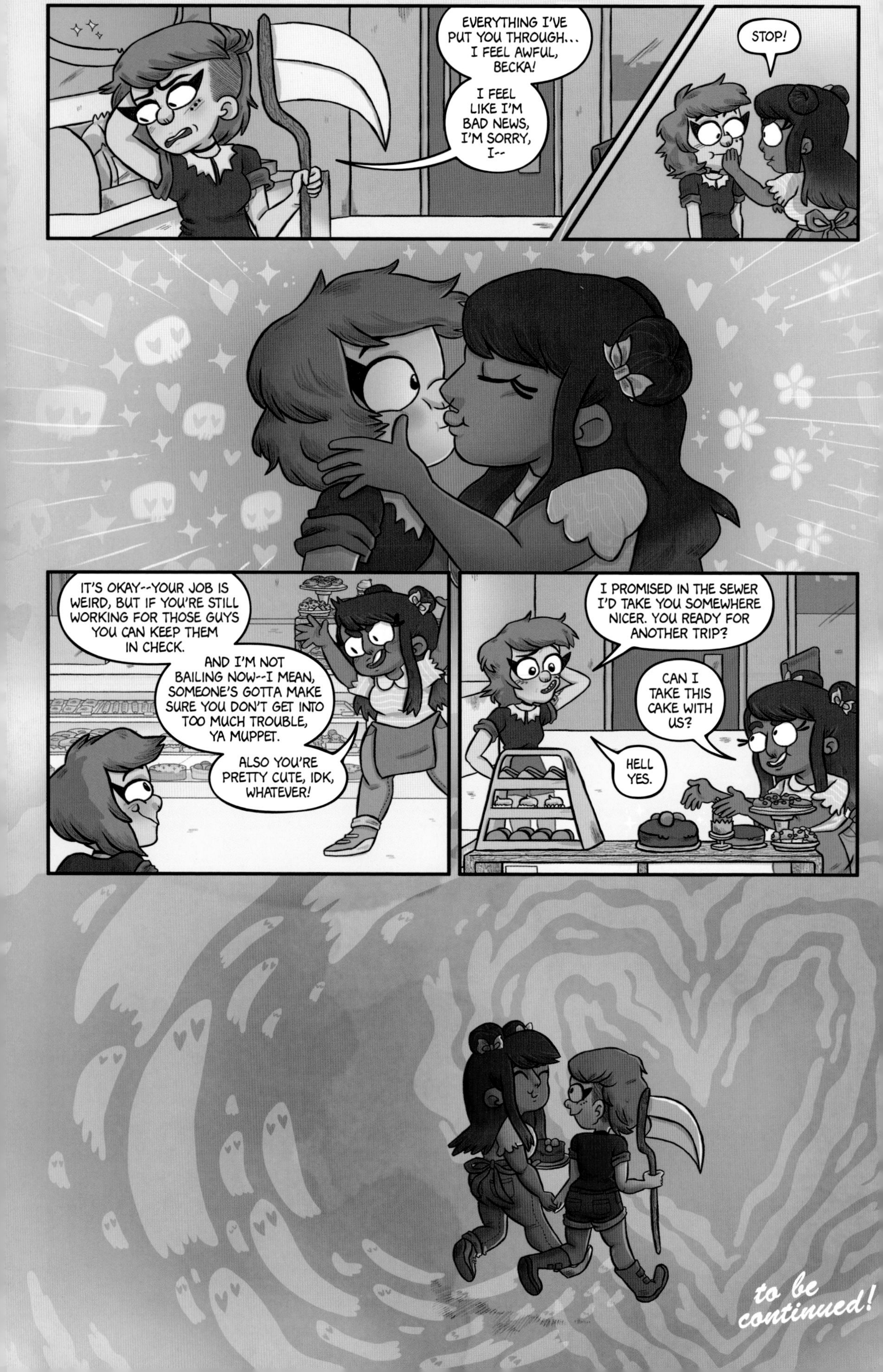
EVERYTHING I'VE PUT YOU THROUGH... I FEEL AWFUL, BECKA!
I FEEL LIKE I'M BAD NEWS, I'M SORRY, I--
STOP!
IT'S OKAY--YOUR JOB IS WEIRD, BUT IF YOU'RE STILL WORKING FOR THOSE GUYS YOU CAN KEEP THEM IN CHECK.
AND I'M NOT BAILING NOW--I MEAN, SOMEONE'S GOTTA MAKE SURE YOU DON'T GET INTO TOO MUCH TROUBLE, YA MUPPET.
ALSO YOU'RE PRETTY CUTE, IDK, WHATEVER!
I PROMISED IN THE SEWER I'D TAKE YOU SOMEWHERE NICER. YOU READY FOR ANOTHER TRIP?
CAN I TAKE THIS CAKE WITH US?
HELL YES.
to be continued!

ILLUSTRATION BY LISSA TREIMAN

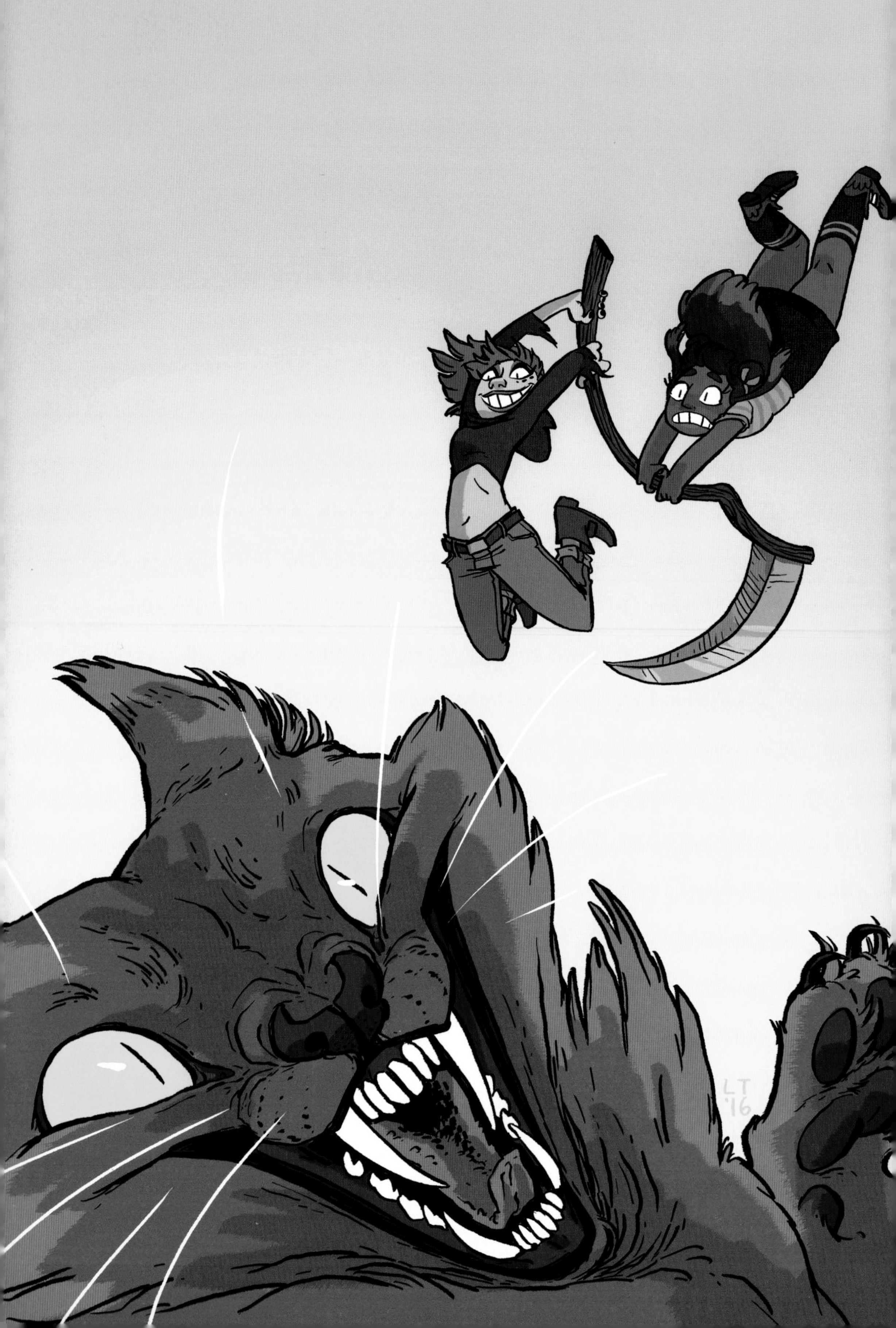
LT
'16

BONUS MATERIAL!

SIGNING TOUR POSTER

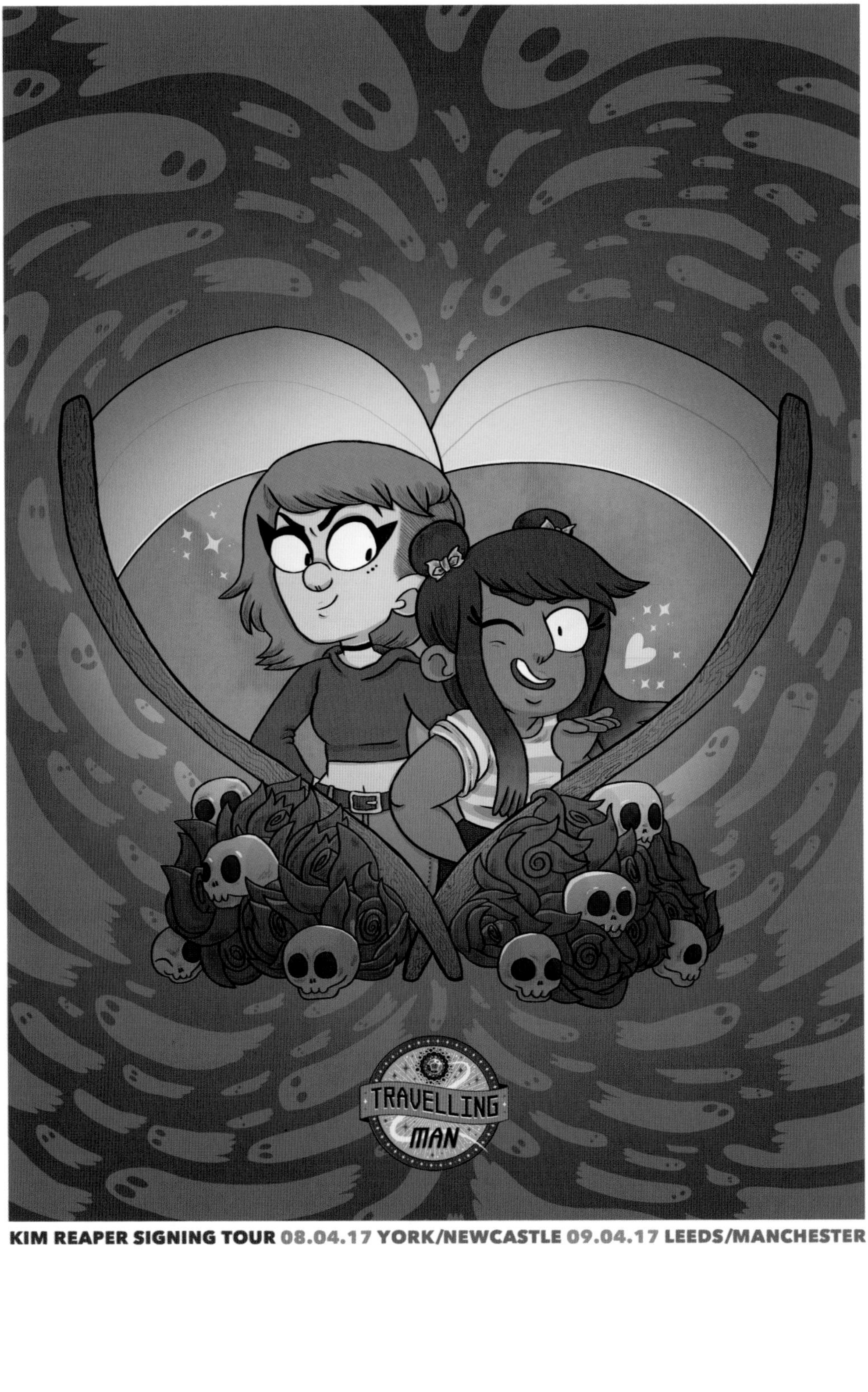
TRAVELLING
MAN

KIM REAPER SIGNING TOUR 08.04.17 **YORK/NEWCASTLE** 09.04.17 **LEEDS/MANCHESTER**

ART PRINT

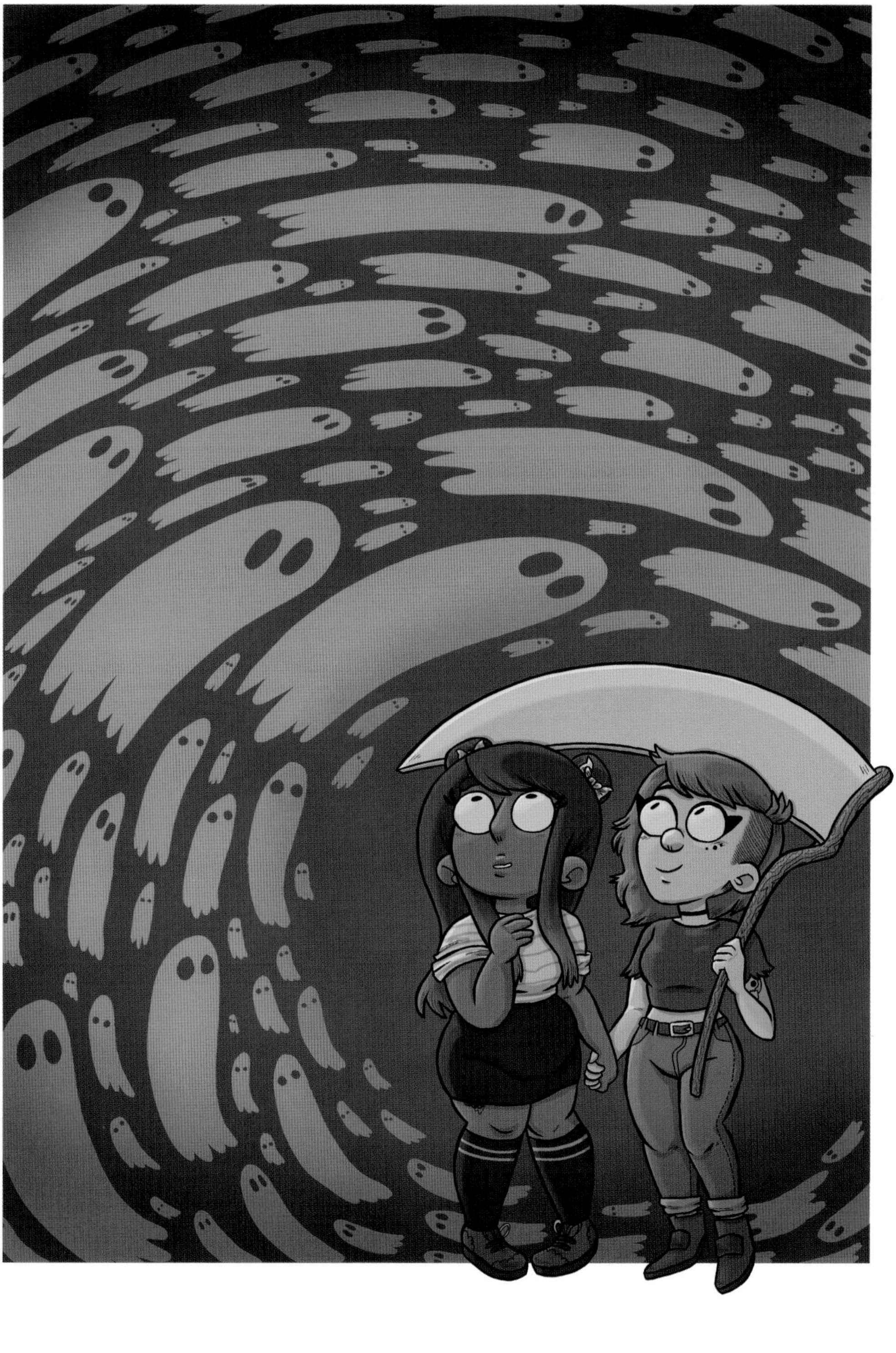

THE PITCH

These images are from my pitch for *Kim Reaper*! The comic was initially titled *Part-Time Grim Reaper*, until my partner Stef suggested the much catchier name *Kim Reaper*. That also meant Kim's name changed from the original Sabrina!

Becka's design stays quite close to the original, but Kim's changes quite drastically. I think I was going for some kind of hooded hair cut to give the vibe of a Grim Reaper's cloak, but it just wasn't working out! Luckily, undercuts are very cute and great so that became Kim's new look.

PART-TIME GRIM REAPER
BY SARAH GRALEY

BECKA

SABRINA

REJECTED COVERS

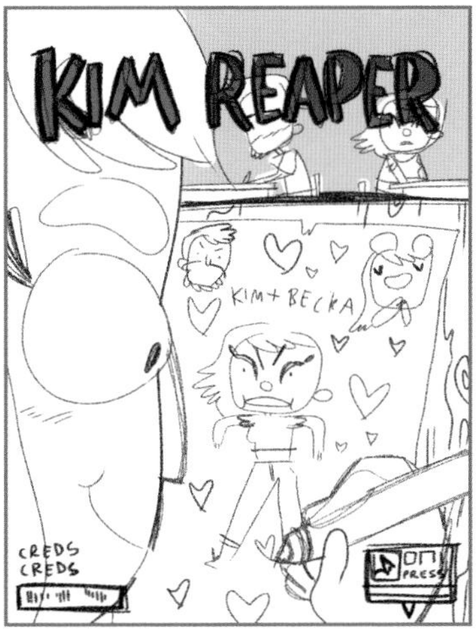
KIM REAPER
KIM+BECKA
CREDS
CREDS
ONI PRESS

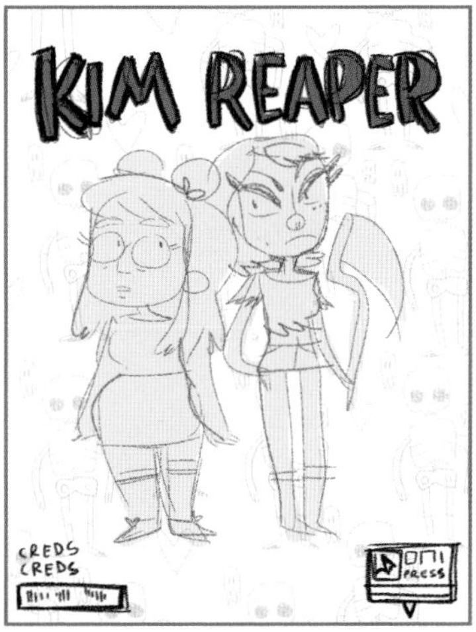
KIM REAPER
CREDS
CREDS
ONI PRESS

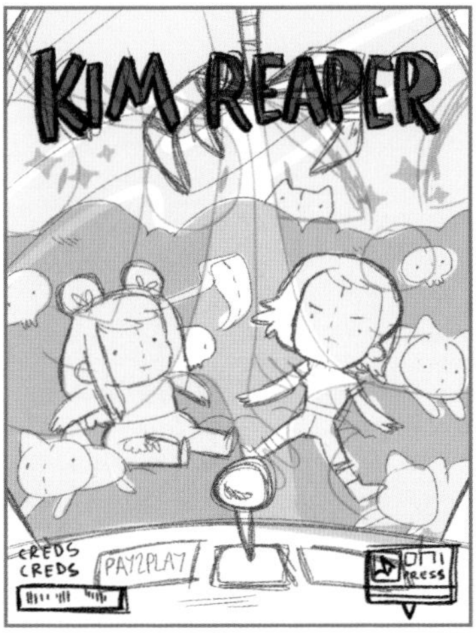
KIM REAPER
CREDS
CREDS
PAY2PLAY
ONI PRESS

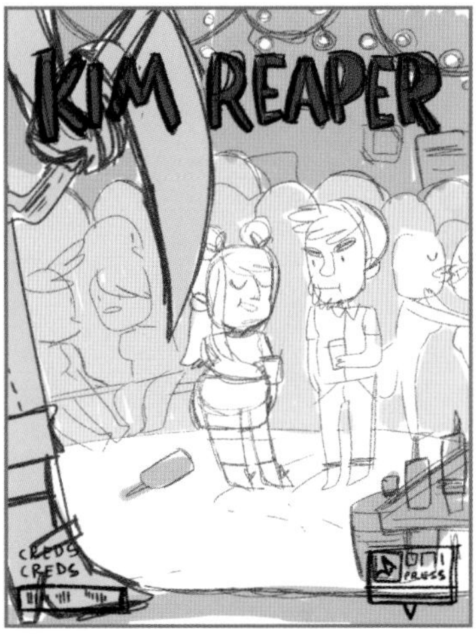
KIM REAPER
ONI PRESS

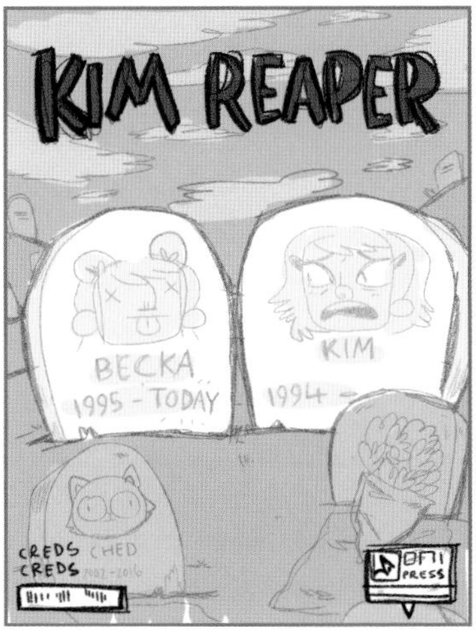
KIM REAPER
BECKA
1995 - TODAY
KIM
1994 -
CREDS
CREDS
CHED
ONI PRESS

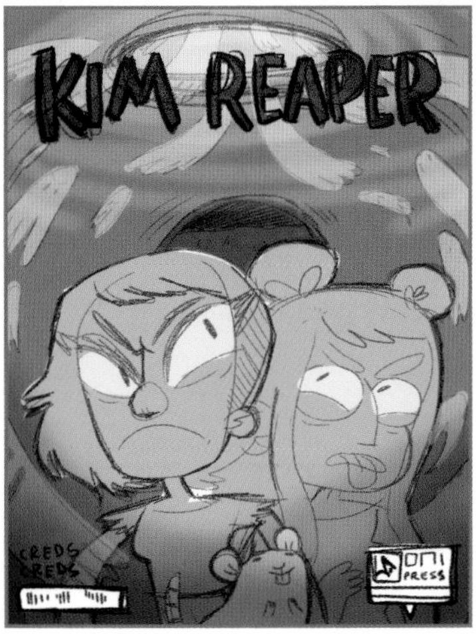
KIM REAPER
ONI PRESS

Here are some of the rejected cover ideas for the series! I think the claw machine is my favorite reject—I'm quite partial to a good claw machine. We went for a cover that was cat-heavy instead, which worked out for me 'cos I also very much like cats. Like, a whole bunch. I have four and it's ludicrous.

SCRIPT

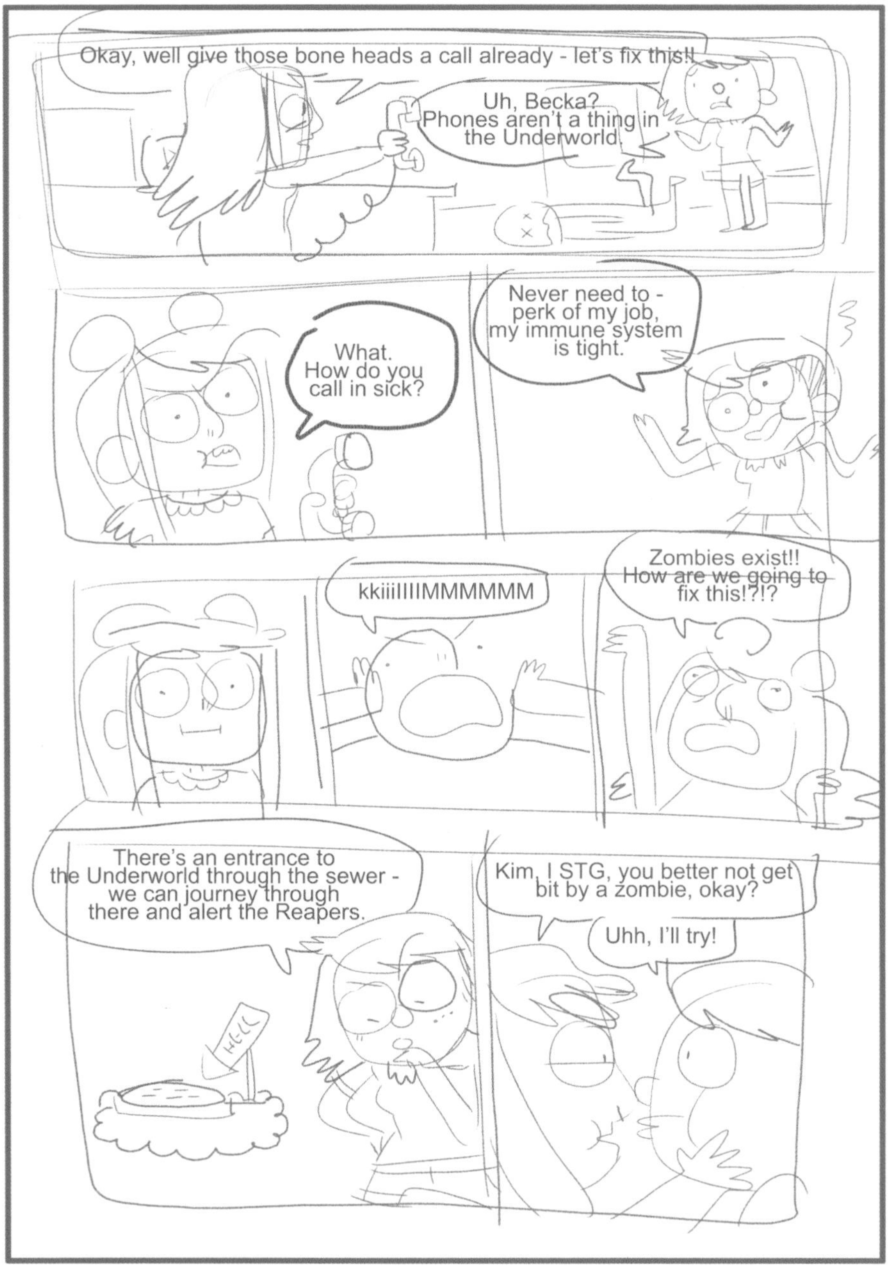
Okay, well give those bone heads a call already - let's fix this!!
Uh, Becka? Phones aren't a thing in the Underworld.
What. How do you call in sick?
Never need to - perk of my job, my immune system is tight.
kkiiiIIIIMMMMMM
Zombies exist!! How are we going to fix this!?!?
There's an entrance to the Underworld through the sewer - we can journey through there and alert the Reapers.
HELL
Kim, I STG, you better not get bit by a zombie, okay?
Uhh, I'll try!

When I write scripts, I tend to make a list of main plot points for the story and then dive straight into thumbnails! I find it helps to have the characters in front of me when writing their dialogue—and it'll sometimes inspire extra stages in the script for my characters to explore before we hit that next plot point.

SKETCHES

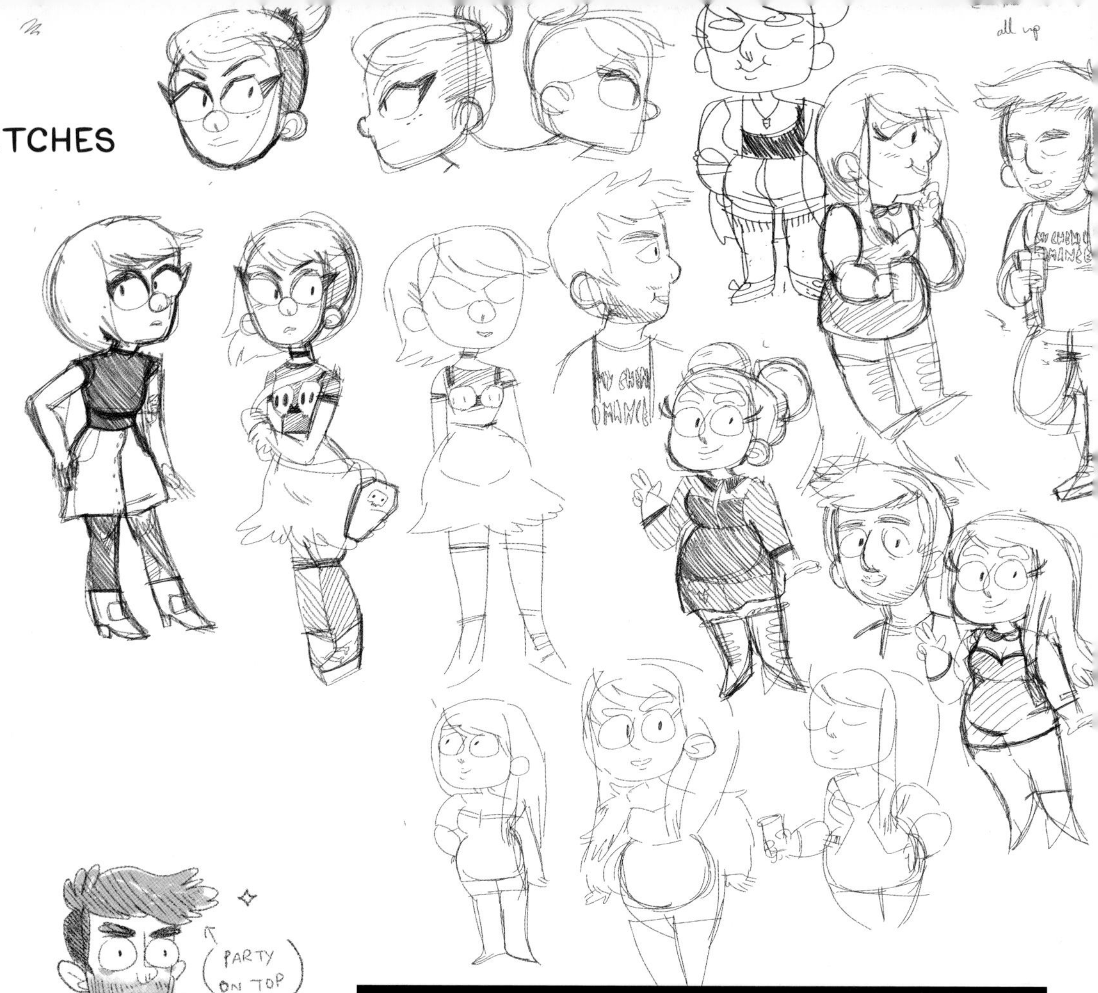

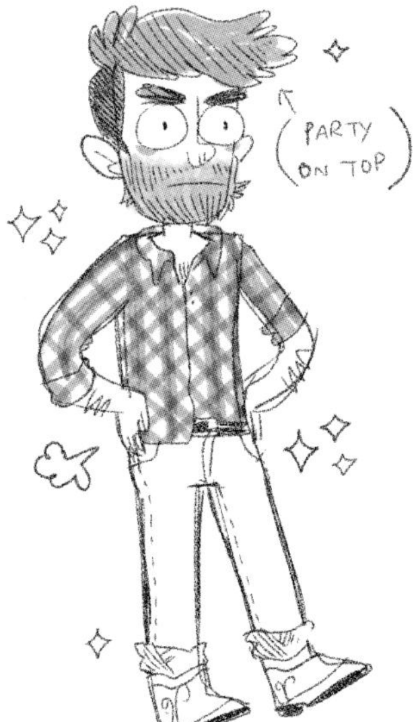
PARTY ON TOP

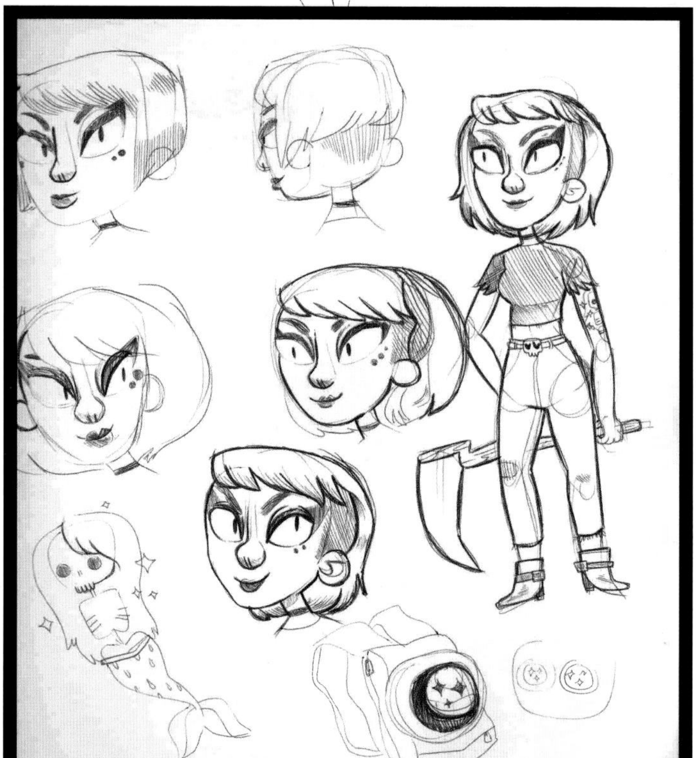

✦ SARAH GRALEY ✦

is a UK-based comic artist and writer, living with four cats
and one cat-like boy. When she's not working on comics about
part-time grim reapers and cuties, she's probably working on other
comics about other cuties! She did that RICK AND MORTY™ series
(LIL' POOPY SUPERSTAR) that one time, and also does a diary
comic called OUR SUPER ADVENTURE. You can check those
out and more at www.sarahgraley.com!

MORE FROM ONI PRESS!

**SPACE BATTLE LUNCHTIME,
VOLUME 1: LIGHTS,
CAMERA, SNACKTION**
By Natalie Riess
ISBN 978-1-62010-313-5

**SCOTT PILGRIM COLOR
HARDCOVER, VOLUME 1:
PRECIOUS LITTLE LIFE**
By Bryan Lee O'Malley
ISBN 978-1-62010-000-4

RICK AND MORTY™: LIL' POOPY SUPERSTAR
By Sarah Graley, Marc Ellerby, & Mildred Louis
ISBN 978-1-62010-374-6

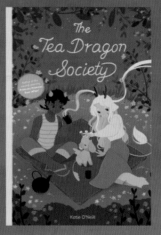

**BAD MACHINERY, VOLUME 1:
THE CASE OF THE TEAM SPIRIT**
By John Allison
ISBN 978-1-62010-387-6

LUCKY PENNY
By Ananth Hirsh & Yuko Ota
ISBN 978-1-62010-287-9

THE TEA DRAGON SOCIETY
By Katie O'Neill
ISBN 978-1-62010-441-5

ONI
PRESS
www.onipress.com

For more information on these and other fine Oni Press comic books and graphic novels, visit **www.onipress.com**.
To find a comic specialty store in your area, visit **www.comicshops.us**.